W9-CLD-863

HEARSE AND BUGGY

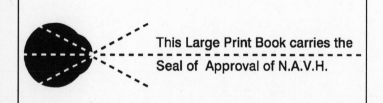

HEARSE AND BUGGY

LAURA BRADFORD

THORNDIKE PRESS
A part of Gale, Cengage Learning

GALE
CENGAGE Learning®

Detroit • New York • San Francisco • New Haven, Conn • Waterville, Maine • London

GALE
CENGAGE Learning®

LIBRARY OF CONGRESS CATALOGING-IN-PUBLICATION DATA

Bradford, Laura.
    Hearse and buggy / by Laura Bradford. — Large print ed.
      p. cm. — (Thorndike Press large print mystery)
    "An Amish Mystery"—T.p. verso.
    ISBN-13: 978-1-4104-5165-1 (hardcover)
    ISBN-10: 1-4104-5165-8 (hardcover)
    1. Amish—Amish Country (Pa.)—Fiction. 2.
Murder—Investigation.—Fiction. 3. Large type books. I. Title.
PS3602.R34235H43 2012
813'.6—dc23   2012021889

Published in 2012 by arrangement with The Berkley Publishing Group, a member of Penguin Group (USA) Inc.

Printed in the United States of America
1 2 3 4 5 6 7 16 15 14 13 12

*For my family, for making
my life extraordinary.*

ACKNOWLEDGMENTS

I loved every moment of writing this book. The characters and the town of Heavenly, Pennsylvania, sprang to life before my eyes, making each day I spent at the computer a true joy.

That said, I want to thank my fabulous editor, Emily Rapoport, and my agent, Jessica Faust, for allowing me the opportunity to spend my days in such a wonderful place — creating this world I hope you'll love as much as I do.

CHAPTER 1

Claire Weatherly looked around the empty stockroom, kneading the small of her back with stiff, tired fingers. Three hours earlier she'd been almost convinced it would take an act of God to clear away the last of the handmade furniture left behind by the previous tenant. Bed frames, tables, chairs, chests, and cribs had claimed the much-needed space for weeks, a glaring reminder of one more task that needed to be completed before Heavenly Treasures would finally feel as if it were truly there to stay.

Because it was.

And so was she.

Sure, there had been times — like three hours ago — when she'd been inclined to give in to the doubts and simply roll over, convinced her fresh start was nothing more than idle daydreams with a hefty dose of delirium thrown in for good measure. Yet she'd pressed on, driven by the same little

9

voice that had prodded her to make some of the best decisions she'd made in years. Including taking a gamble and leaving her ex-husband's harried world in favor of one where she actually fit.

"Miss Weatherly?"

At the sound of Esther King's timid voice, Claire turned and drank in the sight of the young woman in her plain royal-blue dress and white apron.

"Oh, Esther, aren't you a sight for sore eyes!"

A hint of crimson rose in the nineteen-year-old's face. "Sore eyes?"

"Sore eyes, sore arms, sore legs . . . Take your pick."

Esther's soft brown eyebrows rose toward the white head cap secured to her matching brown hair. "Are you sick, Miss Weatherly?"

"No, no — I'm fine. A little tired, perhaps, but fine." She waved her hand around the room. "So? What do you think?"

Esther's gaze followed suit, a shy smile inching her full lips upward. "You did nice. You cleared everything from the room just as you said you would."

Indeed, she had, the last of the items — a beautiful chest — being picked up by one Eli Miller, not more than ten minutes earlier.

She met Esther's eye and held it a beat. "Eli was sorry he missed you."

"Eli?" Esther's hand flew to the cape of her dress and smoothed its way down to her apron. "Eli was here? In the shop?"

Claire knew she shouldn't tease, but she couldn't help it. Esther needed a little spark in her life. "He was. And even though he's rather distracted by everything going on with his sister, he asked about you."

All color drained from the young woman's face. "He did?"

"He did."

Esther took a step back and flopped against the wall. "This is when I miss my cousin Hannah's world. If I had a cell phone as she does, you could have called me, and I would have come sooner."

With a few easy strides, Claire claimed a section of wall to the left of her new friend. "Do you miss it?"

"Miss what?" Esther asked.

"Living the way you did, the way the English do every day."

Esther closed her eyes, her audible inhale filling the space between them. "Sometimes. I mean, I love Mamm and Dat, and I'm glad I made the decision to come back after Rumspringa and be baptized, but . . . sometimes . . . I wish I could do things

Hannah can do."

"Like what?"

"Like be able to tell Eli I like him, rather than wait for him to notice me."

"Then you're not worried about his temper?" The second the words were out, Claire wished she could recall them. Eli Miller was a nice guy. He'd been nothing but polite the few times she'd run across him coming and going from Shoo Fly Bake Shoppe next door. Several times a day, he showed up at the Amish bakery to see if his sister, Ruth, needed anything, and when she did, he attended to whatever it was in quick fashion. That, and the fact that Esther thought so kindly of him, should be enough to drown out any whisperings Claire had heard about his short-fused temper.

"His temper is not good, but he does not deserve so much shunning. What that man did was wrong."

Claire reached out, rested a calming hand on Esther's arm. "I know. And you're right. I can't imagine how a man like Mr. Snow could hurt your community in the way he did. Pocketing money that rightfully belonged to your family, and to people like Eli and his brother, was wrong. He should have been thrown in jail."

And it was true. Walter Snow, the previous tenant, had lured Amish furniture makers to his shop, offered their work on consignment, and then stiffed them of money that was rightfully theirs for months before the Amish had grown wise to his thieving ways. Unfortunately, Eli had taken a stronger stance than the rest of his community, breaking his oath of nonviolence and threatening the shopkeeper with bodily harm if the money wasn't returned.

"How was Eli to know Mr. Snow would leave town in the middle of the night, taking everyone's money and leaving his own wife behind?" Without waiting for a response, Esther continued as she paced around the room, the strings of her head cap dangling in a rare show of independence. "Yet, to hear Eli's brother, Benjamin, and even my own grandfather talk, you'd think *Eli* was the criminal. And he did nothing more than speak his mind."

"I'm sure it will blow over soon. It has to." But even as she put words to the hope she knew Esther needed, Claire knew it wasn't the case. The Amish took their vows very seriously. To break one carried consequences — lasting consequences to those who refused to repent.

A jingle of bells from the main part of the store propelled Claire from her place against the wall. "I'll get —"

"Esther? Are you here?"

Claire glanced at her employee in time to see the girl freeze, midpace. "Yes. Yes, I am here, Mamm. Just one minute. I will be right there."

A charge of excitement made Claire reach out, momentarily thwarting Esther's move toward the main room. "That's your mother?"

Esther nodded.

"I didn't know you'd convinced her to come."

"I did not know either," Esther whispered.

It was hard not to laugh at the mixture of bewilderment and fear on the young woman's face — bewilderment and fear Claire understood yet was equally anxious to ease. "It'll be okay, Esther. You wait and see."

"You do not know Mamm."

"That's about to change." Beckoning for Esther to follow, Claire made her way out of the stockroom and into the main shop, the shelves lining the walls showcasing a smattering of Amish crafts, many of which had been made by Esther. As she rounded the corner, Claire couldn't help but do a double take. For there, in the middle of the room, stood a virtual carbon copy of the young woman at her heels. The hair was the same soft brown shade, the hazel eyes a nearly perfect match, and their height was no more than a centimeter off from one another.

And, like her daughter, Martha King was dressed in typical Amish dress, though, as an older woman, her apron was black and her dress color a bit darker. But the burgundy hue the mother had chosen did little to mute the pretty face that peered back at Claire.

"Mrs. King, I'm Claire Weatherly. I'm honored to finally meet you." She stuck out her hand only to pull it back and opt for a smile instead. "Esther has told me so much about you."

Martha's gaze moved to a red-faced Esther. "She has?"

Claire rushed to explain, for fear the woman would think her daughter had spoken in a boastful manner. "She tells me you taught her how to quilt and how to make many of the items my customers love so much." She pointed toward the shelf that, only yesterday, had been filled with candles of varying sizes and shapes. "Esther's creations are some of our most popular items."

"We are grateful for the money you send home with Esther each week. It has made up for some of what Mr. Snow took

15

when . . ." Martha's words trailed off as she seemed to realize what she was saying. Such matters were not for the women to pay any worry.

"It's money Esther has rightfully earned." She flashed a smile in Esther's direction, hoping some of the tension that seemed to hover around the young woman's shoulders would dissipate. "In fact, your daughter is quite a businesswoman, if I must say so myself. She comes in with a price in mind and holds firm."

Martha eyed Esther closely but said nothing.

Flushed, Esther toed the wood-planked floor.

"I was hoping that maybe you might consider showcasing some of your own crafts here at Heavenly Treasures as well."

A peaceful silence blanketed the room as Martha appeared to consider Claire's request, her eventual response catching both Esther and Claire off guard. "My daughter told me you were interested in speaking to me about this, but I put it off, certain that you would lose interest . . . in this shop and the Amish way. But I have listened to Esther these past few weeks, listened to the things you have told her, and I have changed my mind."

Esther's mouth gaped. "You mean you're going to bring your painted milk cans and wooden spoons here, too, Mamm?"

"If Miss Weatherly will allow, then yes."

"Yes?" Claire echoed.

"Yes. You can pick up some items on Thursday."

It took every ounce of strength Claire could muster not to jump up and down, squealing. Suddenly, the shop she'd opened with little more than hope was showing the kind of potential she'd only dared to imagine.

This time, when she reached outward, she didn't stop, her hand closing over the top of Martha's in a gentle squeeze. "Thank you, Mrs. King. Thank you so much."

"Esther, it is time to go." With barely more than a nod at Claire, Esther's mother marched toward the front door, stopping midway with a glance over her shoulder. "Miss Weatherly? If we are to work together, you shall call me Martha."

And just like that, Claire felt the familiar sting in her eyes. For five long years, she'd been Mrs. Peter Ross — the Wall Street wife who existed simply to attend company dinners and sit home alone the rest of the time. But now, thanks to a healthy dose of courage and her aunt Diane's offer of solace à la

Heavenly, Pennsylvania, Claire was making a life of her own.

With people who wanted to be friends with her because of who she was, not who she was married to.

Swallowing over the lump that threatened to render her speechless, she eked out the only reply she could. "And I'm Claire."

"I will have these things ready for you on Thursday." Taking hold of her daughter's arm, Martha continued on her path to the door, her black-stocking-clad legs freezing in motion mere inches from their destination.

"Mamm?" Esther nibbled at her lower lip. "Mamm, what's wrong?"

Martha stepped to the left and leaned toward the large plate-glass window that overlooked Lighted Way — the road that linked Heavenly's Amish and English communities. Here, the two worlds met, as cars shared the roadway with buggies, and sidewalks were traveled by the hatted and unhatted. Slowly, Martha's finger rose into the air, pressing against the window. "Who is that?"

Claire moved in next to Martha, her gaze following the path indicated. "Oh. I believe that's the police department's new detective. I've not met him yet, but my aunt says he's from New York City, like me." Claire took a moment to study the tall man with the sandy blond hair and broad shoulders she'd seen in the newspaper over breakfast just that morning. More handsome in person, he moved with a sense of quiet authority befitting his new title. "Had I moved to a place like Washington, D. C., or Chicago, I'd have thought nothing of meeting others from New York. Yet here in Heavenly, it always takes me by surprise."

"Do you know his name?" Martha asked.

She searched her memory for the name she'd seen captioned under his photo, her aunt's running commentary on the latest happenings in Heavenly helping to fill in at least part of the answer her mind seemed unable to recall on its own. "Jakob. Jakob something or —"

"Fisher," Martha finished. "Jakob Fisher."

Esther gasped. "*Fisher?* Mamm . . . Wasn't that your last name when you were —"

Grabbing hold of her daughter's arm once again, Martha's gaze dropped to the floor, a flash of pain skittering across her face before disappearing behind a facade that could only be described as stoic. "Esther, we must go. *Now*."

CHAPTER 2

She'd always been of the notion that life changed in bits and pieces, small course variations that allowed a person to navigate more effectively. But now, after the way things had changed in the past few months, Claire knew that wasn't always the case.

Not in her life, anyway.

One minute, she was holed up in the Manhattan apartment she'd shared with Peter, waiting — as she always did — for him to come home from work. The candles had burned themselves down to their bases, the anniversary dinner she'd prepared had gone untouched, and her heart had been broken for the very last time.

Six months later, after caving in to Aunt Diane's offer for some much-needed solace, she was living at Sleep Heavenly, the bed-and-breakfast her aunt owned on the outskirts of Heavenly, Pennsylvania.

She'd come out of desperation and loneliness.

She'd stayed after finding something she'd thought she'd lost forever.

And in the process, she'd learned more about herself than she ever thought possible.

Some of the things were little — like the fact that she enjoyed live music and wandering through bookstores for hours on end. Some were more eye-opening — like the kinds of things that she could use to make life decisions.

Top on the list of things learned, though, was her unearthed passion for simplicity and tradition. She liked counting on herself, and learning to believe she could count on others as well.

Aunt Diane had taught her that. And so, too, had the quiet, God-fearing people who lived their lives in a place as far from New York City and her life with Peter as she'd ever dreamed possible . . .

"Good heavens, Claire, you look as if you're a million miles away." Diane Weatherly breezed into the kitchen, waving a dish towel in her niece's direction. "You're not thinking about that buffoon you were married to, are you?"

Claire ducked out of the towel's path and

returned to the dishes in the sink, the warm soapy suds soothing against her skin. "Guilty as charged."

Diane took a rare moment to stop, her meaty shoulders drooping. "You're not thinking about going back, are you?"

The soup bowl slipped from her fingers at the notion of ever returning to her previous life. "Aunt Diane, there are no circumstances under which I'd ever go back. This is my home now."

The sixty-two-year-old clapped her hands, releasing a happy squeal as she did. "I've been hoping you'd decide to live here with me on a permanent basis."

Claire reclaimed the bowl from the sudsy water and placed it in the water-only side. "I don't necessarily mean here as in the inn, Aunt Diane. I just mean here in Heavenly."

Diane's chin rose upward a notch. "What's wrong with the inn?"

Realizing she'd offended, Claire rushed to explain, pausing from her dishwashing duties long enough to wipe her hands on the cloth she'd tucked into her apron. "I love the inn, Aunt Diane, you know that —"

"I thought I did."

"And I do. But, at some point, once the shop is on solid footing, I'll want to get my own place."

Horror widened Diane's eyes. "But you can't. You're still so young . . . so fragile."

She had to laugh. "I'm thirty-one, Aunt Diane." Stepping two feet to the right, she peered into the mirror her aunt had nailed to the wall above the dish drainer, her blue-green eyes finally void of the wounded quality they'd reflected upon her arrival in Heavenly six months earlier. Even her auburn hair featured a more relaxed look, its former bob cut giving way to one that slipped below her shoulders. "And as for fragile, not so much anymore."

Diane spun on her soft-soled shoes and headed back toward the dining area, a tray of turkey, dressing, and mashed potatoes balanced atop her shoulder. "We'll see about that moving-out part when it's time. Seems silly to get your own place unless you find a nice man. The guests always love you . . . even the odd ones."

Taking one last peek in the mirror, she followed her aunt through the series of doorways that led to the dining area where the paying guests ate each night. As she passed through the final opening, she took a deep breath, commending the scene to memory for use later on, when she was in bed, and her mind started wandering back to darker days.

It was a technique that served her well and allowed her to sleep on nights she might not otherwise have slept.

She supposed some of that was simply the vibes that a group of people, seated together around a table and enjoying a home-style meal, tended to give off. She knew, too, that some of it came from the feel of the room — the dim lighting cast about from the wall-mounted sconces, the large colonial-style table capable of seating twelve during the busy season, the framed black-and-white photographs of Heavenly over the years. It was, in fact, her favorite room in the inn, rivaled only by the parlor, with its full-wall fireplace, floor-to-ceiling bookshelves, and cozy upholstered reading chairs.

"Miss Weatherly, I was hoping you'd come back out." Arnie Streen, the anthropology student who'd taken a room at the inn some two weeks earlier, reached across the table, helping himself to five slices of turkey before Claire's aunt had finished removing all of the platters from her tray. After plunking the meat onto his plate, he exchanged his fork for a spoon and dove into the serving bowl of mashed potatoes as a scrap of his red hair fell forward against his freckled cheek. "I'd like to interview that young woman in your shop tomorrow morning.

Say around nine thirty or so? I've got some questions I need her to answer."

Claire wrapped her hands around the dressing bowl and made her way down one side of the table and then the other, scooping generous helpings onto the other guests' plates before stopping at Arnie's spot. "You mean Esther?"

It was a rhetorical question, of course, since Arnie knew the young Amish woman's name by heart. But like his many other socially inept ways, he seemed to be clueless to the way he rubbed people. Including Claire.

Coughing across the turkey platter, Arnie shifted in his seat, a move Claire had come to recognize as discomfort or embarrassment — awkward emotions the man tended to exhibit in tandem with talk of Esther.

He was an odd man, a self-proclaimed outcast who was fascinated with the Amish.

She supposed it made sense on some level. The drastically different lifestyle of her Amish neighbors probably touched some sort of kindred place in his soul. At least, that's what she and Diane had managed to come away with after sharing a roof with the man for the past fourteen days.

Officially, he was there to observe the Amish culture as part of the thesis he was writing for his master's degree — an education milestone he'd funded by shucking oysters near his Maryland home. The fact that his vast interest in the Amish seemed to stall on Esther the minute he caught his first glimpse of her was apparently beside the point.

"Yeah . . . Esther."

Diane removed the platter of turkey from Arnie's reach and headed back into the kitchen, returning just as quickly with a second, cough-free platter for the rest of her guests. As the robust woman moved her way around the table, she addressed Arnie. "Ruth Miller, the woman who runs Shoo Fly Bake Shoppe, might be a better person for you to talk to, Mr. Streen. Her brother Benjamin is a very respected member of the Amish community despite his relatively young age. Perhaps she can introduce you. I'm quite certain you could learn a lot about the Amish from him."

Then, with a wave of her hand, Claire's aunt dismissed the idea as quickly as she'd said it. "On second thought, with the little problems that keep occurring at the bake shop and Ruth's intense shyness around men, maybe it's best if you find someone else."

Lifting the pitcher of ice water from the

center of the table, Claire topped off everyone's glass. "I take it you heard about the shipment of pie boxes that were stolen from Ruth's store this morning?"

A soft *tsk* emerged from Diane's lips. "I did, indeed. Between that and yesterday's broken milk bottles, the poor thing must be beside herself over all of her bad luck."

"Broken milk bottles?" Arnie asked between bites of turkey.

Claire nodded. "Ruth's brothers deliver fresh milk to her store every morning just before sunrise. But yesterday, all four bottles were smashed when she arrived."

"Sounds like a hate crime to me," Arnie mused as his spoon clattered to the floor. Without so much as a word, the twenty-something plucked the utensil off the ground and dug it into his helping of potatoes, depositing a huge portion into his mouth. If he noticed the remnants that spattered onto his misbuttoned and wrinkled shirt, he showed no indication. "Regardless, Esther will be fine to interview. Besides, I think she kind of likes me."

For the first time since eyeing the evening's menu, Claire was grateful the guests were always served first. If they weren't, she'd likely be wearing her own spoonful of potatoes. She quickly forced her mouth shut, but not before noticing her aunt's eyes rolling. Arnie Streen might be intelligent in some areas, but when it came to the cues of women, he deserved a big, fat F. With a few red circles around the grade for good measure.

Before she could think of a response, Diane dismissed the man's delusion with gentle diplomacy, a skill Claire admired more and more with each passing day. "Esther likes *everyone*."

When Claire and Diane were done serving the meal, a couple from Wichita, Kansas, asked them to join everyone for supper. Upon the echoed sentiment of the newlyweds seated across from the couple, as well as from Arnie, they slipped off their aprons and took a place at the table.

Dinner was a lovely affair, as each guest shared a little about his or her own hometown, interspersed with questions about the Amish. Diane's vast knowledge, gleaned from decades of running the inn, kept everyone enthralled in much the way it had Claire when she first arrived.

Now, however, Claire was beginning to couple Diane's words with her own experiences, thanks to people like Esther and some of her fellow Amish shopkeepers, who were slowly but surely becoming her friends.

Still, Diane knew more. And when she brought out a photo album she'd compiled over the past twenty-plus years, even Claire found herself mesmerized by the pages and pages of pictures her aunt had gathered from various sources — including postcard photographers who tended to stay at the inn while on assignment.

"The tour guide who took us through that Amish village today said they don't keep pictures of themselves around their homes," Gerry Baker said, leaning back in his chair and hooking an arm around his wife, Amanda. The Kansas couple had arrived the day before and were Claire's favorite of the current guests. "The only pictures they have in their homes are on the calendars they seem to have in every room. But even those are just things like bridges and flowers and stuff."

"That's true. They feel as if photographs pay homage to themselves, which is something they don't believe in," Claire explained.

Amanda's brows furrowed. "They don't mind photographers taking their pictures?"

"They don't look at the photographer. Don't keep their own photos around their homes. In fact, most of the pictures you see on postcards and in books were taken without their permission with high-powered zoom lenses. Needless to say, what those in the English world do with them is not their worry." Diane flipped to the next page. "Likewise, most Amish families don't have mirrors in their homes, and if they do, there's only one, and it's generally kept in the kitchen, making it difficult to linger for long. To have it any other way promotes vanity in their eyes."

"That woman could be a fashion model."

Claire glanced at the picture that had claimed Amanda's interest, the beauty depicted impossible to miss. "That's Ruth — the woman who runs the Shoo Fly Bake Shoppe just down the road."

"The photographer who took that shot desperately tried to convince her to abandon the Amish and pursue a career in modeling, but Ruth declined," Diane explained as she readied her page-turning hand. "I wasn't surprised, though. Poor thing is as sweet as they come, which, coupled with her beauty, only makes Nellie Snow all the more hateful."

"Nellie Snow?" Claire moved to the left to escape the flow of Arnie's breath on her ear, the new crop of photos barely registering.

"Hey, that's Esther!"

At the mention of her friend's name, Claire forced her focus onto the picture in front of her before glancing up at her aunt with a different question. "When was this taken?"

Diane leaned forward, a smile playing across her gently lined face. "They look so much alike, don't they? Even I get confused at times."

And then she knew. It wasn't Esther in the picture. It was a young Martha, with her parents and two brothers.

"It's a shame it's been so long since they've seen him. I only pray that changes now that he's back. Maybe they can find a way to forgive."

Her aunt's voice hovered in the air like some distant cloud as Claire studied the face she'd met that afternoon, a face so like one she now called friend.

Arnie paused in the middle of picking his teeth. "Which one didn't come back?"

Confused, Claire looked up at Arnie, then followed the path of his eyes back down to the photo. As she watched, her aunt's finger pointed to the young man standing to Martha's immediate left, his sandy blond hair just visible beneath the rim of his hat.

"That one." Diane pulled her hand from the photograph in front of them and grabbed the day's paper off the hutch. Placing it next to the album, she pointed to the man who had sent Martha and Esther scurrying from Claire's shop that very afternoon. "Who's also the same as *this* one."

Chapter 3

Claire looked up from the novel in her lap and pointed at the rose-colored love seat on the other side of the Victorian lamp. "Aunt Diane, you really need to sit. You've been going a mile a minute since I got back from the shop this afternoon. The guests have been fed and they've all retired upstairs for the night, leaving you with only one thing to do. And that's relax. You've earned it."

"I will relax when it's time for bed." Armed with a dust cloth in one hand and a book of matches in the other, Diane moved from one built-in bookcase to the next, stopping from time to time to straighten a frame or knickknack and light a scented votive. "The Bakers are a lovely couple, aren't they? And the Reynolds? Can't you just see them as they'll look when they come back in twenty-five years to celebrate their anniversary? Why, I've never seen a man look at his new bride with such love and reverence before. It's simply a treat to witness."

Claire turned her head, following her father's oldest sister around the room with her eyes, the soft flickering light creating an almost halo-like effect behind the woman's gray-streaked hair.

Fitting . . .

"Do you ever regret not getting married?" It was a question she'd been tempted to ask often over the past six months yet had resisted until that moment.

The woman paused, a thoughtful expression brewing behind her bifocals. "If I didn't have you, I'd have to say yes. But, since I do, I have been blessed with the chance to know a sense of motherhood without all the red tape. Besides, with the way I tend to run off at the mouth about history and such, I'd have bored some poor fellow into an early grave."

A smile tugged at Claire's lips. "You sell yourself short."

"And you, my dear niece, tend to make me bigger than I am." Diane tucked the dust cloth and matches into her apron pocket and retrieved the day's paper from the rocking chair. "I love my life, Claire. I love cooking, I love gardening, and I love meeting new people every few days or so. Through them, I learn about parts of the country I've yet to visit, and with them, I can share my love for this town and its people."

"And you're very good at what you do." Shifting her novel from her lap to the side table, Claire pulled her feet underneath her body and snuggled deeper into the depths of the upholstered lounge chair. "Do you mind if I ask what happened?"

"Happened?" Diane echoed in confusion.

She pointed to the newspaper tucked beneath her aunt's arm and nodded. "With the detective and his family."

A rush of sadness muted the woman's trademark sparkle, bringing her to sit on the same love seat she'd refused to inhabit just moments earlier. "It's a sad story, really. One I don't see ever changing, even though I wish with all my heart that it could."

"Tell me," she encouraged.

Unfolding the newspaper across her knees, Diane gazed down at the picture below the fold. "Jakob was raised Amish right alongside his sister and his brother. He stayed close to home during his Rumspringa, his experimentation of the non-Amish world extending only to music and a fascination with the local police."

"The local police?" She tugged a throw pillow onto her lap and hugged it to her chest. "How so?"

Diane scooted the paper onto the love seat and pulled her feet from her comfortable-soled shoes, wiggling her stocking-clad toes as she did. "He became friendly with members of the Heavenly Police Department. He'd ask them questions about what they did, listen to their stories, even go for a few ride-alongs when the chief allowed. But, when his year or so was over, he went back to his life and was baptized."

She felt her mouth drop open. "I didn't realize the Amish could be police officers."

"They can't."

"Then how —"

"Sixteen years ago, a member of the Amish community was murdered as part of a hate crime. Jakob wanted a hand in bringing the perpetrator to justice."

Reality dawned as she took in her aunt's words. "He joined the force?"

Diane's capable shoulders rose and fell once beneath her simple powder-blue dress. "He wanted to, but it wasn't allowed. Farming is more than an occupation to the Amish. It's also about their devotion to a commandment from God that says man is to work in harmony with the soil and nature. Police work doesn't fit with that teaching."

Anxious for her aunt to continue, she merely nodded.

"Unfortunately, by the time Jakob made the decision to leave, the suspect had already been found."

"But it was too late for him to go back, wasn't it?" she asked, although she knew the answer all on her own. Leaving the Amish world after baptism was an unforgiveable offense.

"It would have been, if he'd wanted to go back. But he felt that police work was his calling in a way farming never could be." Diane slipped her feet back into her shoes and stood. "He couldn't face the shunning he was certain to encounter, so he enrolled in a police academy in New York and worked there until this past week, when he was hired on as a detective on the Heavenly force."

She considered her aunt's words and compared them to what she witnessed from Martha earlier in the day. "But why come back now? Surely he can't believe things will be different with his family?"

Diane crossed to the bay window that overlooked Lighted Way and the gas-powered lanterns that outlined Heavenly's quaint shopping district. "I suspect his return is more about hope than belief."

Hope.

Claire understood what it meant to steer one's life in the direction of hope. It was what had saved her at a time when simple belief kept her from seeing anything other than what was right in front of her face.

"Maybe he can figure out who's behind the trouble at the bake shop or track down Walter Snow and all that money he owes the Amish," she offered.

"Maybe; maybe not." With one last look out at her beloved town, Diane pulled the thick velvet drapes closed, signaling the end to yet another day. "Either way, Jakob will most certainly have his work cut out for him here."

She looked a question at her aunt.

The woman rushed to explain even as she moved around the room, dusting the last of the knickknacks. "The English may be open to Detective Fisher and his position in this town, but the Amish . . . not so much. Which means that hope that most certainly brought him back here is about to disappear in a cloud of pain."

Claire closed her eyes and leaned her head against the back of the lounge, her thoughts revisiting the moment Martha saw Jakob for the first time in sixteen years. Although she hadn't known what was going on at the time, the disbelief, the shock in Martha's face and voice had been undeniable.

Aunt Diane was right.

By coming back to Heavenly, Jakob Fisher had placed himself in a position to be hurt. Deeply.

She opened her eyes to find Diane staring at her from the foot of the lounge chair. "What?"

"I'm certain he could use a friend or two." Diane sidestepped her way to the side of the chair. "Breakfast will be here before I know it, so I'm going to head up to bed. Would you make sure to blow out all the votives before you turn in for the night?"

She smiled as her aunt's lips came down on her forehead, the warmth and love she felt at that moment bringing a lump to her throat. Swallowing over it, she managed to nod.

"I'm glad you came here, Claire," Diane whispered.

"So am I."

Left alone, Claire was all too aware of the fact that the novel she'd been engrossed in less than thirty minutes earlier no longer held any appeal.

Suddenly, she felt as if she understood this man she'd never met. A man who left the only world he truly knew in order to pursue something that no one in his inner circle would ever understand.

Yet she did.

She'd left her wealthy, high-powered husband for the life of her dreams — a place where she felt important and needed, just as Detective Fisher had left farming behind to protect and serve.

The difference, though, was in where they landed.

She found a family in her aunt and her Amish friends.

He'd pursued his passion but lost his family in the process.

And although she'd had hope on her side when Diane invited her to come and stay after her divorce from Peter, Jakob had none. Not real hope, anyway.

He'd left the Amish after his baptism.

That alone meant his return to Heavenly would go uncelebrated.

Swinging her feet over the edge of the lounge chair, Claire stood, her gaze fixed on the paper Diane left behind. Slowly, she crossed the hand-hooked rug that separated the two pieces of furniture and picked up the *Heavenly Times*. Flipping it around, she stared into the same eyes that inhabited her shop on a near-daily basis, the same eyes that agreed to give her and her shop a chance that very afternoon.

Only these eyes were a little different.

Sure, their shape, their size, their hue were the same. But just as Martha's and Esther's exuded a sense of quiet peace, the pair in front of her held something else — something she hadn't been able to identify until that very moment.

"Diane is right," she whispered. "You're going to need some friends."

CHAPTER 4

Unlike many of its white cinder block counterparts in neighboring towns, the exterior of the Heavenly Police Department was more in keeping with the shops and restaurants along Lighted Way. It featured the same clapboard siding, the same wide front porch, and the same tastefully written sign above the front door.

Yet all of those similarities ended the moment Claire stepped inside the building and became aware of the one thing it *didn't* have.

Everywhere she went along Lighted Way, the Amish were present. Their buggies traveled the street, their people worked in the shops, and their wares were displayed on shelves. Yet there, amid the quiet hustle and bustle of the police department, they were noticeably absent.

At least to the unknowing eye, anyway.

Lifting the blue-and-green-striped gift bag onto the counter, she smiled at the balding dispatcher. "I was wondering if I might be able to have a moment of Detective Fisher's time."

"And you are?"

"Claire Weatherly. My aunt owns —"

"Sleep Heavenly."

Startled, she glanced over her shoulder and into the same hazel eyes she'd seen in duplicate twenty-four hours earlier. Only this pair had a sprinkling of amber flecks that served as the perfect accompaniment to the dimples, which weakened her knees.

She reached out, her hand disappearing inside the non-uniformed man's capable grasp. "Detective Fisher?"

"That's me." His hand lingered around hers a beat longer as he broke eye contact long enough to view her in her entirety. When his visual inspection ended, he continued. "Though any relative of Diane's is welcome to call me Jakob."

Her face warmed under the appreciative scrutiny, making her grab for the comfort of common and distracting ground. "Aunt Diane is a mighty special person, that's for sure."

Jakob nodded. "So what can I do for you" — his gaze dropped to her left hand — "Miss Weatherly?"

"I . . . I wanted to bring you this." She

handed him the gift bag, the gesture-induced shock in his face making her smile. "To welcome you . . ." Her words trailed off as she opted not to refer to his past. If and when he wanted to admit to his previous life in Heavenly, the timing would be up to him.

"Welcome me?" he echoed in a hushed voice.

"To Heavenly."

The play of emotions across the detective's face was unmistakable. So too was the presence of the dispatcher not more than five feet away.

She rushed to lighten the atmosphere. "It wasn't all that long ago that I was the new one in town, myself. And after living in a place like New York City for the past seven years, Heavenly had the added nuance of feeling like another country."

He lowered his bag-holding hand to his side. "You're from New York, too?"

"My aunt talked me into coming about six months ago." With a brush of her fingers, she pushed her hair over her shoulder. "Listening to her was the best thing I could have ever done."

"Oh?"

"It changed my life."

She felt his eyes studying her closely and

was grateful she'd chosen her white trousers and blue-green blouse for work that day. The blouse's color had a way of setting off her eyes.

"How so?"

"Well . . ." She searched her mind for just the right way to describe her life at that moment. "It's made me realize that my passion for simplicity isn't as bizarre as I'd been led to believe, I guess."

"By whom?"

Feeling a familiar lump forming in her throat, she waved his question away. "Let's save that for another day, shall we? Today is a new day."

Hesitation was followed by an encore of dimples. "Which means *what* for Diane Weatherly's niece?"

She met his heart-stopping grin with one of her own. "*Claire* is going to head off to work — a place she's dreamed about for years but only recently found the courage to turn into a reality."

He opened his mouth to speak but closed it as the dispatcher peered over the counter. "Detective Fisher, you've got a call on line three. It's Howard Glick."

"Take his number. Tell him I'll call back —"

"No, it's okay. I really should be getting

to work. Es . . ." She swallowed back the name of Jakob's niece as she glanced down at her watch, the disappointment she felt at the interruption catching her by surprise. "I mean, *my assistant* is probably wondering what happened to me."

Without waiting for a response, she stepped toward the door, the weight of the detective's gaze bringing an odd flutter to her chest. "Please know I'm not terribly proficient at knowing what constitutes a good housewarming gift for a man. So if I'm way off, please accept my apology."

She crossed the street and headed southeast into the late-morning sun, the chirping of the birds and the familiar *clip-clop* of the Amish horse-drawn buggies bringing a smile to her lips. From the moment she'd first laid eyes on Lighted Way, she'd been mesmerized, convinced she'd found her own little Utopia in the middle of Lancaster County, Pennsylvania.

It was the kind of place where she fit. Where her tastes and interests didn't stick out as being hokey or silly. Yet, talking to Jakob Fisher, she'd felt a taste of that old discomfort. Though, if she were honest with herself, it was night and day different from what she experienced with Peter.

Peter made her feel odd.

Jakob made her feel . . . alive.

Raking a hand through her hair, she forced herself to focus on the day ahead, on the candles she hoped to finish, the quilt racks she needed to fill, and the jars of preserves she planned to stack.

Shop by shop she made her way toward Heavenly Treasures — passing Heavenly Scented Brews, Tastes of Heaven(ly), The Toy Factory, and Glick's Tools 'n' More. Each shop, each restaurant paid tribute to the very reason her aunt's bed-and-breakfast was full virtually year-round.

People were fascinated by the Amish.

And they were willing to shell out a sizable amount of money each year to sample their food, their craftsmanship, their way of life.

She was just about in line with Shoo Fly Bake Shoppe when the front door opened and Ruth Miller stepped onto the porch, followed by her twin brother, Eli. Clothed in traditional Amish dress for a young, unmarried woman, Ruth was simply stunning. Her blonde hair, parted severely down the middle and covered with a head cap, set off her wide-set ocean-blue eyes perfectly. Her high cheekbones and perfectly arched brows completed a face more befitting a

47

magazine spread than an Amish bakery.

Yet somehow, despite the beauty that was glaringly obvious to everyone around her, Ruth was oblivious. Maybe even a bit naive. Painfully shy, Ruth tended to prefer staying in the shadow of her headstrong twin.

Claire's gaze shifted to Ruth's left as the pair came to a stop at the edge of the bake shop's front porch. With the exception of the mop of blond hair visible around the bottom of his brimmed black hat, Eli and Ruth couldn't be more different. Where Ruth was quiet, Eli tended to be loud. Where Ruth tended to shrink from anything resembling confrontation, Eli boldly stepped forward, his penchant for angry outbursts landing him in hot water with the Amish more than a few times.

In fact, on any other Amish man, the sight of swollen and splinted fingers would startle, but on Eli it wasn't all that shocking. What wasn't normal, though, was the worry on Ruth's face.

"Ruth? What's wrong?" Claire turned up the walkway to the bake shop and stopped at the base of the steps. "Has there been another incident?"

Ruth nodded yet said nothing.

She looked at Eli and felt the intensity of his anger. "Eli? What happened?"

A flash of red reignited on the young man's face. "Someone is spouting hateful words about my sister. That is what."

"What are you talking about?"

Eli started to speak only to have his words thwarted by Ruth's calming hand on his shoulder. "It is nothing. Really," Ruth whispered.

"It is not *nothing*," Eli spat through clenched teeth. "It is wrong, and it must stop."

She climbed the same three steps that fronted each shop on the street and reached for both Ruth's and Eli's hands. "Tell me. What happened?"

"There was a letter. On my door. It said my baked goods made people sick," Ruth explained as Eli fumed beside them. "I am afraid I have hurt someone."

"You have hurt no one. Someone is trying to hurt you."

Claire's shoulders sagged under the reality of Eli's words. Had the smashed milk bottles or even the stolen pie boxes been the only thing that had happened that week, it was possible it could be chalked up to an accident or mishap of some sort. But to have both *and* a letter . . .

No. Eli was right.

Something was wrong.

She looked toward the door, noting the tape residue that remained. "May I see the note?"

Ruth put words to Eli's head shake. "Benjamin gave it to Mr. Glick."

Benjamin was Ruth and Eli's older brother, a man Claire had yet to meet. His milk runs to the bake shop had him there before Claire arrived. Any deliveries during the day fell to Eli.

"How did Mr. Glick get involved?" she asked as she glanced to her right at the shop that served as a bookend to Shoo Fly Bake Shoppe along with Claire's own Heavenly Treasures.

"He was sweeping the porch when Ruth arrived. He heard her cries." Eli toed the porch floor as his anger intensified still further. "I . . . I was . . . in back when I heard Mr. Glick. I came quickly."

She took in the information, realizing the note must have been behind the call that brought her meeting with Jakob to a close. Releasing Ruth's hand, Claire reached up, tucked an errant strand of blonde hair beneath the young woman's head cap. "It'll be alright, Ruth. Just you wait and see. Detective Fisher seems like a capable man."

Surprise replaced anger on Eli's face momentarily. "You met Jakob?"

"I did." Stepping back, she retraced her way down the stairs. "I better get next door. Give a shout if you need anything, okay?"

"Thank you, Claire."

She looked over her shoulder one last time as she traded Shoo Fly Bake Shoppe's walkway for Heavenly Treasure's, Ruth's sad eyes tugging at her heart.

Ruth Miller was the epitome of goodness. In fact, Eli's twin sister exuded the kind of kindness and generosity that made the world a better place. How anyone could target her with such venom made no sense.

Pushing open the door of her dream come true, Claire willed herself to take comfort in the brightly colored candles that graced the front shelves, the meticulously crafted quilts that covered half of the handcrafted racks, and the sight of her always smiling assistant, Esther.

Only this time, Esther wasn't smiling.

Not by a long shot.

She rushed to the counter. "Esther? What's wrong?"

Bringing her hands to her face, the girl responded, her voice shaky. "Mr. Snow. He was here."

Her mouth gaped. "Walter?"

"I came in from speaking with Eli out back, and he was here." Esther pointed at

51

the very spot where Claire stood. "He was angry."

"Angry? At who? You?"

"And you."

"M-me?" she stammered. "But why? I've never even met the man."

"He spoke of things he left behind. In the stockroom. He grabbed my wrist and yelled for me to tell him the truth. But I could not. I did not know what he was saying." Esther lifted her arm for Claire to see, but any temporary marks had since subsided.

She felt her stomach churn. "Did he hurt you in any other way?"

"He . . . he . . . No. He did not."

"Did you call for help?"

Esther's gaze followed hers to the telephone, the reality of the girl's world answering Claire's question better than words ever could.

Instead, she changed tactics. "What did you do?"

Defeated, Esther sunk onto the folding chair behind the counter. "I did nothing. When I could not help him, he ran out the back way. I waited until ten o'clock to be sure he would not return."

"And then?" she urged, taking in the grandfather clock on the east wall, noting it was nearly ready to chime eleven times.

"I went out the front door to find Eli. He was pacing the bake shop's front porch with his brother, Benjamin. He was very angry. I did not interrupt." The girl dropped her head into her trembling hands. "I came back inside and waited for you. But then —"

"You've been alone in here like this for over an hour?" Claire ran around the counter and grabbed the phone off its cradle. "I'll call Detective Fisher. Have him come and speak to you —"

Esther's gasp sent a chill down her spine.

"What? What's wrong?"

"You can not call the detective. Mamm would be angry."

She stared at her friend. "But Esther, we have to call him. We have to tell him Walter was here. That he scared you."

"Will I need to speak?"

"Of course. He'll want to ask you questions."

"I can not speak to the detective." Esther shook her head fiercely, her voice emerging in a raspy, broken sound. "Please. I must talk to Mamm first. I will do so tonight."

CHAPTER 5

She let herself in through the back door of the inn, her shoulders heavy with worry and regret. All afternoon she'd tried to get Esther to change her mind, to let Claire place the call to Detective Fisher, but to no avail.

The girl had been adamant she speak with her mother and, eventually, Claire resigned herself to the notion of waiting. It was the only way.

Hanging her keys next to the washer, she paused in the middle of the mudroom, grateful for the answering sound of silence. Dinner was still a good hour away, and most of the guests were probably still out and about, enjoying the Amish countryside.

If she moved fast enough, she could finish the candles she'd put into molds before heading out that morning. If all went as she hoped, the colors and scents would sell well in the shop. Particularly the ones that mimicked the aroma of baked goods.

Turning left, she entered the inn's kitchen and headed straight for the table beneath the picture window. There, she found the three dozen votive molds she'd painstakingly filled nine hours earlier, the perfect shape and attractive colors enveloping her in a feeling of satisfaction. The candle-making process, like most things in life, had come with a learning curve. Her first few times at bat had earned her wax burns, off-centered wicks, and the oddest of colors on the rare candle that actually made it through the process unscathed.

She slid onto the closest chair and began to work, peeling the molds back from each candle. Slowly, candle by candle, she made her way through the molds, the fruits of her labor paying off with her best batch to date.

"Whatcha doing?"

Claire spun around. "Oh. Mr. Streen. You scared me."

The freckled redhead shrugged, then reached into the fruit bowl on the counter. "Just looking for something to eat. This seven o'clock dinner hour is rather ridiculous."

She searched for her least defensive-sounding voice and hoped her facial expression didn't give her true feelings away. "That's why my aunt includes the dinner hour in the inn's brochures. So prospective guests who prefer an earlier meal can find accommodations better suited to their needs."

"Whatever." One by one, Arnie pulled each piece of fruit from the bowl, turning it over and over in his faintly scarred hands before finally settling on the first one he'd touched. He bit into the apple, ignoring the juice that dribbled down his chin. "What's with the candles?"

Shaking her head, she willed herself to focus on the question rather than the urge to go at him with a napkin and a bottle of disinfectant. "Uh . . . They're for the shop. They're one of the few things that I make in my inventory."

Arnie paused midbite. "Speaking of inventory, why do you price those blankets so darn high?"

"You mean the quilts?" She felt the rise to her left brow. "Those are Amish made. It is standard to charge double the hours spent making it."

He snorted. "You're telling me those things take three hundred hours to make?"

"Have you seen the detail, Mr. Streen?"

"I have." His bite echoed off the walls of the kitchen.

She folded her arms and met his challenging gaze. "Then you must know they deserve every penny of that money."

A second snort. "For something that's flawed? Give me a break."

"Mr. Streen, if you are going to write your thesis on the Amish, you must know that the notion of the Amish intentionally making a mistake in their quilts as a nod to God's perfection is a myth. Other cultures might do that, but not the Amish. The price tag simply reflects the quality work and attention to detail they put into their quilts. And that's it." She heard the rise to her voice, knew it was something she should try to rein in, but she couldn't.

Wiping the back of his shirt sleeve across his chin, Arnie flashed a smile in her direction. "Gotcha."

She stared at the man, all anger temporarily suspended in favor of confusion. "Excuse me?"

He tossed the core toward the trash container at the base of the counter and missed. "I was just checking to see how much you knew about the Amish goods you sold, that's all." Then, turning on his bare feet, he headed toward the main part of the house only to stop just before he reached the doorway. "If I were you, I'd talk to that Amish guy from the bake shop. His constant mooning over Esther is making her uncomfortable."

"Amish guy — you mean, Eli?"

He waved away the name. "Yeah. How can she do her job if he's continually bothering her?"

She cracked her first smile in the man's presence. "Trust me, Mr. Streen. Eli doesn't bother Esther." Rising to her feet, she plucked a napkin from the holder and crossed to the abandoned apple core. With a pointed look in Arnie's direction, she picked it up and tossed it into the trash.

The man's jaw tightened with visible discomfort.

Point made, she switched topics, her mouth putting words to a question that appeared out of nowhere. "Hey. Did you happen to notice anything funny when you stopped to interview Esther this morning?"

"We didn't get a chance to talk."

"Oh. I thought —"

"Claire? Claire, are you here?" Diane breezed into the room in a soft pink aproned dress, her smile remaining steady despite nearly being knocked to the floor as Arnie headed back toward his thesis. "Oh good, there you are. You have a visitor."

"*I* have a visitor?" she asked.

The woman beamed and whispered conspiratorially. "He's really grown into a handsome man."

And then she knew.

Or, rather, the contingent of long-dormant butterflies in her stomach knew.

She stepped to the side of the sink and peered into the mirror, her fingers gliding their way through her growing hair only to stop as they reached the ends. "I wonder if he's here because Esther and Martha went to Jakob on their own."

"There are no circumstances under which Martha would ever seek out her brother, nor allow Esther to do so, either." A momentary hint of sadness skittered across Diane's face only to disappear just as quickly. "But that isn't for you to worry about, dear. Jakob is here to see you and he seems quite anxious to do so." Grabbing hold of Claire's upper arm, the woman tugged, then pushed her niece toward the front room. "Off with you."

Slowly but surely she made her way through the parlor and into the entryway, an odd mixture of apprehension and anticipation brewing in her chest as she closed in on the man carefully studying her aunt's framed pictures.

He turned at the sound of her footsteps. "Claire."

"Detective Fisher."

He closed the gap she left between them and encased her right hand between both of his. "Jakob, please."

She tried to ignore the tingle that shot up her arm, tried to focus on something else. Something mundane. But it was difficult. "What can I do for you, Jakob?"

With a trace of reluctance, he released her hand, his dimpled smile taking over in the warmth department. "I've come to right a misconception."

"Oh?"

"You're actually quite good at picking a housewarming gift for a man."

She felt her mouth gape ever so slightly and worked to keep it shut.

He glanced down at the ground as a twinge of crimson rose in his cheeks. "Well, at least for this man." Two beats later, he regained eye contact. "The candles and the framed photograph of Lighted Way in the snow couldn't have been more perfect."

She searched his face for any indication he was being less than sincere but found none.

"I . . . I'm glad."

"They will make an otherwise plain home feel a bit less plain." Gesturing toward the parlor, he studied her closely. "Would it be okay if I sat for a moment?"

Startled, she jumped back, a burst of embarrassment making her own face warm. "I'm so sorry. I don't know where my manners are."

His smile spread to his eyes. "Don't worry, I won't tell your aunt."

She had to laugh. "Thanks for that."

He pointed her toward the love seat, then sat a few inches away. "Tell me about the gift."

If she didn't know any better, she'd think she was dreaming the kind of dream she used to have as a little girl. Only instead of some castle in the middle of the woods, she was sitting in the parlor of her aunt's bed-and-breakfast. Peter had never given any of her gifts more than a head nod or a sniff.

Shaking her thoughts free of her ex-husband, she willed herself to focus on the here and now. "I made those particular candles over the weekend, and the picture is one I took the day I arrived in Heavenly."

"You're very talented."

She balked at the label. "Oh no. Any talent I have pales in comparison to your —"

The peel of an unfamiliar jingle cut her off, mercifully thwarting her from a conversational path she didn't mean to take. Mumbling an apology, he pulled a cell phone from his back pocket and checked the display.

He made a slight face and then yanked open the phone. "Fisher here."

She pushed off the couch and wandered around the room, her desire to give him privacy tempered only by the need to offer an apology of her own. Had he known what she was going to say? That she was going to speak of his sister's talent? His niece's?

"Where?"

The abruptness of his words caught her by surprise.

"When?"

She wasn't delusional enough to believe she knew Jakob Fisher beyond their brief encounter at the station that morning and the five or so minutes they'd had so far that evening, but she also wasn't blind. The calm, friendly man she'd seen seconds earlier was gone, replaced by someone who not only seemed tense but maybe even a bit angry.

"You sure it's Snow?"

A feeling akin to ice water splashed across her face as she abandoned all attempts at privacy in favor of out-and-out eavesdropping.

"I'll be there in five." Snapping the phone closed inside his palm, Jakob jumped to his feet, his amber-flecked eyes trained on her face. "Claire, I'm sorry. I hate to run out like this but I've got to go."

She crossed to him, stopping his forward progress with a hand on his arm. "He came back again?"

Regret turned to confusion. "Who?"

She pulled her hand back, unsure of what to say without breaking her promise to Esther.

"Who?" he repeated.

"W-Walter." She heard the stammer in her voice. "Walter Snow."

"Then yeah, you could say he came back."

Bringing her hands to her mouth and looking at him over the tops of her fingertips, she sent up a mental prayer for Esther's safety. "What happened?"

He trotted toward the door, stopping with his hand firmly wrapped around the knob. "It looks as if someone has settled the score with him once and for all."

CHAPTER 6

She pushed the hair from her eyes to afford a better view of the bright-yellow tape pulled taut between the buildings.

Still, it made no sense.

Things like murder happened in big cities with lots of people, not in quiet places like Heavenly, Pennsylvania.

And if by chance they did happen, they most definitely didn't happen behind her shop.

Claire swallowed against the denial that continued to rise in her throat, its presence futile against the billowing crime-scene tape strung across the narrow alley separating Heavenly Treasures from Shoo Fly Bake Shoppe. A crime had, indeed, happened. And judging by the chalk outline on the other side of the tape, it had occurred mere strides from her back door.

Pulling her hand from her hair, she let the wind hamper her vision long enough to find a calming breath. It didn't take a genius to put a name with the outline. Jakob had essentially handed it to her the night before as he hurried from the parlor.

Yet, somehow, despite a meaning that was suddenly crystal clear, she'd actually thought Walter Snow had been on the other end of someone's fist rather than a murderous rampage.

And she knew why.

Heavenly had become her safe harbor — a place where all the heartache of her divorce and the constant feeling of social inadequacy had disappeared, a sense of hope and belonging rising from its ashes. It had been a battle well fought, and she didn't want someone else — dead or otherwise — to come along and mess it up.

Not now.

"It is shocking."

Startled, Claire spun around, the unfamiliar voice accompanying a pair of oddly familiar and deeply penetrating blue eyes beneath the brim of a black hat. The man's strong but callused hands rose into the air. "I am sorry. I did not mean to frighten you."

Before she could speak, Eli Miller appeared on the porch to her left, tipping his own black hat a hairbreadth. "Good day, Miss Weatherly."

She pulled her gaze from the strikingly handsome man in front of her and fixed it, instead, on the object of Esther's never-ending daydreams. "Eli. How's that hand of yours today?"

He lifted his splinted fingers into the air and shrugged. "Soon it will be fine." Looking past her, Eli turned his focus to the stranger. "I have filled the case with Ruth's desserts."

Like a lock yielding to a key, she looked back at the well-built man and inventoried the clean-shaven skin, the erect posture, the hint of dark-brown hair that escaped around the brim of his hat, the masculine version of Ruth's high cheekbones . . .

And just like that, she knew.

"Benjamin Miller?" She thrust her hand in the man's direction and felt the unexpected catch in her throat at the answered warmth and the tingle it sent down her arm.

"I did not mean to scare you, Miss Weatherly."

She rushed to ease the worry etched in his brow. "You didn't, really. It was more a case of me being so wrapped up in" — with a reluctance she vowed to address with herself later, she removed her hand from his and waved it toward the tape that sagged and snapped in the breeze — *"that."*

Her breath caught as his eyes left hers in favor of the chalk outline. "I feel the same way."

"I say, good riddance to the man."

A flash of something resembling disappointment skittered across Benjamin's face. "You shan't talk like that, Eli. A man is dead."

"Walter Snow was no man," Eli hissed. "He was a crook."

"Hush, brother!" Benjamin's words, clipped yet firm, brought a flush to the younger man's face. "That distinction is to be made by no man."

Eli smacked his good hand against the porch railing, then stormed into his sister's bakery, slamming the door in his wake.

"I apologize for my brother's rudeness. He has much to learn and a broken hand to prove it." Benjamin glanced from Claire to the taped-off crime scene and back again. "Did you know Mr. Snow?"

She drew in a breath and let it work its way past her lips once again. "Only what I've heard from others."

"What have they told you?"

"That he stole money from your community." It was a simple answer but true nonetheless. "Eli's anger is understandable."

"It is anger he must learn to keep inside."

She shrugged. "He's human, I guess."

"He is Amish," Benjamin corrected, not unkindly.

She considered his words and offered the only response she could. "I've only been here a few months, but I know this much. Your younger brother is kind. I glimpse him out the window of my shop often throughout the day, and when I do, he is always helping your sister with various tasks. Sometimes he even stops in to see if I need anything. Though I suspect that's as much about Esther as anything else."

A knowing smile crackled behind his blue eyes, making her catch her breath. "Ahhh, yes. Esther. Her name claims my brother's tongue often."

She forced her gaze from his eyes and said the only thing she could think of at that moment. "W-would you like to see my shop?"

He nodded. "I would like that."

Inhaling deeply, she turned and followed the sidewalk the remaining ten feet to the front porch of Heavenly Treasures, the sight of the white clapboard siding and newly hung shingled sign bringing an instant smile to her lips. It was as if the cares of the world stopped at the doorstep, chased from their foothold by the promise of dreams and their power to win in the end. "While I make the candles and a few other odds and ends, the majority of items I sell here are Amish made. Or, to be more specific, Esther-made."

Benjamin reached around her, pushing the door open and allowing her to enter first. "Martha has taught her daughter well," he said above the jingling bells.

Grateful for the common ground that was the Fisher family — or, at least the female arm of the Fisher family — she forged ahead. "She is dedicated and conscientious and everything a shopkeeper could want in an employee." She set her handbag on the counter and looked around. "Speaking of Esther, she should be here by now."

Esther hurried into the room and stopped, her scared eyes widening still further at the sight of Benjamin Miller bent at the waist and studying one of her quilts. With quick fingers, the young girl tied the strings of her white head cap and neatened the apron of her simple dress. "I . . . I am sorry I did not hear you come in."

"Is everything okay?" Claire asked.

Benjamin straightened and turned to face them both.

Esther swallowed. "Did you not hear about Mr. Snow?"

"I heard, or, rather, *saw*."

Nodding, Esther continued, her momentary apprehension regarding Benjamin's presence dissipating in rapid fashion. "How could this happen? And so close to the store?"

Claire crossed the room and rested a calming hand on the young girl's arm. "That's what the police will determine. But everything will be fine, I'm sure —"

The front door of the shop opened, its telltale door-mounted bell announcing the presence of a shopper. Pulling her hand from Esther's arm, Claire turned, her usual customer greeting dying on her lips at the sight of Jakob Fisher in what was obviously an official capacity, judging by the gun on his hip.

"Claire?" The detective's smile slipped from his mouth as his gaze traveled across her head and narrowed in on Benjamin before coming to rest on Esther. He reached out, grabbed hold of a nearby shelf for support. "Martha?"

Esther's gasp brought Benjamin to her side, the Amish man's lean yet muscular stature creating a buffer of protection between Jakob and the niece he'd never met.

"This is not Martha," Benjamin said in a voice suddenly devoid of all warmth.

"But it looks just like her," Jakob whispered.

"It is not."

Anxious to wipe the pain from the detective's eyes, she rushed to fill in the gap Benjamin and Esther left open. "This is Esther . . . Martha's daughter."

"Martha's daughter," he echoed. "My . . . my niece."

"Martha's daughter," Benjamin corrected.

Jakob pulled his hand from the shelf and fisted it at his side. "Which makes her my niece, doesn't it?"

Feeling the tension magnifying tenfold, Claire stepped forward, positioning herself between the detective and his past. "I imagine you're here about what happened . . ."

When he didn't respond, she tried again. "The crime scene out back has to do with Walter Snow, doesn't it?"

It was as if she'd thrown a bucket of ice water over his head, startling him from a long-ago path of regret and anguish and setting him on one he could still master. "That's right. But first I have to ask what you're doing here."

"This is my shop."

"*Your* shop . . ." His words gave way momentarily to a knowing smile. "You mean the place you dreamed about for years but only recently found the courage to grab hold of?"

She felt the pang in her chest at his ability to hear and remember — almost verbatim — their conversation at the police station. What guy did that?

Not Peter . . .

With a quick shake of her head, she willed herself to focus on the man standing in front of her rather than the one clouding her past. She found her smile. "Welcome to Heavenly Treasures."

He looked past her to Benjamin and Esther. "Thank you."

"So what happened?"

Pulling his gaze from his former life, he fixed it, instead, on Claire. "Last night, around six o'clock, this building's former shopkeeper was found dead out back, not more than a few feet from the alleyway between here and the bake shop. He was a victim of foul play."

She brought her hands to her mouth and looked at the detective across her fingertips. "Who? How?"

"The *how* is easy. He was strangled. But we're still actively working on the *who* behind the crime. And that's why I'm here, Claire."

It was her turn to grab for a shelf, her turn to wish Benjamin's strong form would move in to protect her . . .

Benjamin did not disappoint. "Miss Weatherly did not kill Mr. Snow."

Jakob's hand stilled, midflip of his notebook, irritation marring his otherwise-attractive features. "Did I say she did?"

"You are here to question her, no?"

"I'm here to ask her questions. There's a difference, Benjamin."

"I see no difference."

"You never do." Jakob fixed his gaze back on Claire. "The estimated time of death has Mr. Snow's murder within an hour of his body being found."

"Okay . . ."

"I assume your shop closes at five like the rest of the shops on Lighted Way?"

She nodded.

"Well, since you were at Diane's about that time, can you tell me who handled the closing of this place?"

"Esther did."

Jakob peered around Claire. "Then I will need to speak with Esther."

An audible gasp emerged from Esther's mouth. "I can not. Mamm would not allow it."

"I'd be speaking to you as a police officer,

not as your . . . uncle." Jakob raked his free hand through his hair.

Esther stepped closer to Benjamin, worry and fear evident in every nuance of her young face. "Mamm will never forgive me, Benjamin."

"Your mom can be with you," Jakob suggested softly.

"No!" Esther grabbed hold of Benjamin's arm. "I can not do that to Mamm."

Claire rested a hand on Jakob's arm, his tension rising up beneath her fingers as she addressed her young friend. "Esther, would it help if I stayed with you?"

Esther looked from Claire to Benjamin and back to Claire before finally settling on Jakob. "I would like Claire to be with me."

Jakob offered an encouraging smile. "Of course. I don't need to take you to the police station, Esther. I just have a few basic questions that I can ask you right here."

"Basic?" Esther echoed.

"Like this one," Jakob said as he flipped to a clean page in his notebook. "Did you notice anything unusual in the alleyway when you were closing up?"

Esther considered the question. "I did not. I took the trash to the outdoor bin and saw . . ."

Jakob looked up as Esther quit talking.

"What did you see?"

Knowing the answer, Claire encouraged Esther to continue. "Tell him, Esther. It's okay."

Esther peeked at Benjamin through long lashes. "I . . . I saw Eli."

A slight smile tugged Jakob's lips upward. "Benjamin's brother?"

"Yes," Esther whispered.

"How is he?"

"Very well, thank you."

Claire grinned at Esther's sweet reply.

"Did the two of you talk?"

"Talk?" Esther repeated.

"Yes. Did you have a conversation?"

"We did."

"May I ask what you talked about?" Jakob asked.

"He asked about my day. And I told him." Claire stood up straight as a cloud passed across Esther's face. "He . . . He got very —"

Bells jingled over the door once again, preventing Esther from finishing a sentence Claire wasn't sure she should finish. Grateful for the momentary reprieve, she turned toward the fiftysomething woman standing in the doorway.

"Good morning. Welcome to Heavenly Treasures."

Pushing past Claire, the overly made-up woman planted herself between Jakob and Esther, eyes blazing. "Detective Fisher?"

"Yes? And you are?"

"Mrs. Snow. Mrs. Nellie Snow." Bypassing Jakob's hand, the woman pointed at Benjamin. "I want you to arrest that man and his brother, Eli."

Benjamin stumbled backward, shocked. "Why? What did I do?"

"You and that brother of yours killed my husband. You killed my Walter!"

CHAPTER 7

In Claire's experience, a person was hard-pressed to know much about another human being inside twenty-four hours. It simply wasn't enough time to learn the kinds of things that mattered. Those things came with time. Sometimes painfully so.

Jakob Fisher, however, broke that mold.

In fact, the list of things she'd discerned about the detective since dropping off his welcome-to-Heavenly gift at the station the day before was growing. Quickly.

There were the basics, of course — the sandy blond hair, the amber-flecked hazel eyes, the strong arms, the tall form. But there was also the deeper stuff, the kinds of things that Peter had failed to display after five years, let alone one day.

Yet of all the things she'd seen crossing paths with Jakob, the scene unfolding in front of her eyes was by far the most impressive. Sure, his reaction to her gift had been refreshing. So, too, was the way he listened and remembered things she said. But the clarity of thought and bent toward kindness he showed during a high-stress moment said the most. The fact that the same attributes appeared to have been noticed by Benjamin Miller and Esther King, of all people, only served to strengthen his character.

Claire glanced around Esther's chair and studied the woman who had blown into Heavenly Treasures with nothing more than wild accusations and an ax to grind. Nellie Snow was the proverbial wounded soul. Her husband of twenty years had skipped town on her a month earlier amid a hailstorm of finger-pointing from the Amish community. But rather than consider the notion that her precious Walter had stolen thousands and thousands of dollars from these same people, Nellie placed the blame on them.

Walter hadn't stolen their money and run, she claimed.

No, the Amish had concocted an elaborate plan to drive an honest businessman from town for some other nefarious reason. What that reason was, Nellie claimed, was Jakob's job to determine. But when it came to her husband's murder, she had the suspects all picked out.

"Now tell me again why you believe Benjamin and Eli were behind your husband's murder, Mrs. Snow?" Jakob asked, pausing to rake his hand through his hair before listening to a tirade that simply didn't hold water when it came to the Amish.

Nellie took a slow, deliberate inhale, her broad shoulders rising and falling as she did. Then, with pointed finger, she gestured at a wide-eyed yet silent Benjamin Miller. "That man there, he was the one who came into Walter's shop and accused him of stealing money. Why, he said my husband sold their handmade furniture and chests and pocketed all the money for himself."

"That is because he did," Benjamin said, his voice wary yet firm.

Nellie's chin jutted into the air. "If he had, he would have spent it on me. On clothes and fine restaurants, love letters and trips."

"There were letters but not for her," Esther whispered above the soft clatter of her own teeth.

Claire's hand stilled on the young woman's shoulder. "What was that, Esther?"

Esther's eyes widened as the clattering stopped, the rhythmic sound quickly replaced by an insistent shushing meant only for Claire's ears. But the girl was unsuccessful.

"Don't you shush me, Esther King. This

man" — Nellie again pointed at Benjamin — "may have made the original accusation, but his brother — the boy you moon after morning, noon, and night — is the one who hated my Walter enough to kill him."

Benjamin stood erect. "Amish do not kill."

"Do they drink, Mr. Miller?" Nellie spat.

"No."

Nellie's eyes narrowed. "Oh no?"

"No."

"Do they fight?"

"No."

Jakob raised his hands in the air. "What are you getting at, Mrs. Snow?"

"This man says his brother would not kill because he is Amish. Yet he also says that same boy would not drink or fight because he is Amish."

"You've lost me." Jakob looked from Nellie to Benjamin and back again, the confusion in his face surely a mirror of Claire's.

Nellie walked to the center of the store and spun around, her face a study in righteous indignation. "If an Amish man would drink and fight, why wouldn't he kill?"

Jakob pinned Benjamin with a stare. "What is she talking about, Benjamin?"

The Amish man's shoulders hitched upward. "I do not know."

Raising her finger once again, Nellie

pointed in Claire's direction. "She does."

Claire drew back. "Excuse me?"

"Not you, *her.*"

All eyes turned on Esther, prompting the clattering to start all over again.

"Esther?" Claire whispered. "Is there something you need to tell us?"

One by one, tears streaked their way down the young woman's makeup-free face, twisting Claire's heart in the process.

Claire sent a hopeless glance in Jakob's direction and prayed he would understand its meaning.

He did.

"Mrs. Snow, I've heard what you have to say and will want to speak with you in greater detail at the station. But for now, I must ask you to leave as I conduct my investigation."

Rage reduced Nellie's eyes to mere slits. "I've heard about your past, Detective. And I will tell you right now that I will go to every ethics board I can find if this becomes an Amish-protecting-Amish case."

For a moment, Jakob was silent, the only sound in the room his breath as he worked to steady it. "I am neither Amish nor English, Mrs. Snow. What I am is a detective. And I will not rest until the truth surrounding your husband's death has been found.

No matter where that leads."

The tears became sobs as Esther dug her elbows into her lap and dropped her head into her hands, her whispered confession audible to no one but Claire. "I promised Eli I would not tell."

Claire bit back the urge to offer any sort of condolence or encouragement for fear it would be overheard. Instead, she opted to simply keep patting the young woman's shoulder until Nellie Snow and her over-dressed, overbearing self had disappeared down the steps of Heavenly Treasures, leaving a veritable firestorm in her wake.

"What was she talking about?" Jakob demanded.

Esther looked up from her hands yet said nothing, her eyes wide with fear.

Benjamin stepped forward. "Miss Weatherly, if you would allow Esther a break at this time, I will see that she returns when we are done speaking."

"Esther is not going anywhere," Jakob interjected. "Not until I've asked her a few questions."

Benjamin's blue eyes darkened. "She can not speak with you!"

Jakob worked to contain his matching anger. "I am not asking as her uncle. I am asking as the detective who is trying to get to the bottom of a murder. One that has the victim's wife accusing both you and your brother."

Esther's head dropped forward once again, a barely audible moan escaping her plump lips.

"Would it be okay if I asked the questions?" Claire posed.

Silence filled the room as both Benjamin and Jakob considered her offer.

"I will allow that."

"Allow that?" Jakob hissed at Benjamin. "*Allow* that? What are you, Esther's father?"

"In his absence, I will act as so," Benjamin replied.

Claire held up her hands. "Please. This isn't getting us the answers we need." Turning her back to both men, she squatted down beside Esther, covering the young woman's hands with her own and gently guiding them away from her worried face. "Esther? What was Mrs. Snow talking about just now?"

Esther's hands began to tremble. "I promised Eli I would not tell."

"You may hurt him more if you don't tell," Jakob said, not unkindly.

Claire continued. "Did Eli ever get into a fight?"

Esther peered at Benjamin from the corner

of her eye.

"Esther?" Claire prodded.

"He did," Esther whispered. "While on Rumspringa."

Benjamin sucked in a breath. "How did I not know this?"

"Maybe because he feared being treated like a pariah by his friends and family."

Claire glanced over her shoulder at Jakob, saw the hurt that matched his voice.

"Mr. Gussman got him from jail," Esther said.

Jakob drew back. "Eli was arrested?"

"That is not so!" Benjamin yelled.

Esther clamped her lips together and nodded.

"When did this happen?" Jakob asked, jotting something down in his notebook.

"Six months ago."

Jakob took two steps and then squatted on the ground beside Claire, his full attention on no one but his niece. "Do you know where this happened?"

Again, Esther nodded. "I do. But if I tell, Eli will not forgive me."

Jakob reached out and patted Esther's knee. "Then you don't have to tell."

"I . . . I don't?"

Jakob shook his head. "I can find out the particulars on my own."

Esther's shoulders dipped in momentary relief only to tense again just as quickly. "Eli would not kill."

For a moment, Jakob said nothing. Then, slowly, his awkward pat turned into a gentle squeeze. "I will keep that in mind."

Claire rocked back on her heels, soaking in the brief but tender moment between two family members who had been robbed of time together by no real fault of their own.

"Is that all?" Benjamin asked woodenly.

"For now." Jakob flipped his notebook shut and smiled at Esther. "If I have more questions, I'll stop out at the farm."

Esther's gasp was drowned out by the sound of her ankle boots as she jumped from the chair. "You can not come there!"

Claire reached out and tried her best to calm the girl, but it was no use.

"Mamm will not allow it!"

Visibly upset, Jakob rose to his feet, sliding a hand down his face as he did. "This is an investigation, Esther. A *murder* investigation. I'm going to have to question members of the Amish community. People like you, and Eli, and" — his gaze met Benjamin's — "Benjamin's sister, Ruth."

"My sister is too upset to talk."

Jakob met Benjamin's worry-filled eyes. "I will have to talk to her, Benjamin. The body was found between Claire's shop and hers."

"My sister is no killer."

"I didn't say she was. But she may know something that can help me find who is."

A sigh of resignation filtered its way between Benjamin's lips. "I do not know, Jakob."

Claire crossed the room to stand beside Esther. "We'll figure it out. One way or the other." She reached out and tucked a stray lock of hair back under Esther's head cap. "In the meantime, if it's okay with you, Detective, I'd like to let Esther take the rest of the day off. She's been through quite a lot."

After a pause, Jakob surprised her with a nod. "Okay. But there will be more questions."

Esther opened her mouth to protest but closed it as Claire took charge. "Esther will be back at work tomorrow. If you have any further questions, you can find us here."

Esther dropped her normally quiet voice to a whisper. *"Us?"*

"Us," Claire confirmed.

Benjamin closed the gap between his spot by the wall and Esther, grabbing hold of her arm and guiding her toward the front door. "I will see that Esther gets home."

She felt Jakob stiffen as he moved in

beside her, but his thoughts, his feelings, were nothing more than a guess.

CHAPTER 8

By the time Claire walked through the back door of Sleep Heavenly, she was nearly spent, the emotion-filled day taking more of a toll than she'd realized until that moment. Suddenly, the thought of chopping vegetables and filling salad bowls alongside Aunt Diane held none of its normal appeal. Neither did the notion of making chitchat with the guests before and after dinner.

It wasn't that she didn't love helping, because she did. And Lord knew she'd met some amazing people around her aunt's dining table. But just this once she wanted nothing more than to escape to the parlor with a glass of wine and the parade of thoughts that had nagged at her all afternoon, making it difficult to concentrate on anything but the mess surrounding Walter Snow's death.

Tossing her purse onto the catchall table just inside the doorway, Claire took a moment to soak up the sights and smells of the haven she'd come to treasure. Diane's kitchen was everything a person dreamed of when it came to such a room. The vast counter space and state-of-the-art appliances were a cook's dream, yet somehow her aunt had managed to create the kind of homey feel that conjured up images of long talks across a plate of homemade chocolate chip cookies.

And they'd surely had their share of those since she'd made her escape from the city in favor of a new life.

She lifted her nose into the air and sniffed, the hearty smell of her aunt's beef stew wafting out from the lid of an enormous Crock-Pot situated on a counter beside the stove.

"Mmmm . . ."

"I thought I heard you come in, dear." Diane breezed into the room by way of the swinging door that separated the dining room from the kitchen, where she was no doubt in the throes of preparing the table for the guests' evening meal. "How was your day?"

"Exhausting, confusing, heartbreaking — take your pick." Flopping onto one of two breakfast bar stools, she laid her head on the cool countertop.

89

Diane stopped midstep, worry creasing her brow. "What happened?"

She blinked once, twice. "You haven't heard?"

"Heard what?"

"You always know everything that goes on in this town," she mused in shock.

"The Bakers are heading home to Kansas in the morning, and they insisted I accompany them for lunch in Breeze Point." Diane's hands found her hips. "What happened?"

She lifted her head, processing the information as she did. Breeze Point was a small farming community, three towns over, known for its old-fashioned cooking and delightful fruit and vegetable stands. It was no wonder Diane had left her precious Heavenly for a few hours . . .

"They've found Walter Snow."

"They did? Oh, that's wonderful news." Diane reached over, plucked an apple from the fruit bowl, and thrust it in Claire's direction. "Eat this. You look a bit peaked."

She took the apple from her aunt's outstretched hand and simply stared at it, her appetite virtually nonexistent despite having skipped lunch.

Her aunt prattled on. "It's about time he developed a conscience and returned all that money he stole from the Amish."

"He won't be returning anything to anyone."

Diane stared at her. "Why on earth not?"

"Because he's dead."

Diane gasped. "Dead?"

Setting the apple down in front of her, she nodded.

"Where did they find him?"

Claire inhaled slowly, searched for the best way to break the news. Unfortunately, her lack of energy made locating any tact virtually impossible. "Behind my shop. Near the alley between Shoo Fly and Heavenly Treasures."

The woman grabbed hold of the closest counter. "But how? He wasn't more than, what? Forty-five? Maybe fifty?"

"Murder is a bit less age discerning than regular death." The second the words were out, she wished she could recall them. Just because her day had been the stuff of nightmares didn't mean she had to take it out on her aunt.

"Did you say *murder*?"

She pushed her stool back from the counter and swiveled her legs to the side. "I'm sorry, Aunt Diane, I shouldn't have told you like —"

"That can't be," Diane balked. "This is

Heavenly. We haven't had a murder here in sixteen years."

Oh how she wished that were true.

For her aunt.

For Esther.

For Eli.

For Ruth . . .

Reaching into the pocket of her skirt, she pulled out the same heart-shaped piece of construction paper she'd been staring at since shortly after Jakob left the shop. She looked down at the now-familiar words and felt the telltale churn to her stomach at their meaning.

"We do now," she whispered.

In an instant, her aunt was by her side, holding her close. "Why didn't you call? I'd have come right away."

She blinked against the tears that threatened to escape the corners of her eyes. "Everything got crazy. Fast. And then, when things finally settled down enough that I was able to breathe again, I found this . . ."

Pulling back from her aunt's warm embrace, Claire opened her hand to reveal the carefully cut piece of paper that had haunted her thoughts for the past few hours.

"What is this?" Diane took the note and squinted at the masculine writing it featured. "What does it say?"

Claire leaned over and handed a pair of reading glasses to her aunt. "I need you to read it yourself."

Diane's confusion disappeared behind ten-dollar glasses as Claire silently read along.

My Sweet Amish Love,
Roses are red, violets are blue, you need me, and I need you.

All my love,
W.

"Where did you find this?" Diane asked when she was done, the bewilderment on her face surely a mirror of Claire's the first umpteen times she read the same words.

"Crumpled up and shoved under the register."

"What register?"

"My cash register." Even now she still couldn't fully wrap her mind around the notion that had come to her in one heart-stopping moment at the shop.

"How on earth did it get there?"

"Someone hid it there, I guess."

"Who's *W*, and who would hide this under your . . . ?" Her aunt's voice disappeared briefly as their eyes met in a moment of frightening clarity. "You don't think this is

Esther's, do you?"

She shrugged. "Who else would shove something under the register?"

Diane seemed to consider her words, her head shaking side to side after the briefest of moments. "But this says *W* . . . not *E*."

"I realize that."

"Do we know any Amish men whose names start with *W?*"

She traced the pattern on the counter with her forefinger, hoped the gesture would soothe her somehow.

It didn't.

"Not any *Amish* men, no."

Diane's eyes narrowed on Claire. "You think the person isn't Amish?"

"If he were, why would he address her in the way he did?" Again, she held the note out for her aunt.

"Okay, so he's not Amish."

She couldn't stand it anymore. She blurted her fears out in the open, where they could be discarded by a woman with far more sense than Claire possessed. "I think *W* stands for *Walter.*"

"Walter?"

"As in Walter Snow."

She waited for the laugh, watched it build momentarily only to disintegrate away just as quickly. "I suppose it's possible. It certainly wouldn't be the first Amish girl he's taken an interest in. But why Esther? She wasn't working when he owned the shop —"

"Diane? Claire? Are you in there?"

Spinning on the balls of her feet, Diane ran a quick hand down her apron. "Yes, Gerry, we're in here."

The door pushed open to reveal Gerry Baker and his wife. "I'm sorry to interrupt, but there's a fellow out in the parlor looking for Claire. Said his name is Jakob Fisher."

"Jakob is here? To see me?" she asked before glancing at her aunt and noting the slow smile that appeared on the woman's face.

"That's what he said." Gerry hooked his arm through his wife's and turned toward the hallway. "Now, if you'll excuse us, we're going to have a last walk around this delightful town before it's time for yet another meal designed to make me gain weight."

Quickly, Claire crumpled the note inside her hand and shoved it back inside her skirt pocket. "I can't imagine what Jakob could possibly want with me . . ."

"I can." Turning to focus on her niece once again, Diane reached out and tucked a renegade strand of auburn hair behind

Claire's ear. "I don't want you worrying about dinner tonight. The bread is cooling, the stew almost done, and the salad bowls are already filled and in the refrigerator. In fact, there's enough extras that the two of you can take supper on the front porch if you'd like."

"Come to think of it, I'm sure he's simply here to follow up on everything that happened today. Walter Snow's body *was* essentially found outside my back door." Still, she couldn't keep from taking a quick peek in the mirror. Satisfied with what she saw, she headed toward the swinging door, stopping as she reached it. "Can we talk more about the note later?"

"Of course." Diane pulled open the door of the floor-to-ceiling cabinet that housed the evening's dishes and pulled out five — two for the newlyweds, two for the Bakers, and one for Arnie. "But don't rush, okay? Enjoy your time with the detective."

Her time with the detective . . .

"You're incorrigible, Aunt Diane. You know that, don't you?"

"No, I just have a keen sense of reality."

Claire paused, her hand on the door. "And what reality would that be?"

"The detective has noticed."

"Noticed?" she asked, studying her aunt

closely. "Noticed what?"

"You, dear."

CHAPTER 9

She peered at Jakob across her wine glass and silently marveled at her aunt's ability to orchestrate an entire evening with nothing more than a smile and a well-timed head tilt. It was a gift, quite frankly. A gift Claire herself hadn't been bestowed.

"This is the best beef stew I've ever eaten." Plucking his napkin from his lap, Jakob set it on the table beside his plate and pushed his chair back a few inches. "Do you cook like this, too?"

"I kind of got away from cooking when I lived in the city, but it's coming back now, thanks to Diane."

"Oh?"

Claire nodded. "She's even let me take the lead on a few of the meals."

"No, I mean, what made you get away from it when you lived in the city? Didn't your apartment have a kitchen?" Jakob teased.

"It had one. But cooking for two and always eating alone has a way of making takeout look attractive." Claire pushed her hands into the air above her head, then let them drop back down to her lap. "But helping Diane cook for all her guests and having them appreciate our efforts in the way that they do has brought a little of the fun back."

"He thought you odd for liking simplicity, and he didn't come home for dinners you prepared," Jakob said, tracing his index finger around the mouth of his wine goblet. "So what drew you to this guy in the first place?"

"That's hard to remember these days." It was a simple answer but no less accurate. "Which is why I'd prefer to focus on my now. Less second-guessing that way."

"Ahhh. Second-guessing. I know about that." Pushing his wine glass to the side, Jakob leaned back in his seat, his eyes taking on a faraway quality before narrowing back on her. "You must be wondering how I can be Esther's uncle and not be Amish."

"I think I've put two and two together."

"If I'd left during Rumspringa, they wouldn't have shunned me the way that they did. But I didn't. I came back. And then, after I was baptized, I decided I had to be a cop. I couldn't spend my life farming when bad things were happening."

She listened to his words, tried them on for size. "How old were you when you left?"

"Nineteen."

"Nineteen," she repeated softly. "So Esther was what? Three?"

"Almost four."

Tipping forward, he reached into his back pocket and retrieved his wallet. He flipped it open and turned the empty sleeve of pictures for her to see. "With the ban against pictures I had growing up, I was left to just my memories all these years."

She swallowed over the pain that rose up in her throat. "You're a brave man, Jakob Fisher."

A bitter, almost sarcastic laugh emerged from the detective. "Brave?"

"Far braver than I am, that's for sure."

Cocking his head to the right, he studied her closely. "Why do you say that?"

"Because I was running from my mistakes when I came here to Heavenly." Slowly, deliberately, she reached past the last swallow of wine that remained in her goblet and grabbed hold of her water glass. "You, on the other hand, knowingly charged into enemy territory when you came back here."

He shrugged. "Maybe. But at least by being here I can see my loved ones' faces once in a while."

"Are you content with that?" she asked.

"I have to be."

She considered arguing but knew it was futile. The Amish had rules, and Jakob had broken them. Mostly, she just felt bad for him.

"I made my choice to come back here, and now I have to live with it. I just didn't realize how my past would make it so difficult to do my job."

She thought back to that afternoon, to the tension in the air at the simple notion that Jakob would have questions to ask of the Amish. "I could help, you know."

"Oh?"

"I'm close to Esther, and, through her, Eli. I just met Benjamin, but he seems nice, and —"

"Looks can be deceiving, Claire." An unmistakable cloud rolled across Jakob's face, taking with it any semblance of warmth.

She drew back. "So that . . . that whatever it was between you and Benjamin in my shop was more than just your being shunned?"

"Much more."

"I . . . I mean I just met him today, but he seemed so nice." She heard the incredulousness in her voice but could do little to stop it. His words and his attitude just didn't mesh with what she knew. "Why, he drops off fresh milk for his sister every morning before any of our shops are even open."

Jakob grabbed his goblet, downing the last of his wine. "That's Benjamin Miller for you. Always helping. Always nice. Always doing everything better than the next guy." A momentary pause gave way to a weary shake of his head. "Gosh, I sound bitter, don't I?"

"You must have your reasons." She pushed back her chair, stood, and felt the flutter in her chest at the instantaneous disappointment on his face.

"Hey, I'm sorry. I didn't mean to get all heavy on you."

"You didn't. I just feel like sitting on the swing. Will you join me?"

The corners of his mouth lifted upward as he, too, vacated his chair and crossed the porch to Claire's favorite piece of furniture. Together, they sat down, the weight of their bodies and the synchronized motion starting them off in a swing. "It's a beautiful night, isn't it?"

Resting her head against the back of the swing, Claire closed her eyes and inhaled, the last of Diane's stew wafting its way onto the porch from the parlor's open window. "It certainly helps lighten the day a bit."

Jakob sighed. "It sure was a doozy, wasn't it? I'm in town less than a week, and Heavenly has its second murder? Only this time, rather than an Amish man being killed, it appears as if an Amish man was behind the crime."

She sucked in her breath as her eyes flew open. "You can't truly believe what that woman said about Eli, can you? I mean, he's hot tempered, sure, but he's got a big heart."

Running a hand through his hair, Jakob released an actual moan. "Yeah, but Esther was right. He was arrested about six months ago outside a bar in Breeze Point."

She closed her eyes again. "He's not allowed to be in bars, is he?"

"Outside his Rumspringa, no. But at that time, it happens."

She shifted on the swing enough to afford a better view of Jakob's face, worried lines and all. "So if it happens, how does that point to the possibility he might have murdered Walter Snow?"

"It doesn't. The reason he got arrested, does."

She waited for him to fill in the gaps.

"He smashed a glass bottle over the head of an Englishman during an argument. Guy had to get five stitches."

"So he had a fight."

"Witnesses interviewed at the bar said it was unwarranted. That Eli Miller simply exploded. And that's what has me worried."

"You think he could have exploded on Walter?" she asked.

"Why not? That man swindled his family of money. Money they rightfully earned. And from what I heard around town today, Eli made some mighty powerful threats against Walter just before the man skipped town. That's not allowed by the Amish, either. So why would murder be any different for him?" Jakob extended his foot to stop the gentle sway of the swing and stood, his troubled gaze looking out over the distant fields of his childhood. "The only real thread of hope I have is that Millers are smart people. Eli had to know that if he killed Walter, the chance of ever getting the family's money back would be slim to none."

"That's good."

Jakob turned around, perching on the top of the porch rail. "It certainly bodes better for him than a fit of jealousy or a bent toward revenge would."

"Jealousy?" she echoed.

"Less chance of thinking something like

that through before acting."

Jealousy . . .

Instinctively her hand moved to her skirt pocket as a new scenario attached itself to the note inside. A scenario that chilled her from the inside out.

"Claire? You okay?"

She looked up and saw the concern in the detective's eyes. But try as she might, she couldn't tell him about the note. Not yet, anyway. Not until after she'd spoken to Esther.

"I . . . I'm fine. I guess I'm just worried about my friends. The Amish are such peaceful people. I hate to see the stress of the outside world invading that." And she did. Truly. It just wasn't the whole truth . . .

Jakob crossed back to the swing and reclaimed his spot as Claire brought the suspended bench to a stop. "My niece is lucky to have a friend like you."

She blinked against an unexpected burning in her eyes. "I'm lucky to have her."

Silence fell over them as they looked out over the setting sun and the glorious shades of red and orange that spread over Heavenly like gentle fingers.

It was Jakob who finally broke the quiet. "Do you ever see her mother?"

She had to smile. "Martha? She's lovely. I

just met her the other day. She's going to be making things for my shop now, too."

Jakob stiffened beside her. "How . . . How is she?"

The sadness intermingled with the faintest hint of hope she heard in his voice reminded her of the why behind his question, prompting her to lay a gentle hand atop his. "She seemed good to me. Very protective of her daughter yet not in a stifling way."

He seemed to consider her words even as he flipped his hand over and held on to hers.

She stared at their hands intertwined, his voice filling the space between them. "I miss many people from my Amish life. But none as much as I miss my sister."

It was hard to know what to say. In five years of being married to Peter, he'd never shared his feelings as openly as Jakob was at that moment. It was everything she'd always wanted yet nothing she knew how to handle.

She withdrew her hand from his and extended her own foot. When the swing stopped, she stood and crossed to the same porch railing where Jakob had perched just moments earlier. Only instead of sitting, she merely shielded her eyes from the sun's remaining rays. If she leaned slightly to the left and looked to her right, she could make out the beginning of Lighted Way and the road that linked the English and Amish worlds. They were different no doubt. Different in everything from transportation and clothes to customs and beliefs. But, in the end, they were all people. People with hopes and dreams and memories held dear.

And if Jakob was missing Martha, she had to believe there was a part of Martha that missed Jakob as well.

She said as much to the detective.

"I wish I could know you're right, Claire. Not because I want my sister to hurt but because I'd know I wasn't alone. But the Amish are steadfast in their beliefs first and foremost. And I broke those."

Slowly, she turned around, her mind processing everything Jakob said against what she had learned so far about her friends. Sure, she didn't know Martha well — the bulk of Claire's information was based only on stories Esther shared during quiet moments at the shop. But what she did know cast a shred of doubt on the man's words.

"I'd like to help if I can," she whispered.

"If today was any indication of the walls I'm going to hit with this investigation, I might have to take you up on that." Jakob rose from the swing and came to stand beside Claire.

"I wasn't talking about that."

His shoulders dropped ever so slightly. "You weren't?"

She rushed to explain. "I mean, sure, I'll do my best to be a liaison of sorts with the Amish if that's what you need while you get to the bottom of what happened to Walter Snow. But I was talking about something more than that."

He studied her face closely, the warmth of his eyes sending yet another unexpected tingle through her body. "Oh?"

"I'd like to help you get close to your sister again."

She'd have to have been blind not to see the way her words impacted the detective, to see the flash of hope that flickered behind his eyes before disappearing altogether.

"I appreciate that, Claire, but it will never happen."

"Never," she repeated. "That's a word I used a time or two when things seemed bleak. But Aunt Diane showed me how that word lies again and again. Now I guess it's my turn to show you the same thing."

CHAPTER 10

The moment the tires of Aunt Diane's car left the tourist-friendly section of Lighted Way, Claire felt the change. The pace slowed, storefronts gave way to wide open fields, and occasional buggy sightings became the norm.

Slowly, she inched the borrowed car around one curve and then the next, her focus alternating between the road and the farms as she soaked in her surroundings. She'd been so busy acclimating herself to the shop and helping at the inn that the closest she'd gotten to the Amish side of Heavenly had been via her day-to-day contact with people like Esther and Ruth. But now, as she left the slightly whitewashed version of Amish life and headed smack-dab into the middle of their reality, she couldn't help but feel her excitement brewing.

Sweeping farmland as far as her eye could

see was parceled into fields of varying colors. From Esther, she'd learned that typical crops for the Fisher family and their Amish brethren were things like hay and wheat, barley and rye, corn and soybeans. Vegetables grown often ended up as wares in an every-once-in-a-while roadside stand that served as yet another way to feed their large families.

She glanced to her left, her gaze playing across a small sheep-tended cemetery with several rows of simple headstones, then to the right at a team of mules hitched to a piece of steel-wheeled farm equipment and pulling a man clad in black suspendered pants, a collared shirt, and a straw hat through thick alfalfa.

In the distance, cattle grazed in lush fields while a homemade wheel turned round and round in a nearby creek, delivering a constant source of water to the landowner's home. A smattering of windmills dotted the horizon, tasked with the job of providing an alternate source of power that wouldn't connect its users to the outside world.

Easing off the gas, she inched her way around a horse-drawn buggy, the orange triangle affixed to its back a reminder to English drivers to use caution when approaching. Two small children, no older than six, peeked through the buggy's back flaps, offering the faintest hint of a smile in response to her wave.

She couldn't help but marvel at their surroundings and compare it to that of her own childhood. Did they play with dolls and toys the way she had? Or were they tasked with chores that had them cooking and cleaning and farming from one end of the day to the next? She could only guess, and guess she did.

Yet, no matter how much she imagined or how much she learned about the Amish from Esther, Claire still found it difficult at times to accept the existence of a world so different than her own less than two miles from her aunt's doorstep.

Glancing from the farm on her right to the description Esther had scrawled on a piece of paper, Claire pulled onto the finely graveled driveway and cut the engine. The farmhouse was ample in size and very well kept, the presence of two separate clotheslines and dozens of garments in various sizes the only outward indication that a family of seven lived inside. A smaller home situated slightly to the right was where Esther's grandparents lived. Claire knew from their many conversations that elderly members of the community did not go into nursing homes. Rather, they turned the family farm over to their children and assisted in ways their increased age allowed.

Securing a plate of her aunt's best cookies in her hand, Claire stepped from the car, her pace quickening as she approached the wide front porch and its smattering of empty chairs — chairs she knew would be occupied after chores had been attended to and the final meal of the day enjoyed.

A rustling off to her left made her stop in time to see Esther step out from behind the same light-green dress the young woman had worn the day before, its simple bodice drying in the sun.

"Oh. You are here."

She transferred the plate to her left hand and embraced Esther with her right. "I told you I would be. Is your Mamm home?"

Pleased with herself for remembering the Pennsylvania Dutch way of saying *mom,* she smiled.

Esther looked right then left, her voice barely above a whisper. "Please. You can not tell Mamm."

Claire drew back, confused. "Tell her what?"

A hint of crimson rose in the young woman's face. "About her . . . about Jakob."

"But she knows, Esther," she reminded.

"Remember? She saw him outside the shop on Monday."

"She does not know we spoke."

"But you had to," Claire insisted. "You really had no choice."

"She would be angry."

Claire considered refuting that claim once again but opted to let it go. She was a newcomer to all of their rules and beliefs anyway.

"I won't say a thing. If and when you share that with her is your choice, not mine."

"You believe I am wrong?" Esther asked.

She shrugged. "I just know that your uncle is a nice man. And I think, if you allow yourself a chance to see him for the man he is, you'll realize that, too."

The front door opened, and Martha stepped outside, a pint-size Amish girl at her feet. "Good day, Claire."

"Hi, Martha. I brought you some cookies."

The toddler's eyes widened, yet she said nothing, opting instead to look up at her mother with hope-filled eyes.

Martha nodded and took the plate, smiling down at her youngest child before looking back at Claire. "That is very kind. Thank you. Please come in."

With Esther only steps behind, Claire followed Martha and her little girl into the house, stopping just inside the door to soak up the sights. To her right was an ample-sized kitchen painted in a glossy, soothing green. A large wooden table was placed dead center with eight chairs and a single high chair surrounding it on all sides. The walls contained no photographs or knick-knacks except one lone calendar depicting the month against a mountainous backdrop. A solitary window over the sink afforded an unobstructed view of the family's crops and livestock. An old-fashioned sewing machine sat on a smaller table in a far corner of the room, with a pocket-ridden wall-hanging affixed to the wall above. Each pocket held an item helpful to the home — scissors, needles, clothespins, and the like, stressing function over frivolousness.

Martha set the cookies on the counter and then gestured Claire to follow her into the next room, a large wide-open space with nothing more than a chair or two.

"This is such a big room," Claire mused.

"It is where we worship when it is our turn," Esther explained. "When it is, the men bring long benches."

She nodded as an image befitting Esther's description formed in her thoughts. "How many people come at that time?"

"Twenty families," Martha said.

Claire did the mental math, taking into account the fact that most families were probably as large as Martha's. "That must be a very busy morning for all of you."

"Busy day. We share lunch, too."

She stopped herself mid–head shake. What seemed so hard to grasp for her was the norm for these people. She had no right to make it seem odd.

"I have items for you." Martha crossed the room to a table that spanned the space between two windows on the southern wall. "I made dolls, an apron, and two bonnets."

Claire followed behind Martha, picking up first one doll and then the next, the plain faces taking her by surprise.

Esther rushed to explain. "We do not believe things should be made in our likeness. To do so would be boastful."

Turning them over, Claire examined the careful stitching. "What a wonderful taste of Amish tradition for our customers. These are perfect, Martha."

A slight smile teased at the corners of the woman's mouth. "Next week, I will have more things. I thought I would have finished painting the skillet, but that was not to be last night."

Esther shot a worried look at Claire. "Mamm heard news of Mr. Snow."

"Oh." She contemplated what she could say without giving away any of Esther's secrets. "What a shock it was to realize he'd been found behind my shop. In the alley between Heavenly Treasures and Shoo Fly Bake Shoppe."

"I do not know why people murder," Martha said. "God decides man's fate."

"Because some people find it hard to wait for that day, I guess." It was all she could think to offer by way of explanation. It was lame, she knew, but it was something.

Martha's head bowed forward. "Mr. Snow was not a good man. He had no worry for anyone but himself."

A strangled noise from Esther's side of the room prevented Claire from offering any sort of agreement, leaving her, instead, to mentally revisit the love letter, which she'd left on her bedside table the night before. A love letter that left a cold feeling in the pit of her stomach.

Esther jumped forward, her hand pushing aside the modest curtain. "Look, Mamm. Benjamin and Eli are here."

The relief in Esther's voice was unmistakable, though the reason behind it wasn't quite so clear. Sure, the girl was smitten with the younger Miller brother, but the timing of his arrival also served to eliminate any questions that may have transpired as a result of her odd reaction to her mother's assessment of Walter Snow.

Claire, however, simply filed it away for a quiet moment at the shop when questions didn't have to be censored in quite the same way as they did in Martha's presence. Maybe the love letter was none of her business, and maybe Esther would tell her so, but she had to at least ask. Especially if there was a chance it could implicate Esther in some way.

"Dat left a hammer for Benjamin on the porch. That is why he is here, I am sure."

Esther stepped back from the window, and then, when she was sure her mother wasn't looking, she tried to make out her reflection in the glass.

"You look beautiful," Claire whispered. "That lavender dress is quite pretty with your skin coloring."

Esther blushed under the praise, her lips forming a silent thank-you.

The young woman's behavior, coupled with the anticipation on her pretty face, gave every indication that Eli Miller was at the center of her thoughts and dreams. Yet the love letter Claire had found crumpled and hidden beneath the register painted a very different picture. One that left Claire more than a little confused.

The open-top buggy carrying the Miller men stopped behind Claire's car, the horse tasked with pulling them not the slightest bit fazed by the more traditional form of transportation parked just in front of its nose.

The sight made her smile. The odd little flutter in her chest, however, didn't begin until Benjamin jumped down from the buggy and strode toward the house.

"I'm surprised Benjamin is not married. I thought Amish men married young." The second the words were out, she wished she could recall them, the question making her sound quite a lot like a busybody.

"Benjamin is a widower," Martha stated matter-of-factly. "His wife died two months after the wedding."

She heard herself gasp and rushed to stifle the reaction. "Oh, I'm so sorry."

"He has remained unmarried for nearly thirteen years."

It was a part of Amish culture she was unfamiliar with, a part she'd question Diane about that night after dinner. In the meantime, she simply trailed Martha to the door and watched as the men approached the Fisher home.

Eli was first, his boyish smile evident the moment he saw Esther. If Martha was surprised by his reaction, she did not show it. Moments later, Benjamin entered the home, his warm eyes making note of each face before noticeably brightening at her presence.

"Miss Weatherly. This is a surprise."

She nibbled her lower lip inward, buying herself time as she searched for a voice that would sound natural. "Martha has made things to be sold in my shop on consignment." Raising the dolls to eye level, she forced herself to focus on the woman's talent. "They're wonderful, aren't they?"

"God is wonderful," Martha protested. "Those are just dolls."

"It is more than I can do," she answered softly.

"Everyone can do as God allows."

Eli shifted from foot to foot, his smile disappearing behind the weight of an entirely different emotion. "And some do things that are for no God."

Esther studied her love interest. "Eli?"

"They steal and they lie and they try to change hearts. That is not God's way."

"Change hearts?" Claire echoed curiously,

casting a sidelong glance at Esther as she did.

Esther blushed.

"That is for God to address, Eli." Benjamin's firm yet gentle statement pulled her focus back on the Miller men and the exchange happening between them. "And He will."

Eli fisted his left hand at his side as his slow boil began to grow. "When they die, He will. But that must happen first."

"Eli, that is enough!" Benjamin thundered. "We must go."

Tipping his head at the women, he pushed the front door open and waited for Eli to exit. When he did, Benjamin followed, the authoritative step of the older brother overtaking that of the sullen younger sibling.

Once they were gone, Martha eyed her daughter closely. "It is time to return to your work, Esther."

Esther nodded, then disappeared onto the front porch as the Millers' buggy turned and headed back toward the road.

Martha looked at the floor but said nothing, her silence heavy with something Claire couldn't identify.

"Martha? Is everything okay?"

Slowly, the woman's covered head tilted upward until her gaze met Claire's. "Mr.

Snow's death brings the police, yes?"

Claire swallowed.

Uh-oh.

"Yes." It was all she could think to say. Anything else might betray her promise to Esther.

"Was it the new detective?"

Her heart ached for the pain she saw on her new friend's face, a pain she knew was shared by the man in question. Again, she gave the simplest, most true answer she could give. "Yes."

"How is he?" Martha whispered. "Is he well?"

CHAPTER 11

Rising up on the balls of her feet, Claire secured Martha's bonnet to a hook visible from the sidewalk along Lighted Way. The pale-yellow fabric, coupled with the simple lace border, was sure to appeal to vacationing grandmothers. And if the bonnet didn't, the handcrafted Amish dolls propped just inside the display window were sure to fit the bill.

The males who vacationed in Heavenly were drawn to shops like Yoder's Fine Furniture and Glick's Tool's 'n' More. The notion of someone crafting a desk or corner cabinet by hand tended to stir some sort of like-minded desire in men of all shapes and sizes, claiming their attention long enough to allow their female counterparts to shed any possible guilt about spending ten or twenty minutes in a shop like Heavenly Treasures.

Her inventory had truly blossomed over

the past few weeks as Esther brought more and more of her talents to the shop. Now, a smattering of quilts, pillows, aprons, and hand-painted spoons were displayed around the shop alongside Claire's candles and decorated picture frames. Martha's contributions would only serve to take Heavenly Treasures to the next level — the kind of place people sought long after their vacation was over, calling in orders from various parts of the country to coincide with birthday and holiday gift giving.

The notion was still a year or so out, but standing there, imagining it to be so, was the next best thing to actually having it happen.

"How much for that smile?"

She whirled around, nearly knocking over her carefully arranged dolls in the process. "Jakob. I . . . I didn't hear you come in."

"The bells jingled," he said, pointing at the rope above the door.

Her face warmed. "I didn't hear them."

Jakob wandered over to the window and studied the new items. "I was guilty of the same thing this morning. The chief walked in my office to ask a question, and I didn't even realize he was there until he'd cleared his throat a half-dozen times or more." Reaching out, he gently fingered the pale-yellow bonnet and the faceless dolls below. "Only I kind of doubt I was smiling the way you were just now."

"Why not?"

He fixed his gaze on hers. "I guess I was wrapped up in the case."

"Have you figured out who killed Walter Snow?" she asked quickly.

"No. Just asking a lot of questions and playing possible scenarios out in my mind. But I'll find who did it, of that I have no doubt."

Coming from any other person after less than a week on the job, Claire would have found the claim to be rather cocky. Yet, somehow, it didn't come across that way with Jakob.

She suspected some of that was because of the quiet confidence he exuded when he spoke. Some, too, was due to the way he listened — carefully, as if every word someone uttered mattered. And, in a murder case, it probably did.

"I hope you catch who did it soon. I hate to see such wonderful people on eggshells."

Jakob shrugged. "The only one walking on eggshells should be the one responsible."

It was a tough point to argue.

And a point that made her more than a little nervous.

"Claire?"

She glanced up.

"I wanted to thank you for dinner last night. I guess I hadn't realized just how badly I needed a little bit of mealtime conversation. Haven't had that in a while, and it was really nice."

"I enjoyed it as well." And she had. Very much.

Jakob gestured around the shop. "So what was the million-dollar smile about just now when I walked in?"

She made a face. "I don't know, I guess I just like rearranging the window display from time to time."

"You do a good job." He lifted one of the dolls in his hands and turned it over, his expression difficult to decipher. "When I was little, I never thought it odd that my sister's dolls didn't have faces. It was normal, you know?"

"And now?"

"I don't know." With a gentle finger, he traced the edges of the doll's head cap, lingered his touch on the simple Amish dress. "One moment I question why Amish kids can't look down at a doll and see it smile back at them. But then I remind myself that they don't know any better."

"I guess the part I find so endearing is

that they're made with love." Reaching past him, she lifted one of Martha's dolls into her own hands. "I mean, how neat would it be to have your mom make you something like this?"

For a moment, he said nothing, his gaze traveling over every nuance of the hand-made doll. When he was done, he looked up, their gazes mingling with one another. "Did Esther make these?"

She considered giving him the easy answer, knowing the truth might create awkwardness where there was none. But, in the end, she said the only thing she could. "No. Her mother did."

In a flash, the carefree, if not wistful, smile disappeared from his face, in its place a pain so raw she felt an answering burn in her eyes. She swallowed.

"Would you like to keep that one?" she whispered.

Dropping his eyes downward, Jakob studied the doll once again.

"Because you can have it if you want."

He cleared his throat — once, twice — then set it back on the raised platform. "Martha wouldn't want me to have it. Not anymore, anyway."

She heard the words, even recognized the detachment with which he spoke them, yet the pain behind them was as visible as ever.

"She asked about you this morning." There, she said it.

He froze. "Excuse me?"

"Martha asked about you this morning," she repeated.

Somewhere, in the back of her head, a faint warning bell sounded. And she knew why. Jakob's relationship with his sister was none of her business. Their estrangement had begun sixteen years earlier, before she'd ever met either one of them. But although she could justify her silence by embracing the fact that their rift was by no fault of her own, she couldn't shake the nagging feeling that it wasn't really by their own doing, either.

"She did?"

Claire nodded, the smile making its way across Jakob's mouth mirroring its way across hers, too.

"Did you tell her I was well?"

"I did," she said, cringing inwardly at the lie. But she couldn't help it. She couldn't smash his hope with reality. Besides, just because Martha had held up her hands and retracted the question before Claire could answer didn't negate the fact that the woman had asked it in the first place.

At least that's what she told herself as

Jakob closed his eyes and inhaled sharply through his nose. A moment later, he spoke. "You must think I'm an idiot, getting so worked up over such a simple inquiry. But to know she asked about me, to know she still cares, I guess that's kind of" — he walked toward the register, then doubled back — "encouraging."

"I'm glad —"

The front door of the shop opened, the jingle of the bells redirecting her focus toward the familiar redhead they announced.

"Good afternoon, Mr. Streen."

Arnie's head bobbed ever so slightly. "Is Esther here?"

She tracked his gaze around the room and saw it linger on the bowl of butterscotch candies she'd set beside the register for her customers. With hurried strides, she positioned herself between her aunt's sloppiest guest and the counter. "Today is Esther's day off."

"Darn." Taking two steps forward, Arnie reached around Claire and plucked a candy from the bowl, his fingers making short work of the little yellow wrapper and dispensing it straight to the floor. "I've written as much as I can without talking to her, but I can't keep waiting around."

She bent down and plucked the wrapper from the ground, keenly aware of Jakob's narrowed eyes assessing the situation. "Well, you'll have to wait a little longer. She's not working today."

Jakob extended his hand. "I'm sorry, I don't believe we've met yet. I'm Jakob Fisher. *Detective* Jakob Fisher."

Arnie's mouth stopped working the candy long enough to allow a thorough once-over of the lean yet well-conditioned body of the man just off to his left. "So you're the one who broke the rules, huh? Wow. That took some guts, eh?"

Realizing a shake wasn't going to happen, Jakob retracted his hand and widened his stance. "I'm not sure what you're talking about, Mr. — I'm sorry, I didn't catch your name."

Claire crumpled the wrapper inside her hand and shoved it in the front pocket of her navy trousers. "Jakob, this is Arnie Streen. He's a guest at Sleep Heavenly as he works on his thesis for grad school. It's on the Amish."

A lightbulb flashed behind Jakob's eyes, but before he could say anything, Arnie prattled on. "You think maybe you'd be willing to talk about your shunning?"

Jakob's mouth tightened. "No."

"You sure?" Arnie asked before reaching around Claire for yet another piece of candy. "It might feel good to unload some of that anger in a productive place."

Sensing the tension simmering below Jakob's surface, she picked the second wrapper off the floor and gestured with it toward the front door. "I'll let Esther know you were in and asking about her." It was a lie and she knew it, but it was the only way she could think to get the man out of her shop before Jakob blew a fuse.

Arnie poked a finger within inches of Jakob's chest. "I imagine this murder case has to be a bit like payback for you."

"Oh?" Jakob's right eyebrow hitched upward. "How is that?"

"You know, throwing one of them in the slammer after getting all high and mighty with you."

"One of *them?*" Jakob repeated between clenched teeth.

Wiping the back of his hand across his face, Arnie nodded. "One of the Amish. I mean, they act so perfect, yet there are some incidents in just the last year alone that show the Amish across this country are capable of things like drug trafficking and even murder."

Jakob quieted Claire's gasp with a raised

index finger. "No, Mr. Streen is correct. There was a case in Ohio where an Amish boy, fresh off Rumspringa, was arrested for trafficking drugs across state lines. Dealers had stowed it in the back of the young man's buggy."

"You make it sound like he didn't know they were there," Arnie mused.

"Because he didn't," Jakob said without hesitation. "I have a friend on that force. He told me about the case."

Arnie rolled his eyes and snorted. "Yeah . . . okay. But what about that Amish guy out in Indiana? The one who killed an intruder?"

Jakob met Arnie's challenge. "He was protecting his family."

"If you're so up on Amish crimes, then you have to know about the one in upstate New York four years ago where the guy killed some little kid. You gonna have an excuse for that one, too, Detective?"

"No. It was cold-blooded, and he's locked away in prison now for the rest of his life."

"Which proves my point, doesn't it?" Arnie shoved his index finger in his mouth and picked at the underside of his molars, extracting remnants of the butterscotch candy.

Claire looked from one man to the other,

frustration making her hands shoot up in the air. "Look, Mr. Streen, you've obviously found some cases where a small handful of Amish have made bad choices. But you can't deny the fact that it's not the norm."

"Just as Detective Fisher, here, can't deny the fact that murder at the hand of the Amish is not completely out of the question," Arnie mumbled around his finger.

"I will go wherever the facts of this case lead, Mr. Streen."

A muffled ring permeated the confines of Arnie's back pocket. He reached back, extracted his phone, and glanced down at the display. "Awww darn. I gotta take this call. It's my professor." He took three steps toward the door, then flipped the phone open and covered it with his hand. "Hey, Claire? If you talk to Esther before tomorrow, tell her I'll be by sometime after eleven. And that I like her lavender dress best."

The jingle of the door, signaling Arnie's long-overdue departure, was met by utter silence broken only by a low whistle.

"Wow."

She shook her head, then retrieved the wrappers from her pocket and tossed them into the wastebasket behind the counter. "I'm sorry you had to deal with that."

"How long has he been at the inn?" Jakob

inquired, wide-eyed.

"Coming up on three weeks, I think."

A second, longer whistle followed. "Your aunt deserves a medal."

Crossing back to the front window, she looked out on Lighted Way and inhaled deeply, the gentle cadence of the horse-drawn buggies alongside the relaxed pace of vacationing tourists slowly ebbing the knot of tension ushered in by Arnie Streen. "I don't understand why so many people feel the need to tarnish what is good. It's like it makes them feel better about themselves somehow if they do."

Jakob moved in behind her, his proximity and his quiet calm making her feel inexplicably better. "You know what? I'd rather have an open and honest discussion with someone like that guy who's taken the time to uncover facts. It's the other ones — the kind who make assumptions — who are most damaging to the Amish and their reputation."

Slowly, she turned, his words and his experience educating her to things she wished the whole world could hear.

"So many people think that because the Amish keep to themselves that they don't pay taxes. And that's not true. They do . . . just like everyone else. The only difference is they don't utilize the services that come from paying them. And for as odd as our life is to outsiders, the vast majority of Amish return home after Rumspringa. Says something, don't you think?"

When he was done, she met his gaze and held it. "You miss it, don't you?" she finally asked.

"Every single day."

CHAPTER 12

When Claire first tiptoed her way down the stairs and into the parlor, she'd hoped reading a few chapters of the paperback mystery novel her aunt had recommended would finally entice sleep to her doorstep. Yet, six chapters later, she was as awake as ever, her attention now fixated on the flickering glow of candlelight as it wiggled and danced along the ceiling.

She'd made a valiant effort at sleep when she retired to her room shortly after ten o'clock, the evening's dinner dishes and dessert plates freshly washed, dried, and set aside for the next day. But as tired as she'd thought she was, her mind proved otherwise, driving her from bed as midnight loomed.

Insomnia was something she knew well from her time in New York. In the beginning, it had been out of hurt as she listened for Peter's key in the doorway after yet another late-night business dinner or cocktail party to which she hadn't been invited. Then, as time passed, it had been a result of the mental chastising and second-guessing she subjected herself to as the sham that was her marriage became too hard to ignore.

Moving to Heavenly had changed that, though, until now.

And, once again, it came down to mental chastising and second-guessing. Only this time it had nothing whatsoever to do with her ex-husband and everything to do with the people and the town she'd grown to love over the past six months.

"I thought I noticed a light coming from down here, and I figured it was probably you." Diane padded across the wood-planked floor in her favorite fuzzy white slippers and struck a match to a second, larger candle. "Do you want to talk about it?"

Claire peered over the top of the couch. "I'm sorry, I didn't mean to wake you."

"You didn't. My kidneys did." Diane extinguished the match with a quick shake and then blew on it for good measure. "I noticed the light when I stepped into the hall."

Claire watched as the light from the new

candle joined with the first in its ceiling dance. "I couldn't sleep, so I figured I'd read a little bit until my eyes got tired."

Diane's gaze shot to the unopened book on Claire's stomach. "Oh?"

"It didn't work."

"I can see that." Diane crossed to the couch, stopping at Claire's outstretched feet. "Would a snack work? I think there are some cookies left, and I'd be happy to put on a pot of tea if you'd like."

Swinging her legs onto the floor, Claire patted the empty sofa cushion to her right. "Could we just talk awhile, instead?"

A smile lit the corners of the woman's otherwise tired eyes. "Of course." With a tug of her bathrobe's sash, Diane sat down and guided Claire's sock-clad feet onto her lap. "So what's troubling you, dear?"

"How do you know something's wrong?" she asked.

"Because you're not smiling."

She inhaled deeply as her aunt's hands began to massage the tops of her feet, the rhythmic motion more than a little comforting. "C'mon. I don't *always* smile."

"Since you moved here, you do."

She couldn't really argue the point. Moving in with Diane, opening her very own shop, getting back to the basics of life . . . It was everything she'd ever wanted even if she hadn't realized it until it happened.

"I love it here." It was a simple statement yet no less accurate. "It suits me."

Diane nodded, her gaze never leaving Claire's. "So then what has you so down in the mouth?"

"Because I don't like seeing bad things happen, and I don't like seeing good people hurt."

"Where is this coming from?" her aunt asked, pausing her hand on Claire's feet. "Who's being hurt?"

"Being hurt, hurting . . . It's all the same thing." She knew she was being vague, but she couldn't help it. Her mouth was having difficulty keeping up with her thoughts.

Diane rested her hand on Claire's calf. "You've lost me, dear."

She tried again, this time doing a better job of filling in the gaps. "First, there's the whole Walter Snow murder thing. His wife is convinced Eli Miller is behind it all."

Diane brought her hand to her face, her eyes wide. "Eli?"

"Eli," she confirmed. "She even pointed to a drunk-and-disorderly arrest he had a few months ago as proof that he has it in him to stray from Amish life."

Shaking her head, Diane wiggled out from

underneath Claire's feet and stood. "Does Benjamin know?"

"He does now."

Diane paced across the floor and back. "Al Gussman took care of Eli and got him out of jail. It was all fine."

"Wait. You knew about that?"

"I did. Al called me, and I met him at the station."

Claire sat up and scooted toward the edge of the couch. "Why didn't you just tell Eli's brother? Or his parents?"

Diane stopped midstep and stared at Claire. "Do you realize the shunning that young man would have endured if his family had known of his drinking and his fighting? We couldn't let that happen. Especially in light of the fact he was defending them."

"Defending them?"

"Well, the Amish, anyway."

She played with a loose thread on the knee of her pajama pants and considered her aunt's account of the event Esther had been reluctant to share out of loyalty to Eli. "And that wouldn't have made a difference to Benjamin or the rest of the family?"

"Fighting is never condoned by the Amish. Under any circumstances."

"Well, Mrs. Snow found out about that somehow, and she's pointing to that as proof that Eli is some sort of hothead capable of snapping."

Diane opened her mouth but said nothing, the silence more powerful than any word she could have uttered.

"You think she's right?" she whispered. "You think Eli could have killed her husband?"

"No. Of course not. I . . ." Diane stopped, her cheeks growing pale in the candlelight. "He *did* publically threaten the man if the money wasn't returned. That's why Walter took off for the hills in the first place."

Claire took in the information, compared it with what Esther had told her. "Eli got in trouble with the Amish for making those threats, didn't he?"

"He was shunned at home and in the community until he acknowledged what he'd done," Diane relayed. "From what I've been told, he struggled with accepting fault, but he gave in because he couldn't stand his family — and Esther — not being allowed to talk to him."

"Then why would he run that risk by doing something even worse? The stolen money has probably been spent by now, anyway. So what would Eli gain by killing the guy?" They were reasonable questions. They were also the same ones that had contributed to her bout of insomnia in the first place.

Before Diane could respond, she continued.

"Unless he wasn't dealing from a place of logic to begin with." She hated that she'd given words to the fear that had trumped all the questions and driven her from bed in the middle of the night. But it just kind of came out.

And went right over her aunt's head.

"Ahhh. Now I understand the part about being hurt and hurting. You're worried about Eli. That's commendable, really, but there's more, isn't there?"

She paused, torn between tackling the path she'd just turned down and leaving it for private exploration at a later time. On one hand, the nagging fear that had driven her from bed was just that — a fear. On the other hand, that fear was based on speculation rather than cold hard facts. If she talked it out, maybe it would be better.

Shaking the troubling thoughts from her mind, she focused on the third and final reason she was sitting in the parlor rather than sleeping in her bed. "I guess I feel badly for Jakob."

Diane's left eyebrow rose. "Oh?"

"He misses his family terribly. You can see

141

it in his eyes and hear it in his voice every single time they come up in conversation or he sees something that reminds him of them."

"I can only imagine how much harder it must make things for him to be back here." Diane crossed back to the couch and sunk onto the cushion beside Claire. "It's wonderful to see him again, but I can't help but feel he made a mistake coming back."

She rushed to defend Jakob's decision, crafting reasons based on conjecture. "Maybe he wanted a chance to be a part of their lives again. To get to know his nieces and nephews . . ."

"Neither of which can ever happen."

"But why can't it? Those people are his family. He wanted to make a difference in the world. How can they truly fault him for that?" She heard the intensity in her voice and worked to soften it. "I'm sorry, Aunt Diane, I really am. I'm not angry at you. I'm just frustrated."

Diane reached for Claire's hand and lovingly pressed it between hers. "I find it sad, too, dear. I truly do. But he knew what was expected of him when he was baptized. And he knew what would come of his decision to leave. He chose to leave."

"To be a cop! To help people like the

Amish!"

"It's just the way it is, dear."

"It shouldn't be," she said, the wistful quality of her voice evident to her own ears.

"Some things just can't be changed."

"Maybe. But that doesn't mean I can't try." Slowly, gently, Claire extricated her hand from Diane's. "I have to, Diane. For Jakob. And for Martha."

For a moment, Diane said nothing, her large thoughtful eyes studying Claire intently. If she had any protests to offer, though, she kept them silent. Instead, the woman leaned over and planted a kiss on her niece's forehead. "I wish I could say I know you'll succeed, but —"

Claire held up her hand, stifling a yawn as she did. "Let's just leave it there, okay? I don't do hopeless very well."

CHAPTER 13

Claire lifted her face to the morning sun and slowly inhaled the very heart of Heavenly, Pennsylvania. Lighted Way not only served as a thoroughfare between the Amish and English sects of the town but also provided the place in which both groups interacted, each true to its own way of life. Cars and horse-drawn buggies lined streets walked by people in outfits from tank tops and jeans to long-aproned dresses and head caps. Here, one did not gawk at the other. It was simply life — a quiet, peaceful existence that suited Claire just fine.

One day soon, she hoped to get her own place. Something small and quaint that could be the kind of home she'd been dreaming about for years.

She knew Aunt Diane would be heartbroken when that day came, but it was the next logical step in Claire's personal makeover. Moving to Heavenly had been the first step, while opening Heavenly Treasures had been the second. Both had proven to be two of the smartest things she'd ever done. Getting her own place and turning it into the refuge of her dreams was the next and final step. Hit that one, and she could overlook the fact that she was single.

Or, at least, pretend to.

Sidestepping a young boy on a scooter, she glanced in the direction of Glick's Tools 'n' More and offered a smile and a wave at the proprietor, Howard Glick. Like Claire, Howard took pride in his shop and the Amish items it offered. In fact, he'd found customers' questions about various implements so interesting, he'd begun to fashion his business around various hands-on demonstrations so the English could learn even more about the Amish. It was a smart idea, really, one she had in the back of her head for her own shop in the future.

She stepped off the sidewalk and crossed the mouth of the alley separating Glick's from Shoo Fly Bake Shoppe, the aroma of Ruth's freshly baked pies and cookies wafting onto the street through the open windows and quickening her pace exponentially.

"Good morning, Ruth." Stopping at the base of the bakery's porch steps, Claire smiled up at the young Amish woman, who spoke little yet smiled often. "You're putting me to shame making your windows gleam like that."

Ruth's rag-holding hand paused on the large plate-glass window highlighting some of the many home-baked goodies inside. Without turning around, she mumbled something Claire couldn't quite pick out.

She climbed the steps and moved closer. "I'm sorry, Ruth, I didn't quite catch . . ." The words trailed from her mouth as her gaze fell on the splash of white paint across the glass. "Ruth? What on earth happened here?"

The tall blonde turned around, her big blue eyes wide and sad beneath her simple white head cap. "I do not know. Someone must have spilled a can of paint."

Claire looked around the porch, taking in the exterior wall and trim. "Were one of your brothers getting ready to paint? Because everything looks fine to me."

Ruth shook her head, then resumed the painstaking task of trying to remove paint from glass. "It is not from them. It is someone else who spilled paint."

Turning around, Claire eyed the main sidewalk some three steps and ten feet away. "I'm not sure how spilled paint could have gotten on your window all the way up here."

"I do not know."

She stepped closer to the window, reality impossible to ignore. "Ruth? I don't think someone spilled that. I think they *threw* it."

The rag began to move faster, Ruth's hand making smaller yet more forceful movements despite any sign of progress.

"Ruth?"

Slowly, Ruth brought her hand to a stop, her shoulders slumping beneath her pale-green dress. "I do not want my brothers to see this."

"But why? Surely Benjamin will know how to get this off, and Eli —"

Ruth spun around, her rag-holding hand now clutched to her chest. "Eli will be angry. He will get in trouble. He is in too much trouble already without" — Ruth gestured to the mess behind her — "*this* making things worse."

"But, Ruth, this was wrong. People can't just deface one of our shops and go unpunished. It's not right."

"I do not know how, but I have upset someone." Dropping onto a single rocking chair to the left of the front door, Ruth stared down at her hands. "First, the note on my door the other day, and now . . . this?"

"Note?" She opened her mouth to challenge the young woman's words but shut it just as quickly as the cloud that was Walter Snow's murder lifted long enough to allow a quick jog of her memory. "Wait. Benjamin took that to Detective Fisher, didn't he?"

"He gave it to Mr. Glick. Mr. Glick gave it to the detective."

"And?" she prompted. "What did Jakob say?"

"He said it was probably a prank."

"What did the note say, again? I never got to see it."

Ruth's cheeks turned crimson. "That my food made people sick."

She had to laugh at the ludicrousness of the statement. Shoo Fly Bake Shoppe was a favorite among locals and tourists alike for one reason and one reason only — Ruth's baking prowess.

Based on the note alone, she could see why Jakob had chalked the note up to a prank. No one in their right mind would ever write, or believe, such a thing about Ruth. But now, with the paint splashed across the window, she had to wonder . . .

And wonder she did.

About the paint . . .

About the note . . .

About the missing shipment of pie

boxes . . .

And, last but not least, the shattered milk bottles.

All things that could be pranks on their own but, coupled with one another and an absence of similar incidents with any of the other shopkeepers on the street, could be an indication of something much less innocuous.

Squatting down next to the rocking chair, she placed a gentle hand on Ruth's knee. "Ruth, you need to say something. If not to Benjamin or Eli, then you need to tell Detective Fisher. Way too much stuff has been happening around your store to be brushed off as a simple prank." A second thought occurred to her, and she gave it voice. "And what happens if Mr. Snow's murder is somehow tied to the stuff happening around here? That's something the police need to look at and consider."

Ruth sucked in her breath. "But I barely knew Mr. Snow."

"No. No, I'm not saying his murder is your fault, Ruth. I'm just saying that maybe it's all tied in together somehow." Seeing the worry only deepen on the woman's face, Claire tried to backpedal, to lessen the stress already weighing on her shy friend. "Look. Would you like it if I spoke to the detective myself, since you don't want your brothers to know what's going on around here?"

Worry turned to a flash of hope as Ruth grabbed hold of Claire's hand. "I would be so grateful. I do not want Eli to know of this."

She considered Ruth's words. "Then I have an idea. How about I take a picture of the window to show the detective, and we ask Mr. Glick for help on how to remove the paint? If we move fast enough, maybe we can get it off before Eli comes to fetch you this afternoon."

"Oh, Miss Weatherly, that would be good. Very, very good."

"Then let's get to it, shall we?" Straightening to a stand, Claire pulled her cell phone from her purse and switched it to the camera function, snapping pictures of the paint-splattered window from various angles as her thoughts revisited a different place and a different conversation.

"I will speak with Mr. Glick." Ruth rose to her feet and started toward the steps, stopping to look back at Claire as she reached the bottom. "You will talk to the police next?"

She snapped the last picture, then slipped her phone back into her purse. "I will talk to them, yes. But there's someone I want to talk to first. Someone who might be able to shed a little light on what's been going on around here lately."

He walked in the door at exactly one minute past eleven, his eyes darting around the store before coming to rest on Claire. "Is she here?"

"If by *'she'* you mean Esther, no. She's not. She's at home working on a few projects for the store." Claire plucked her notebook from a shelf beneath the register and set it on the counter. Flipping it open, she bypassed the first few pages, which contained notes about the store — items she wanted to offer, questions she had for Martha, and customer trends she was seeing — and stopped on the one she'd started less than an hour earlier. This page had nothing to do with the store and everything to do with questions she wanted to ask the man standing in the middle of Heavenly Treasures. "I'll let her know you were in and asking about her."

Arnie Streen pushed a grubby hand through his disheveled crop of red hair and groaned. "The clock is ticking on my paper. I really need to ask Esther a few questions."

Propping her forearms on the counter, she leaned forward. "I'm sure I can find another member of the Amish community to speak with you."

"When is she gonna be back?"

"She's on the schedule for tomorrow morning."

"Wasn't she on the schedule for today, too?" Arnie challenged, frustration evident in his voice.

"She was. But I opted to have her work from home, instead. She'll get more done if she's not distracted by customers coming in and out all day long."

He reached into the candy bowl beside the register and extracted two wrapped caramels, unwrapping the first and popping it into his mouth with lightning speed. "People really get into this Amish stuff, don't they?"

"I'm not sure what you mean," she said as she reached down and retrieved the caramel wrapper from the floor. Tossing it into the trash, she followed the anthropology student around the store.

Arnie grabbed hold of one of the faceless dolls and held it up for Claire to see. "Like this. What little kid truly wants to play with a doll that has no eyes and no mouth? Yet grandma after grandma is going to come in here and buy one of these for their grandkids back home in Iowa or Wyoming or wherever it is they're from, aren't they?" He tossed it back onto the shelf and moved on, his hand already reaching for something else.

"It's a look at another culture. Something to share with loved ones who weren't here," she countered, replacing the discarded doll in the correct spot. "And, when I was a little girl, I would have loved a doll like this."

"If you say so." Arnie spun around holding a painted wooden spoon. "And this? What on earth is someone going to do with a spoon like this?"

Claire took in the delicately painted Amish countryside with its farmhouse and silo nestled in the middle of gently rolling fields. "It's a decoration. A souvenir."

Arnie snorted. "It's not about souvenirs; it's about having something to take back home and use to mock people who are different."

She pried the spoon from his hands and returned it to the display hook from which it had come. "Excuse me?"

"It's like all those people who rubberneck their way past traffic accidents and stand around staring while some poor slob is dying of a heart attack at the beach." He flicked his hand across a nearby quilt stand. "They buy this stuff so they can say they were there . . . where the Amish live. You know, those weird people who don't have televisions and radios."

His assertion brought her up short. "I don't think that's true . . ."

"I do." Arnie stopped along the back wall to inspect a handmade clock, his gaze intent on the impeccable craftsmanship even while his mouth was still trained on the conversation with Claire. "How else can you explain vacationing in a place where the main thing you do is gawk at other people?"

"People vacation here to learn more."

"About people they see as freaks." Arnie doubled back, nearly knocking into Claire as he did. "It's the way this world works. You don't think I notice the way those people stare at my hands around the dinner table every night? But do they ask? No. They'd rather gawk than take the time to learn why they're all scarred up. Do they ask about what I'm doing while they're out all day long posing for pictures that'll end up in some dusty old photo album on some basement shelf? No. They'd rather see me as the geeky stranger who keeps to himself — the weird one. And why is that? Well, that's easy. When someone marches to a different drum, it's to be mocked not celebrated."

From the moment Arnie had shown up at Sleep Heavenly and booked a room for an entire month, Claire had found his fascination with the Amish curious. Yet, in that moment, it all made sense. The only thing that didn't make sense was how long it took her to see it.

Arnie's decision to write his thesis on the Amish was based on an understanding, a kinship. This young man, who was as odd as odd could be, identified with these people he insisted were seen as freaks by the outside world.

She cast about for something to say, something to let him know she got it even if she didn't entirely agree. "Maybe there's some truth to what you say, Arnie, but you can't make a blanket statement about everyone. I think an awful lot of tourists who come here come because they admire people who can live such a simple life."

If he heard her, he said nothing, opting, instead, to grab a handful of mixed candy from the bowl and shoving it into his pocket. "You sure Esther will be in tomorrow?"

"I'm sure."

"Then I'll be back." Arnie started toward the door, then stopped at a bin of Amish reference books. "I didn't know you had these."

She moved in beside him and reached for her favorite. The twenty-page picture book covered many of the basics people liked to know about the Amish — home life, religion, farming, clothing, beliefs. "This one gives some good background. Though, living here for a month, as you are, you'll probably be able to go a bit deeper."

He nodded. "My research started months ago. Being here is just the final step in the process. It makes it come alive, you know?"

Glancing at the counter, she set the book back in the bin and gestured toward her notebook. "I've been wanting to talk to you about something regarding your research. Do you have a minute?"

Surprise flickered in Arnie's eyes, and he turned from the book bin. "You want to talk about my thesis?"

"More about something you said at dinner a few nights ago. About hate crimes and the Amish."

He shrugged. Bypassing the candy in his pocket, he reached for the bowl and yet another caramel. Only this time, he placed the wrapper on the counter rather than the floor. "I remember. Only the particular case that was discussed was the one that precipitated your boyfriend leaving his Amish roots in favor of police work."

"My *boyfriend?* Jakob Fisher is not my boyfriend. I barely know the man." She hated the defensive note to her voice the second she heard it, but it was too late to recall it without looking even worse.

"You looked mighty chummy out on the porch the other night. Dinner for two usually implies a relationship in my book."

"Not in mine, it doesn't."

Arnie flashed a devilish grin. "You don't have to get all touchy. I just made a statement."

She inhaled to a silent count of ten. When she reached the last number, she regained control of the conversation. "In your research for your paper, have you come across other hate crimes against the Amish?"

His eyes narrowed on her face. "Why are you asking?"

"Curiosity, mostly. I guess I equate hate crimes to people who feel threatened by a particular group of people and so they lash out. Something that seems implausible where a group like the Amish are concerned."

"Oh, it's plausible alright. Happens all the time in and around Amish communities all across this country." Arnie turned around, braced his back against the counter, and hoisted himself onto it, planting his now-seated body smack-dab in the middle of everything. "There are documented cases in Ohio, Indiana, Wisconsin, here . . . You name it. If there's an Amish community somewhere, there's been at least one hate crime committed against them."

"But what on earth is there to hate? I mean, they don't cause trouble. They don't get involved in other people's affairs."

"Some people simply hate anything that's different."

She leaned against the register and considered Arnie's statement. "You think that's all of it?"

He shook his head. "No. But it's some."

"And the rest?"

"And the rest comes down to ignorance, plain and simple." He gestured toward the front window and the horse and buggy that passed from view. "Ever been in a hurry to get somewhere and been trapped behind one of those? They're slower than molasses compared to a car."

"So a person takes it out on the guy driving the buggy?" she asked.

"It's not always a big act of aggression, Claire. Sometimes it's a simple case of gunning a car around the buggy and then cutting in really quick and spooking the horse into an accident. Stuff like that has killed everyone in the buggy more than a few times."

She gasped.

"Then there's the people who think the Amish don't pay taxes. They assume, quite ignorantly, that because the Amish don't utilize city services and government-funded schools that they aren't paying the same taxes everyone else is paying. So, rather than educate themselves to the reality, they lash out through vandalism, theft, and a boatload of other ways."

"That really happens?"

Pushing off his hands, Arnie jumped to the ground. "Just ask your friends next door. I believe your aunt said they have broken milk bottles and stolen pie boxes to prove it, didn't she?"

All she could do was nod. If there was any truth to what Arnie had said, the brains behind the shenanigans at Ruth's bakery were ill-informed at best. "So how does it stop?"

"My guess is, it doesn't. You can lead a horse to water, but you can't make it drink." Arnie shuffled over to the door and yanked it open, the jingling bell overhead doing little to bolster her mood.

"Meaning?"

"Meaning, people will believe what they want to believe regardless of the facts staring them in the face. It's easier, somehow."

"Thanks, Arnie. I really appreciate your help." And she did. She just wished he hadn't emptied out her candy supply in the process. "Stop by again tomorrow. I'm sure Esther will be happy to talk with you."

He stopped, one foot on the porch, one foot in the store. "It's hard to miss that fact, ain't it?"

She cocked her head, trying to retrieve whatever conversation piece she'd obviously missed, but she came up short. "Miss what fact?" she finally asked.

"That she digs me. Only, in my case, it's reciprocated."

It took everything she could muster not to laugh out loud or rewind the conversation a few sentences to the one where Arnie himself had talked about people who couldn't accept simple facts. To do either, though, would be an exercise in futility. Instead, she simply waved good-bye and reached for the last remaining caramel in the bowl.

CHAPTER 14

From the time Claire had first moved to Heavenly, Aunt Diane had insisted that her niece claim a night to herself — a night to bury herself in a book, take a long soaking bath, or while away the hours watching sitcoms on the small television in her room. In the beginning, she'd balked, seeing the various tasks around the inn as her way of paying the woman back for allowing Claire to stay with her in the first place.

But when she'd opened Heavenly Treasures a few months later, she'd conceded that one night off each week was probably a good idea. And so Tuesday became that night.

More times than not, she spent her evening off performing tasks for the store. Candles were made, inventory was scoured, and the financial books were brought up to date. The fact that she could do them in front of the TV helped them feel less like a chore.

Occasionally, she spent a Tuesday reading in the parlor or sitting on the front porch talking to guests. When she opted for the latter, her aunt simply shook her head, convinced that Claire wasn't truly enjoying the hard-earned respite her niece needed.

What Diane didn't fully understand was how isolating Claire's time in New York had been. That despite living in one of the most famous cities in the world — where people were in abundance — she treasured Heavenly for the human contact she'd desperately needed.

Tonight, though, was different. Tonight she wanted to be alone, to try her best to make sense of everything happening around her. Which is why, after locking up the shop, she turned right instead of left.

It was a perfect evening for a walk, thanks to the faintest hint of an autumn chill that seemed oblivious to its too-early arrival. And, thanks to the evening hour, Lighted Way was less crowded than normal, the bulk of the cars and horse-drawn buggies heading home for the night.

Still, she couldn't help but release a sigh as her feet left the commercial district and headed toward the quieter, more peaceful side of town, where buggies were the norm and cars the exception. Though, with the fast-approaching dinner hour, buggy sightings were growing rarer as well.

She envied the Amish families who were preparing to share the evening's meal with loved ones. It was like dinner at the inn, only better because the people at those tables didn't leave after a few days. They stayed. For life.

Or, at least, most did.

Jakob was an exception.

She followed the finely graveled road as it wound to the left and headed down into a valley of farmland, the peace and tranquility of her rapidly approaching surroundings allowing a sense of true contentment to seep in past the worry she'd felt lapping at her heart all day long.

So much of what was weighing her down really wasn't her concern. Yet, because it affected people she cared about on some level or another, she simply couldn't shirk it away. It was the way she was, the way she'd always been. And it was why the whitewashed world she'd been living in for so many years prior to coming to Heavenly never truly fit.

A slow *clip-clop* just over her left shoulder made her stop and turn, her hand instinctively rising to block out the last of the evening's rays.

"Good evening, Miss Weatherly. May I offer you a ride to wherever it is you are going?"

She stepped into the shadow of the buggy as it stopped beside her, the now-clear view of the driver and his knee-weakening blue eyes making her wish for a fan or a sudden acceleration to the breeze that cooled her face. "Hi, Benjamin. I . . . I appreciate the offer but I'm not really going anywhere in particular."

His brows furrowed beneath his black hat. "Oh?"

"I guess my brain just needs a break from work. I didn't even really know where I was going until I locked up the shop and my feet took me in this direction."

Benjamin looked down the road stretched out before them, the brim of his hat shielding the sun from his view. "But there is nothing this way except Amish land."

She followed his field of vision and felt the last of the day's tension disappear from her body. "I know. That's why I'm going this way."

His gaze left his people's land and focused again on her. "I do not understand."

Inhaling deeply, she tried to verbalize what

Benjamin's lifestyle did for her, how it made her feel alive and hopeful. "Very often, a person has a place he or she likes to go to regroup. To relax. To think. I've come to realize that this place" — she stretched her arms in front of her — "does that for me."

For a moment she was afraid she'd said something stupid, something he didn't understand or maybe even found silly, but after a long pause he proved differently. "I have such a place."

She wasn't sure why his admission surprised her, but it did. Somehow, she'd assumed a person living such a simple, uncluttered life wouldn't need a place to reflect or regroup. Then again, he was human. Just like she was.

"Perhaps if I show you such a place, you will like it as well?" he asked, surprising her still further.

Shifting from one foot to the other, she stared up at Benjamin, dumbfounded by both the suggestion and the notion that such a quiet man, whom she'd just met, would make such a generous overture in her direction.

"Are you sure? Don't you have to get home for your meal?" It was a fair question, based largely on Amish traditions she'd learned about from Esther.

He let the reins slacken as he reached up and tipped the brim of his hat upward just a bit. "I live alone and, at times, dine alone."

And, just like that, she was transported back to Martha's home and the unexpected news that Benjamin Miller was a widower. Suddenly, this quiet man's need for a place to ponder life made perfect sense.

"If you have the time and you'd like to share your special place with me, I'd be honored. Truly." Reaching up, she grabbed hold of the buggy's edge and lifted herself onto the seat beside him, the beat of her heart vacillating between fast and slow. "Thank you."

With a slight nod of his head, Benjamin jiggled the reins, prompting the horse to resume his previous pace, the *clip-clop* of his hooves lessening the severity of their sudden silence. She looked to her right, and then her left, the farmland she'd viewed from her car window not more than three days earlier more alluring than ever.

"When I was out here the other day, the fields were filled with people working. And now . . . they're so quiet."

"The workday is over."

It was such a simple sentence, yet, after spending nearly five years with a man who was either not around to talk or dominated the conversation when he was, she found it more than a little refreshing.

She pulled her focus off the scenery and fixed it, instead, on Benjamin. "What do the Amish do once the evening meal is over?"

"We visit with family. In the summer months, we sit on the porch."

She leaned her head against the side of the buggy and peered out at the first home they passed, a modest white farmhouse with several clotheslines and a wide front porch. "That sounds nice."

"What do the English do?"

"At my aunt's, where I live, we visit in the parlor. We talk about our day, discuss books we are reading, and enjoy our guests."

"Guests?" The horse and buggy continued down the road, passing one farmhouse and then the other.

She nodded. "My aunt owns Sleep Heavenly at the English end of Lighted Way. It's a bed-and-breakfast. People who stay there come from all over the country, and, sometimes, their stories of home allow us to experience places we've never been."

"Do you like that?" he asked as he cast a sidelong glance in her direction, his deep blue eyes lingering momentarily on her face.

"I like getting to know people. I like learning about them."

"Do you let them learn about you?"

The question caught her up short, its depth not something she would have expected from any man, much less one who was Amish. "I . . . I don't know. I think I listen more than I talk."

With the barely perceptible tug of his hand, Benjamin steered the horse and buggy to the left, taking them up a long climbing hill and through a one-lane covered bridge and out the other side. Where the road narrowed still further and wound off into the woods, he pulled to a stop and swept his hand to the right. "We are here."

She peeked out the side of the buggy and sucked in her breath, the lush green fields of the Amish stretched out before them as the sun began its descent. "Oh, Benjamin. It's beautiful."

The outer edges of his mouth spread outward, and he nodded his head ever so slightly in agreement. "I come here when I am troubled. As I am about Eli." Releasing the reins, he stepped down from the buggy before crossing around to the other side and offering Claire his hand.

Unsure of what to do, she shyly deposited her hand in his and vacated her seat, walking alongside him until they reached a large, flat boulder. "Is Eli alright?"

"He has a temper. He does not always do as he should."

"But he has a good heart." She perched on the edge of the rock and looked out over land that Benjamin himself farmed each day. "He keeps a close watch on your sister, helping her in whatever ways he can. He is polite and kind."

"He has been shunned many times." Benjamin leaned against the rock and glanced down at his hands, his tone hard to read. "He always repents and always forgets."

"He's still young, Benjamin."

"Not that young." He met her gaze and held it for a few beats. "People form opinions of a man. Those who are respected and trusted are looked to for guidance. Those who are not are seen differently."

She weighed his words against the facts as of late. "Are you afraid this talk surrounding Walter Snow's death will affect people's perception of your brother?"

"I do not know how to protect him from himself. Yet it is hard to wash my hands of him. He is my brother."

"Why would you wash your hands of him?"

"His action brings shame, and now it may bring heartache to friends."

She looked a question at him, the answer coming before a single word ever left her mouth. "Is it so wrong for Esther and Martha to come in contact with Jakob?"

"Yes."

"But he loves them," she insisted.

"Jakob made his choice."

"And he's made the choice to come back."

"He can never come back." The statement, while simple, reverberated around them with heartbreaking finality.

"Do you think that's fair?" she finally asked.

"It is our way."

She considered telling him his way was wrong but let it go. It wasn't her right to judge someone else's beliefs, someone else's way of living. Instead, she said the only thing she could. "Walter Snow was found behind my shop, mere feet from the alley between your sister's bakery and my shop. Jakob will need to ask questions of English and Amish alike. It is his job. But if I can help as some sort of middleman, I'm happy to do so."

"That is very kind."

She looked off into the distance and tried to pick out Lighted Way, the lines of the shops and the lampposts working their familiar magic on her heart. "I love being here, in Heavenly. And I love this spot, too. Thank you for sharing it with me."

"I found it after my wife passed on."

"I'm sorry for your loss."

"It was God's will."

"Can you remarry? Is that allowed?" The words were barely through her lips before she was shaking her head at her insensitivity. "I'm sorry. I had no right to ask that."

"I can," he replied softly. "I do not know if I will."

All she could do was nod. "My aunt Diane says that anything is possible if you simply open your heart to everything and everyone around you. I'm not sure I always believe that, but I certainly think it's worth a try."

Feeling the intensity of his eyes as he studied her from the side, she smiled and looked away, her mind a swirl of thoughts she couldn't quite pin down. Life was confusing no matter how you lived. The Amish had worries just like everyone else. Yet, somehow, the dawning of that reality held little comfort.

CHAPTER 15

It was close to eight o'clock when Benjamin dropped her off at Sleep Heavenly, the melodic *clip-clop* of the horse's hooves fairly successful at drowning out the occasional rumble of hunger from one or both of their stomachs.

"I had nice time, Miss Weatherly."

"Claire, please," she reminded as she stepped down off the buggy and turned to face him once again. "Thank you for such a nice evening."

"Was the spot good?"

She grinned. "That spot was spectacular; the company even better."

He glanced down at the reins in his hand, a slight flush of his face barely visible in the decreasing light of day. "Yes. It was."

She felt the answering warmth in her own face. "Are you sure you wouldn't like to come in? I'm sure Aunt Diane has some leftovers from dinner we could eat."

Benjamin shook his head. "I am home each night. I must check in with Eli and Ruth so they do not worry."

"Then please tell them I said hello." She lifted her hand to wave, then pulled it back down when the buggy remained in the same spot. "Is something wrong?"

"I can not leave until you are inside."

"Oh, then I guess I'll say goodnight." She turned toward the inn and made her way up the sidewalk, the answering swish of the curtain in the front hallway window catching her by surprise, first pausing and then quickening her step to the door. When she reached her destination, she offered one final wave to Benjamin Miller and then stepped inside, anxious to put a face to the unidentified snoop.

But there was no one there.

Slowly, Claire worked her way out from the window in question, peeking into various corners and nesting spots sprinkled around the inn. Her first human sighting, though, didn't come until she was in the kitchen off the back of the sprawling Victorian home. She took in her aunt's soapy hands and the stack of dishes in the drainer and announced her presence, earning herself a curious smile in response.

"Where did you disappear to this evening, dear?"

Claire plucked an apple from the fruit bowl and a dish towel from the rack and headed over to dry. "I went for a walk after work only to have it turn into a buggy ride."

Her aunt's left eyebrow rose upward. "Oh?"

She took a quick bite of her apple and then set it on the counter, her stomach gurgling in protest. "I just got back a minute ago." Reaching for a plate, she ran the dish towel around the outer edges and worked her way toward the center. "You wouldn't have any idea who might have been watching me from the front hallway, would you?"

"Watching you?" her aunt echoed before extracting the plate and the towel from Claire's hands and gesturing toward the apple with her chin. "This is your night off, remember?"

"You don't get a night off."

"Because this is my business, not yours." Diane stared at the apple until Claire picked it up and took another bite. "As for your question, I can't imagine who would have been in the hallway just now. Arnie is upstairs working on his thesis."

"And the lovebirds?" she asked playfully.

"Not standing in a hallway watching you,

I'm quite certain." Diane finished wiping the dish Claire had started and set it on the counter to the right of the dish drainer. "Perhaps it was our new guest."

She paused midbite and studied her aunt. "So where is this one from?"

"Here."

"You mean Pennsylvania?"

Diane grabbed the next dish and added it to the growing dry stack with quiet efficiency. "No, here as in Heavenly."

"Heavenly? Why on earth would someone stay here if they live in Heavenly?" She winced at her choice of words and did her best to lessen any sting they may have caused. "Wait. I don't mean it like that. I mean, I can't imagine anyone *not* wanting to stay here, but isn't that kind of wasting money when you already live in the same town?"

"She's staying here to get away from the memories, I guess."

Claire opened her mouth to speak only to shut it at the sound of tapping on the kitchen door. Tossing the dish towel atop the stack of clean dishes, Diane crossed the kitchen and pushed the swinging door open to reveal a familiar face.

Only the Nellie Snow standing less than twenty feet away seemed much different than the Nellie Snow who had marched into Heavenly Treasures a few days earlier, demanding Jakob arrest Eli for the murder of her crooked husband.

Gone was the anger she'd spat through clenched teeth.

Gone was the aura of suspicion.

And gone was the feeling that Nellie Snow was standing on a mountaintop looking down on everyone else.

In its place was a woman who looked tired — like she'd backpacked around the world all by herself.

"Ms. Weatherly, I was wondering if I could have a glass of water for my bedside table." Nellie pulled the flaps of her silk robe more tightly against her body and peered around the kitchen, her tired eyes coming to rest on Claire. "Oooh, I know you, don't I?"

She dropped her apple core into the trash container and joined the women by the door. "We met very briefly the other day."

Nellie covered her face with her hands. "I'm sorry. I'm having a hard time keeping track of anything since my husband was killed." When Claire didn't react, Nellie stole a peek over the tips of her fingers. "He was . . . *murdered.*"

"I know. And I'm sorry." Claire patted the woman's silky sleeve. "This must be an awful time for you."

The woman let her hands drift back to her sides in lieu of a dramatic nod. "Everywhere I looked around the house, I saw Walter's face, Walter's smile. It simply became too unbearable." Claire watched Nellie's eyes follow Diane to the cupboard, the sink, and back to the door before continuing her tale. "Ms. Weatherly was kind enough to offer me a deal on a room, knowing that I'll make up the difference when Walter's finances are released."

"I imagine the money he stole will have to be returned first." She hadn't meant to say it, to utter the thought aloud, but it had just come out, prompted no doubt by her evening with Benjamin Miller, one of the people most affected by Walter Snow's thievery.

In a flash, the Nellie Snow of earlier came back with a vengeance, the woman's tired eyes crackling to life. "I'm fairly certain the court will be more interested in putting an Amish murderer behind bars than making sure Walter's books are squared."

She swallowed back the urge to defend Eli out of respect for her aunt, but it was hard. It was obvious that Nellie Snow had made up her mind as to the identity of her husband's killer. And it was also obvious —

based on what Claire had witnessed the other day — that Nellie was going to do everything in her power to keep the Heavenly Police Department focused on the same suspect.

Fortunately, Jakob Fisher was a smart man, determined to find the truth no matter where it led. He just needed the Amish to cooperate in order to do his job . . .

"The problem is how closed-mouthed those people are. Everyone seems to believe they are so peaceful, so quiet, so law abiding. But it's all a farce." Nellie took the tall glass of water from Diane's outstretched hands and clutched it between her own. "They fight. They drink. They —"

Diane rested her hands on her hips. "Now, Mrs. Snow, I've lived in this town long enough to know when something is true and when it's not. The Amish do not drink."

"Eli Miller does."

"He was on his Rumspringa."

"He is still Amish, isn't he?" Nellie challenged.

"When on Rumspringa, he is no different than an English college student exploring the world around him. Which means he can drink."

"Rumspringa." Nellie rolled her eyes. "As if all their ill behavior is confined to that year. Please. I've seen enough in this town to know that the Amish engage in all sorts of behaviors people think they avoid. But I'm here to tell you both that it's not true. Not even close."

With each new word, each new accusation that filtered between Nellie's lips, Claire could sense Diane getting tenser.

"They take things that don't belong to them and —"

"Like what?" Diane demanded, her voice adopting an unfamiliar shrillness.

Nellie stared at Claire and her aunt. "Like goods that were left in my husband's store when he . . . when he went away for a little while."

Claire took a step forward, successfully cutting off her aunt's response. "The goods that were left in your husband's store didn't belong to him in the first place. They belonged to the people who'd made them. Which is why I returned each and every item to its rightful owner."

Nellie's eyes narrowed on Claire. "You're the woman who opened that shop in Walter's space?"

"You mean the space Walter had rented before skipping out on the landlord without a word?" She didn't wait for a response, choosing, instead, to stick to the facts. "I left the stockroom untouched for weeks in the event he came back ready to square things away. When he didn't, I went through it with a fine-toothed comb, returning each handcrafted item to its rightful owner. Perhaps you should do that with the money that is rightfully theirs, too."

Nellie's jaw tightened in anger. "And their women? Are you going to defend them as well?"

Diane gasped. "What are you talking about?"

"Everyone thinks they're so innocent in their little bonnets and simple dresses. But they're not. They think nothing of prancing around and flirting with just about anything that crosses their path — Amish, English . . . married or unmarried. It makes no difference."

Reaching behind her back, Diane untied her apron and draped it over a stool. "Mrs. Snow, I understand that you are finding it difficult to stay in the home you shared with your husband in light of everything that has happened. But Sleep Heavenly is not the right place for you, either."

"You're kicking me out?" Nellie spat.

"I'm afraid so."

"You did the right thing, Aunt Diane."

Diane looked up from her spot on the couch, instinctively moving to the side to make room for her niece. "I didn't see you standing there."

"I know. You've been staring at that spot on the wall over there for the past ten minutes." Claire bypassed the empty sofa cushion in favor of the ottoman. "Are you okay?"

Her aunt's shoulders hitched upward ever so slightly in the flickering candlelight. "I've never asked someone to leave before."

She grabbed hold of the woman's hands and held them tight. "People stay here because they've come to learn about the Amish. Nellie Snow would be detrimental to that."

"I can't believe those awful things she was saying. That they drink, steal, flirt with married men . . . I can't remember the last time I was so angry. About anything." Diane pushed off the couch and wandered around the room, stopping to straighten a hanging frame or fix a cockeyed book. "I mean, can you imagine accusing the Amish of such things? After her husband bilked them of their money?"

"No, I can't." She shifted on the ottoman to afford a better view of her aunt. "I think the part that really pushed me over was the accusation about the women."

"That was like everything else with her — a way to make reality more palatable." Diane released a pent-up sigh and then retraced her way back to the couch. "You know what? I don't want to talk about Nellie Snow anymore. I'd much prefer to hear about this buggy ride of yours."

She couldn't help but smile at her aunt's ability to shut off the negative on a dime. It was certainly a skill worth learning. "I ran into Benjamin Miller while I was out walking, and we spent a little time together." Feeling her aunt's gaze, she twisted her hands together in her lap. "He told me a little bit about his life, I told him a little bit about mine. It was . . . nice."

"He's Amish, Claire."

Surprised by the implication, she snapped her head up. "What's that supposed to mean?"

"You don't think I noticed that sparkle in your eye when you came into the kitchen this evening?"

She felt her face warm. "What sparkle?"

"The kind that comes from a connection. Like I saw after your dinner with Jakob."

She wanted to argue, to call her aunt crazy, but she couldn't. Nor could she explain to herself why. Instead, she simply shrugged. "Benjamin is nice, and he's a good listener."

"And Jakob?"

She closed her eyes at the image of the Amish-turned-English detective and the odd feeling he, too, stirred inside her heart. "Jakob is also very nice."

"I'm glad. I'm glad to see you settling in and making Heavenly your home. I think it's a perfect match for you, dear. I just don't want to see you get hurt again, that's all."

"Hurt?" she echoed.

Diane nodded, her gaze never leaving Claire's face. "Benjamin is, and always will be, Amish. So long as you remember that, you'll be fine."

CHAPTER 16

Claire turned the hand-painted coal bucket around in her hands and marveled at the detail of the winter cabin it depicted, her mind actively considering and discarding various display options.

"I had no idea your mother could paint like this. I mean, look at this stuff." She swept her hands above the crowded countertop. "It's amazing."

Esther leaned against the counter, her expression lacking the awed shock Claire knew her own face revealed. "Mamm likes to paint."

"Likes to paint?" she babbled, taking in the hand-painted handsaw and milk can Esther had placed on the counter upon her arrival, the scenes they portrayed more befitting of an expensive frame than regular everyday items. "Saying she likes to paint implies a basic interest, Esther. There's nothing the slightest bit basic about your mother's work."

Reaching down beside her feet, Esther grabbed hold of a bag and handed it to Claire. "There's more."

"More?" she whispered.

Esther nodded. "Some pillows."

"She made some pillows?" Claire stuck her hand inside the bag and extracted a soft quilted pillow, the pleasing feel of the material bringing a smile to her lips. "Ohhh, Esther, this feels wonderful."

"Watch." Esther took the pillow from Claire and unfolded it, the soft material transforming itself into a blanket. "And see? A pocket to keep your feet warm."

Claire leaned forward, mesmerized. Sure enough, the blanket had a special place for feet. "I had no idea. I thought it was a pillow when I pulled it out."

"It is that, too." With a few easy motions, Esther folded the blanket into itself once again, re-creating the original pillow in the process. "See? The English call them quillows."

She looked from the pillow to the hand-painted items and back again. "Your mother is a genius, an absolute genius."

Esther's eyes widened. "She is just Mamm."

She wanted to argue but thought better of

it, her aunt's ongoing tutorial on the Amish and their humility looping its way through her thoughts. "You will thank her for me, won't you?" she finally said.

"I will do so." Esther scooped up her mother's creations and peered at Claire. "Where do I place these?"

Glancing at the clock beside the register, Claire shook her head, curiosity and an awareness of Arnie's pending arrival pushing the latest inventory additions to the background. "I was hoping we could talk for a minute instead."

Slowly, Esther set the items back down on the counter. "Is there something I am doing wrong?"

"No! Having you here is working wonderfully." She took hold of Esther's hand and guided her toward the solitary stool propped behind the counter. "It's just . . . Well, I found something the other day that I don't think you wanted me to see."

Esther's eyebrows dipped downward. "I have nothing."

Claire reached into the front pocket of her trousers and pulled the crinkled heart-shaped note from its depths. Holding it outward, she studied her employee's horror-filled eyes. "You have this."

Esther gasped and grabbed the paper, her

slender hand balling it up and shoving it beneath the register once again. "Please, please, please do not speak of this. Eli can not know."

"I'm not trying to hurt Eli," she explained. "I'm just worried about you. About what this note means."

"It means nothing."

"Then why are you worried about Eli? It can't hurt him if it means nothing."

"Not hurt. Anger. Much, much anger."

"Walter Snow wrote it, didn't he?" she asked.

The bell above the door sounded, sucking all remaining color from Esther's face. "Please," she whispered. "I can not speak of this now."

"But I don't understand. You said he grabbed your arm. That he yelled at you when he came in that last day. Why would he do that if he had feelings for you?"

Esther drew back, shock widening her eyes still further. "I can not explain that. He . . . he just did."

She opened her mouth to speak, to offer to listen when Esther was finally ready, but it was too late. Arnie Streen was on the scene, notebook in tow.

"Esther! I've been looking for you for days."

Esther shot a worried look in Claire's direction. "I am sorry. I did not know."

She rushed to explain the man's presence. "You remember Arnie Streen, don't you? He's staying at my —"

"Of course she remembers me," Arnie boasted as he plucked a pen from his shirt pocket. "Isn't that right, Esther?"

Esther nodded slowly. "Mr. Streen is a good customer. He comes in often."

It took everything she had not to laugh out loud. Esther was so innocent, so sweet, that she had absolutely no clue the freckle-faced redhead graced the confines of Heavenly Treasures for one reason and one reason only.

And it had absolutely nothing to do with Amish-made crafts.

"Mr. Streen is working on a paper about the Amish for school."

Esther's eyebrows rose. "I do not understand."

She searched for a way to explain what the man was doing but came up empty. Instead, she let Arnie do the talking as she set about the task of finding spots for all of the new merchandise, her thoughts bouncing between Esther's reaction to the note and her own confusion on how to proceed with the handful of nothing she knew.

Her gut told her the note was something Jakob might want to know about, but her heart told her to stay out of it. One only had to look at Esther to know she had a crush on Eli Miller. And it was that crush that surely explained Esther's reluctance to share the existence of the note with the young man.

But if it was Walter's feelings for Esther that brought him back to Heavenly in the first place, wasn't that something Jakob should know? And if he did, where would that knowledge lead?

It was that last question, coupled with the answer it conjured in her own mind that made her hesitate most.

A shy laugh from Esther broke through her woolgathering. Glancing over, she couldn't help but smile, too. Arnie, who finally had Esther all to himself, was putting his best and least socially awkward foot forward, taking only one candy from the bowl at a time and actually depositing the wrappers on the counter instead of the floor.

It was progress, even if it was only temporary.

For a moment she simply watched the two interacting, the differences between them vivid. First, there was Arnie. Somewhere around six feet tall, the anthropology student's khaki trousers had seen a few too many hot-water washes, and his pale-blue button-down shirt was in desperate need of an iron. His red hair stood on end in some places, while several sections appeared matted to his head.

Across from him stood the always-neat Esther — a young woman who hand washed her simple clothes on a daily basis and was up at the crack of dawn to help around the farm before putting in her time at Heavenly Treasures. Coming in at just over five feet three, Esther was a nonstop ball of energy wrapped in a very unassuming package. To the outside world, she was quiet, maybe even meek. But to those who knew her, Esther was a dreamer.

Unfortunately for Arnie, Eli was at the center of those dreams.

Their conversation was fairly quiet, with breaks every once in a while for Arnie to consult his notebook and Esther to peer forlornly toward the bakery in the hope that Eli's buggy might be parked in the alley.

She could make out the occasional questions pertaining to Amish beliefs and customs, but, for the most part, she could only guess at their words. There was a part of her that wanted to pull up a chair and listen, to learn even more about the group of people who had grabbed hold of her heart. But she resisted.

What she still wanted to learn about the Amish would unfold in time. At the hands of people she considered friends. Like Esther and Ruth, Eli and Ben —

The jingle of bells resonated around the room, forcing all eyes toward the front door.

"Good afternoon, Claire" — Jakob's eyes darted around the room, stopping on the twosome by the counter — "and Esther . . . and Mr. Streen, isn't it?"

A quick nod was all the answer the detective received as Arnie turned back to a suddenly flustered Esther.

Anxious to ease the tension that ignited in Esther every time her uncle was near, Claire stepped back from the hand-painted milk can she'd positioned in the window and spread her arms wide. "So? What do you think?"

Jakob closed the gap between the front door and the window display in short order, his hazel eyes riveted on the forty-eight-gallon can. "Where'd you get this? It's beautiful."

Before she could answer, the detective reached out and traced the autumn-based farm scene with his finger. "My sister did this, didn't she?"

A quiet gasp from the other side of the room went unnoticed as Jakob's voice took on a faraway quality. "I remember our Mamm using a paintbrush once for something I can't even remember. We were sitting around the table after the evening meal. Martha picked up the brush and just started painting. Within minutes, there was a horse, and then a buggy. It was so good that it looked as if you could step inside the picture and go for a ride."

And then, as if sensing the question that hovered over his niece, he added, "She was about your age at the time, Esther."

Claire stole a peek in Esther's direction and saw the tentative curiosity behind her friend's brown eyes. Not wanting to see the connection end, Claire grabbed hold of the still-unplaced handsaw propped against the wall and held it up for Jakob to inspect. "Look at this one. Can you imagine actually using this to cut something?"

Jakob leaned forward and sucked in his breath.

She lowered the saw and pinned him with a worried stare. "Are you okay?"

Without saying a word, he took the saw from her hands and studied it closely. "This pond is where we swam as kids. It is where my sister and I played together."

She blinked against the tears that pricked the corners of her eyes, the wistful tone of the man's voice tugging at that same place in her soul that desperately wanted to mend fences for this man and his sister.

A faint rustle made her turn to find Esther not more than three feet away.

"It is where Mamm took me to swim as a child," Esther whispered. "She said it was a special place."

Jakob nodded, his focus never leaving the painted landscape he held in his hands. "Because it was."

Claire held her breath, afraid to break the spell.

Esther had spoken to Jakob. A real, honest-to-goodness sentence.

"Hey. You can't do that."

Esther spun around to face Arnie. "Mr. Streen?"

The redhead pointed at Jakob but addressed his Amish niece. "You're not allowed to speak to one who has been shunned, remember? It's against the Ordnung."

And with those two simple sentences, the spell was broken.

CHAPTER 17

She knew she should be pleased at the sales for the past week, but it was hard to focus on anything besides the image of Jakob Fisher's face the moment Arnie opened his mouth and ruined a long-overdue moment. The detective's hurt had been so raw and so fresh that it had been agonizing to witness.

In fact, if he hadn't shaken her anger off, she'd have thrown Arnie out on his ear. Since he had, though, Arnie and Esther had resumed their private conversation, and Jakob had made some lame excuse that allowed him to retreat back to the police station.

By the time Arnie had finished with his elongated interview, she opted to cut Esther loose for the day, citing the quiet foot traffic along Lighted Way as a reason for the decision. But it hadn't been the truth. Not really, anyway.

She just wanted to be alone — to go through the books, wander the store, and maybe even plan a way to reclaim the tiny inroad Jakob had almost made with his estranged niece before her aunt's boarder had stepped in and ruined everything.

Sure, she knew her aunt wouldn't approve. The rift between Jakob and his family was a lost cause in Diane's eyes, a casualty of a culture that was unbendable. And maybe it was.

She just wasn't ready to write it off yet.

"Miss Weatherly?"

She looked up from the old-fashioned roll-top desk to find Benjamin Miller standing in the doorway of her makeshift office. "Oh, Benjamin. I didn't hear you."

"I knocked. You did not come." He gestured toward the hallway from which he'd come. "Should I go?"

"No." Pushing her paperwork and calculator toward the side of her desk, she gave the man her full attention. "I guess I didn't realize I left the back door unlocked."

She followed Benjamin's gaze as he took in the envelope of money with Martha's name sprawled across the front, the expression he wore difficult to decipher.

"Benjamin? Is something wrong?"

"I have something for you."

Her focus dropped to Ben's empty hands. "Oh?"

"Come."

She rose from her rickety chair and followed the man down the hallway and out the back door. "What's wrong? Did you find something?"

"I did not find it. I made it." He sidestepped a team of matching horses and made his way to the back of an open wagon carrying a few small pieces of furniture. "Esther tells Eli of your honesty."

Leaning forward, he reached across the wagon bed and wrapped his hands around the base of an unfinished rocking chair, depositing it on the cobblestoned ground at her feet. Next to it, he placed a small side table and a child-sized footstool.

She ran her hand across the back of the rocker. "Is this for the store?"

He nodded.

An unexpected burning pricked at the corner of her eyes, and she blinked it away. The last thing she wanted to do was cry in front of this stoic man. Especially when she knew she'd sound foolish trying to explain the reason behind the tears. Instead, she swallowed — once, twice. "Benjamin, I'd be honored to display these in the store. They're beautiful."

A slight smile played at the corners of his mouth, and again he nodded. "I can make more."

"How long does it take you to make a rocker like this?" she inquired. "The spindles alone must take forever."

"If I work each night, it goes fast."

She met his eyes. "But you're in the fields all day long. How do you find the energy to do this, too?"

"I do it after the evening meal. It keeps me busy."

It made sense now. Having been married, Benjamin lived alone. And although his house was on the same farm as his parents' and grandparents' homes, he surely felt his wife's absence at mealtime and beyond. Woodworking surely eased that absence in much the way candle making eased Claire's occasional bouts of loneliness.

The difference was, she had Diane to talk things over with when the candle making didn't cut it. Benjamin, on the other hand, had a rock and a view . . .

"I . . . I want to thank you for last night. Seeing your special place, talking with someone close to my own age . . . It was more needed than I realized."

For a moment he merely studied her face, his thoughts a mystery. But just as she began to think she'd said too much, he grabbed the rocker in one capable hand and the side table in the other. "I will bring them inside for you."

"I'll get the footstool," she mumbled before trailing him back through the door, across the stockroom, and into the shop. "Every Wednesday, I put Esther's and now Martha's consignment money in an envelope for a Thursday payday. When any of your work sells, I will do the same for you."

"I trust you."

Overcome by yet another round of emotions, she forced herself to focus on the best possible location for Benjamin's pieces. "I'm not sure where the best place to put everything is just yet."

Benjamin strode across the room and placed the side table and rocker in the section with other items for the home. Then he retraced his steps long enough to commandeer the footstool from her arms and place it alongside the bin of Amish dolls and hooks of baby bibs. When he was done, he turned to face her once again. "I have a new rolling pin for Ruth. But she left with Eli, and I did not bring the key."

"I think I can help with that." Beckoning him to follow, she made her way over to the counter. "The register and that tiered display stand in the front window are the only two things I hung on to when I took over this space. And, by default, that means your sister's spare key, too." She slid her hand along the side of the register until she felt the magnetized key holder on its side. "If it weren't for Eli helping me carry in my candles on that first day, I'm not sure I would have ever noticed it back here."

"I will bring it back in one moment." He reached out and grabbed hold of the key, his fingers lingering on hers a beat longer than necessary.

She held her breath, unsure of what to say or how to respond — or even whether it was all in her head. But before she could make sense of any of it, his hand was gone, and he was walking toward the hallway off the back of the shop, completely oblivious to any spark of attraction her desperate little mind had conjured.

She was just repositioning the footstool amid the items geared toward children when she heard his footsteps. "I bet Ruth is going to be thrilled with her new rolling pin."

"Rolling pin?"

She spun around, surprised by the voice that answered. "Oh . . . Jakob, I'm sorry. I thought you were someone else." She shifted her weight from one foot to the other as her thoughts traveled back to their earlier meeting. "I'm really sorry about what happened today. If I could have stifled Mr. Streen's words with a roll of duct tape, I would have."

"You and me both." He wandered over to his sister's coal bucket yet kept his hands in his pockets, the smile on his face anything but natural. "But he was right. And Esther knew it."

"No one had to know."

"Esther knew. That was enough."

"What did Arnie mean about the Ordnung?" It was a question she'd intended to ask Diane that evening, yet was better suited to present company.

Jakob leaned his right shoulder against the nearest row of shelves. "The Ordnung is really an unwritten code of order that's been handed down over generations. It essentially interprets the laws of social and spiritual behavior Amish are expected to follow."

"But if it's unwritten, doesn't that leave room for exceptions?"

A strangled sound emerged from his lips before he shook it off. "No. And that is why the Amish have existed in such strong numbers for so long. They know what is expected of them, what kind of life they are to lead. It's when exceptions come into play that things eventually fall apart."

It was hard not to ache for this man who still championed the same lifestyle that had turned its back on him, and she said as much to him.

"The Amish do not baptize children. They wait until one is mature enough to make a conscious choice. That choice, should they make it, binds them to the Amish life, for they have committed to obeying the church rules. They know that if they sin, they will be excommunicated and shunned until they confess their sins and seek forgiveness in front of their congregation." He took an audible breath as he brushed at the faintest hint of stubble on his chin. "I was baptized. I said I understood. And then I left. That can't be forgiven."

"How can you be so . . . so okay with it?" she whispered.

"I'm not. It hurts every day. But I knew the consequences of my actions when I left, and I left, anyway."

"But why can't your sister talk to you? Or even Esther, for that matter?"

"Because they follow the Ordnung."

"I'm not Amish, and they talk to me," she argued.

"You did not promise to be Amish and

then leave."

She didn't know what to say. Her head got what Jakob was saying — it really did. But her heart just couldn't wrap itself around the hurt.

"I made my choice, Claire."

"Then I guess I just can't understand why you came back." She sat down on the edge of Benjamin's rocker. "The hurt must be so much stronger here than it was in New York. At least there you could try to forget. At least a little."

"I left so I could help people like my family. I can't really do that in the city."

"There are other Amish towns, where you wouldn't be treated like a pariah . . ."

She followed his gaze as it moved from the handsaw to the milk can and back again, his thoughts as much of a guess as the expression on his face. "But this is where I want to be."

"What happens if you run up against a case that forces you to lock up a member of the Amish community?"

"You mean like Eli if it turns out he murdered Walter Snow?"

"My brother did not murder!"

Claire jumped from her chair, nearly knocking Jakob to his feet. "Benjamin, I didn't hear you."

Benjamin pointed Ruth's spare key at Jakob. "I heard him. And he is wrong!"

"He didn't say Eli murdered anyone." Claire made her way around various display tables and freestanding pieces of furniture to stand in front of Benjamin. "He was just responding to a hypothetical situation I posed. I'm sorry."

"He should not use my brother!" Benjamin thundered.

Jakob closed the gap Claire had created between them with several long strides. But his change in proximity only intensified the tense atmosphere that suddenly gripped Heavenly Treasures with an ironclad fist. "You have to realize your brother is a suspect, Benjamin. That's a simple fact that would exist whether I was on the force here or not."

Benjamin's jaw tightened.

"I realize the Miller boys can do no wrong in the eyes of people like my father, but I am trained to see the facts in front of me." Jakob's hand tensed into a fist at his side only to release just as quickly along with a burst of air from his lips. "Actually, you know what? Forget it. Forget all of this. I don't have to defend myself to you. Think what you want, Benjamin. You always have anyway."

Turning on the heels of his simple black work boots, Benjamin placed his sister's key on the counter and nodded his head in Claire's direction. "I must go."

And, just like that, he was gone, his suspender-clad form disappearing down the back hallway once again.

"I'm sorry you had to witness that."

She toed the floor in search of something to say. Twice in the same day, Jakob Fisher had opened up about his past, with no expectations. And twice he'd been shot down in her presence. "I'm sorry I walked you into that. I . . . I didn't mean any harm."

An unbelievable warmth spread down her arm as his hand touched her skin, the sensation so unlike anything she'd ever felt that it nearly took her breath away. "Claire, what happened here was not your fault. This was set in place over sixteen years ago. Old wounds and all, you know? The only issue that truly matters anymore is Eli Miller's possible involvement in a very real murder. That can't be swept under the carpet by anyone . . . even me."

CHAPTER 18

For the second night in a row, Claire found herself following Lighted Way as it made its way past the popular yet quaint shopping district and branched out toward the Amish side of town. Only this time, she was accompanied by someone who knew life from the perspective of both the Amish and the English.

"I traveled this road on bare feet more times than I can count." Jakob reached into his pocket and extracted a pack of gum, holding it out to her first. "It was certainly a different upbringing from the one my friends in New York gave their kids."

"What was it like?" she asked, her curiosity in overdrive.

"By the time I was two, I was helping around the farm — gathering eggs, weeding in the garden, helping with the wash — you name it."

"Wow. That's young."

"We didn't know any better." They meandered down the road, stopping from time to time to admire the picturesque setting created by the Amish farms and their neatly planted crops. "That's not to say, though, that it wasn't fun. Because it was. We got to visit with friends and relatives on Church Sundays, and we got to play with homemade scooters and wagons."

"And you got to swim when you were a little older," she reminded, despite the nagging internal voice warning her to steer clear of the potentially hurtful topic. "That watering hole on the milk can Martha painted looked like a mighty special place."

If the subject bothered Jakob, he didn't let it show. "Did you happen to notice the tree along the outer edge of the pond that overhung the water near the center?"

She closed her eyes briefly as she tried to recall the painted setting, the tree in question revealing itself fairly quickly. "I did. Why? Did you jump off it or something?"

Dimples appeared in his cheeks just before he laughed. "You better believe we did." With a gentle hand to the small of her back, Jakob guided Claire off the road and down a narrow gravel path. "We'd run down this very path, spread our arms wide, and jump right in . . . See?"

They rounded a grove of trees and there, on the other side, was the watering hole Martha had so expertly depicted with a paintbrush and a palette of paint. "Oh, Jakob," she whispered. "This is lovely."

"It is, isn't it?" He jogged over to the tree on the edge of the pond and pointed upward. "And this is the tree . . . the one we jumped off."

She stared up at the tree and tried to imagine a young Martha and a young Jakob swimming and playing there. The Martha part wasn't hard. All she had to do was think of Esther. But Jakob? He was a little harder to picture.

"You don't have any childhood photographs do you?"

"Nah. No pictures. Just memories. But they're plenty clear."

"For you, maybe," she said, making a face. "But it's a little tough for someone like me to picture you as a kid."

"I was cute. Real cute."

It felt good to laugh, the sound echoing in the still evening air and wrapping her in a much-needed bear hug. "I bet you were a little pistol with those dimples."

"And you'd bet right." Wrapping his hands around the branch overhead, he let his body hang for a few seconds before dropping to the ground once again. "Can I ask you something?"

She tried her best to hide her surprise at the sudden tone shift, but she wasn't all too successful. "Uhhh, okay, sure."

"Unlike so many others in this town, you didn't grow up in Heavenly. Therefore, it stands to reason that you've made assessments of folks based on the here and now rather than who they might have been a decade ago."

"I suppose." She leaned against the tree trunk and did her best to answer as truthfully as possible. "Though, in all fairness, I had a slight window as to who everyone was and how they fit based on things my aunt told me."

"What kinds of things?" Jakob bent over and rummaged around on the bank of the pond until he found a flat rock. Clasping it between his thumb and index finger, he straightened and looked across the water, the last of the sun's rays making the amber flecks of his eyes dance.

She watched as he pulled his arm back and then, with a flick of his wrist, released the rock, skipping it once, twice, three times before it disappeared into the water. "Basic things, like who owned the bakery and who owned the toy shop. Who was Amish and who was English. Who was chatty and who kept to themselves. That sort of thing."

He stared out at the water before turning his back on it to look at her. "What's your read on Eli Miller?"

Pushing off the trunk of the tree, she wandered over to the shoreline and scanned the ground for a suitable rock of her own. When she found what she thought would work, she gave it a toss and watched it sink at the site of its first hit.

His answering laugh was warm. "Looks like someone needs a course in rock skipping."

"Are you offering to teach it?" she asked, the playful words escaping her lips before her mind had even fully registered what she was saying.

He bent over once again and retrieved a rock from beside his feet. "Now hold it in your hand, just like this." The warmth from his earlier touch duplicated itself tenfold as he moved in behind her, grabbed hold of her hand, and bent it around the rock. "Feel that?"

"What?" she whispered.

A momentary hesitation let her know he felt it, too. It was an unexpected confirmation that kicked off a flurry of nerves she struggled to tamp down.

"Pull your arm back, like this." He guided her arm into the desired position and then held it firm. "Now flick — hard — with your wrist."

Grateful for the opportunity to think of something other than the feel of his hand, she did as she was told, the rock sailing across the water before hitting the surface once, twice. She squealed in pleasure. "I did it!"

"Yes, you did."

She glanced back, surprised by the sudden rasp in his voice. "You okay?"

"Yeah. Just dealing with a few mixed emotions."

When he didn't elaborate, she turned the conversation back to his question. "I don't know Eli all that well. But what I do know is that despite his work in the fields, he still shows up in the alley periodically throughout the day to check on his sister. Sometimes he stays and helps, particularly when she has even more customers than normal because of a tour-bus stop. He even helped me one day when the hinges on the shop's back door came loose."

He nodded but said nothing.

"We always know when Eli arrives because his horse releases a very distinct snort when Eli parks the buggy. Esther knows the sound, too."

Jakob's eyebrow rose. "Esther?"

"Esther is crazy about Eli."

Understanding lit his eyes, softening his stance in the process. "Ahhh. So that's why she is so protective of him."

"That's certainly some of it." She led the way over to a nearby stump and sat down. "But I think some of it is also the simple fact that she thinks he's a good person."

"Tell me about his temper."

She took a deep breath, then let it slowly release, her heart acutely aware of the harm her words could bring to someone she cared about very much. "I've heard stories from others but I've not seen it with my own two eyes all that often."

He squatted in front of her. "But you *have* seen it then?"

Oh how she wanted to say no. To tell him that the only version of Eli she knew was the kindhearted one who looked after his twin sister with obvious love.

But she couldn't.

She glanced down as his hand covered hers, the warmth of his contact making it difficult to speak. "Once . . . maybe twice."

"Tell me," he urged.

Tell him. It sounded so simple. But it wasn't. Especially when she knew why he was asking and what it could mean for Eli and Esther.

"Please, Claire."

"The first time came the day I signed the lease. Mr. Gussman, the landlord, had just handed me the key when Eli rode up in his buggy." She closed her eyes as her words provided the accompaniment to the scene playing out in her thoughts. "I waved and said hello. Told him who I was and why I was there."

"Go on."

She opened her eyes to find Jakob grimacing ever so slightly. Scooting a bit to the right, she patted the empty portion of stump to her left and continued. "It was like watching a thunderstorm roll in across these fields until the sky is completely black and you have no doubt what's coming."

When Jakob said nothing, she offered a translation. "He got real angry and asked if I was going to rip off the Amish like my shop's former tenant did."

"Walter Snow," Jakob muttered.

"Eli said that Mr. Snow was a crook and that he'd fooled a lot of people . . . including him and his family."

Jakob cupped his hand over his mouth and then let it slide down his chin. "The guy *was* a crook."

She stared out over the water, the peaceful scene giving way to the memory of what came next, a memory she was hesitant to share.

"Claire?"

"He — he said that it took them a while to catch on to what Mr. Snow was doing but that they did. And he would pay . . . dearly."

Jakob sat up straight, his gaze fixed on her face. "But Snow was gone when you took over the shop, wasn't he?"

Looking down, she swallowed. Hard. "Eli pointed that out. But . . ."

Hooking a finger beneath her chin, he guided it upward just enough to bring her focus back on him. "Tell me, Claire."

"He said he suspected Mr. Snow would come back one day. And that when he did . . . Eli would be waiting to" — her voice dipped to a barely audible whisper — "settle things once and for all."

A deafening silence enveloped them, broken only by the occasional chirp of a cricket and the on-again, off-again roar of guilt in her ears. "I just hurt her, didn't I?" she finally asked.

"Hurt who?"

"Esther."

"You answered a question with the truth.

If Eli is not responsible for Snow's murder, Esther will be fine."

"And if he is?"

"Then she's better off knowing before she wastes the rest of her life on a man who isn't suitable for her."

It made so much sense when he said it like that, but still . . .

"So tell me about the other time."

"Other time?" she echoed.

"You said there were two times you saw Eli's temper." Jakob dropped his hand to his side but kept his focus firmly planted on Claire. "Tell me about the other one."

"It happened the day before I came to the station to meet you. I'd gone into the shop early because I was finishing up in the stockroom. Mr. Snow had left a ton of merchandise behind, and I'd finally whittled it down to a manageable level that I could get it cleared out once and for all."

"Okay . . ."

"Anyway, I heard some noise outside in the alley, and I went out to see what it was."

"Eli?"

She nodded. "He was furious over a shipment of pie boxes that went missing."

"Pie boxes? Why didn't I hear about this?" Jakob threw his head back and stared up at the sky. "Wait. Don't answer that. I know why I didn't hear about it."

She resisted the urge to touch him and, instead, stayed on task. "When I asked Eli what happened, he punched the bake shop's back door so hard I cringed. When I went to help him, he said it was all Mr. Snow's fault. He was convinced Walter was back . . . seeking revenge on Eli's family for outing him as the crook he is."

"And little more than thirty-six hours later, Walter Snow turned up dead in that very same alley." Jakob released a sigh big enough for the both of them. "Wow."

Wow was right.

So, too, was the renewed sense of dread that came from sharing her memories of Eli's temper aloud.

She looked out over the water. "Can I ask you a question, Detective?"

"Of course. What's on your mind?"

Inhaling sharply, she made herself face him on the stump. "How did he die?"

"You mean Snow?" At her nod, he offered a quick shrug. "He was strangled."

"I know that part but I don't know *how*. Did they use a rope or something?"

"Nope. The killer used his bare hands."

She sucked in a breath. "But how could someone do that? Wouldn't that take . . ." Her sentence petered out as she looked at the water once again, an image playing in her thoughts while Jakob provided the narration.

"Someone would have to be mighty angry to strangle the life out of another human being like that."

Oh, Esther . . .

A muted vibration made them both jump. Standing up, Jakob reached into his pocket and pulled out his phone. "I'm sorry, Claire, but I've got to take this. It's the station."

At her nod, he flipped it open and held it to his ear. "Detective Fisher."

She tried to look away, to give him a measure of privacy as he spoke, but it was hard. There was a certain quality about the man that drew her in and made her want to know him better.

"How bad?"

Something about the tone of his voice broke through her woolgathering and made her sit up tall.

"I'll be right there." He snapped the phone closed in his left hand and reached for Claire with his right. "C'mon. We've gotta go. There's been a fire at Shoo Fly Bake Shoppe."

CHAPTER 19

The acrid smell of smoke permeated her nose as she stood on the sidewalk watching firefighters enter and exit Shoo Fly Bake Shoppe with decreasing urgency. The shell of the store looked fine, as did the front window and much of what she could see, thanks to the old-fashioned gas-powered streetlamps that bordered Lighted Way. But still, she worried.

Ruth Miller had been through enough the last few weeks, the vast majority of which she'd shouldered alone rather than seek support from her overprotective twin and their older brother. The only reason Claire had become privy to the trials the young Amish woman faced was a simple matter of timing.

"Miss Ruth isn't going to be able to keep this from her brothers." Howard Glick rocked back on his heels and shook his head. "There's nothing in my store that can make remnants of a fire go away before morning."

"If only there was." But even as she said the words, she knew the truth was long overdue. Putting isolated incidents off as pranks only worked so long before the cumulative picture became too hard to ignore.

The *clip-clop* of a horse off to their left grew steadily louder until it ceased altogether not more than ten feet from where they stood.

"Here come the real fireworks," Howard mumbled as Eli's gloved hands released the reins, and the brothers jumped down from their buggy.

"What happened?" Benjamin barked. "How is there fire?"

Howard stopped Eli's passage with a firm hand and a soothing voice. "You can't go in there yet."

Claire stepped forward and supplied what little information they had. "From what Mr. Glick and I can see, it looks like the fire department has things under control."

"There was no reason for fire." Eli pulled his arm from Howard's grasp and paced in a little circle. "I check every day when I come to collect Ruth."

"I'm sure Detective Fisher will tell us

what he can when he comes out."

Benjamin's gaze left the shop long enough to size up Claire. "Jakob is here?"

Before she could answer, the front door of the bake shop opened, and Jakob stepped onto the porch, beckoning for them to come closer. When they did, he gave his assessment. "Thanks to Mr. Glick's expert nose and the fast action of the Heavenly Fire Department, there is very little damage. What there is is basically confined to the kitchen in back, where it started."

Eli repeated his earlier assertion. "There was no reason for fire. I check every day when I collect Ruth."

Jakob sat down on the top porch step and held up his hands. "It didn't start like that, Eli."

Benjamin's eyes widened beneath the brim of his hat. "Then how?"

"We believe it was started with gasoline."

They were seven simple words but, when put together, they brought a collective gasp from everyone gathered.

Claire and Howard exchanged alarmed looks, while Eli and Benjamin said nothing. "Any chance someone spilled a little bit while filling a lawn mower or an automobile?" Howard finally suggested.

Keeping his gaze locked on the Miller

brothers, Jakob gave a quick shake of his head. "Not unless that lawn mower or automobile happened to be sitting inside the kitchen when someone tried to fill it."

The implication wasn't lost on Claire or Howard.

Benjamin shifted his weight away from Jakob, confusion evident in every facet of his handsome face. "I do not understand."

"Is someone angry with your sister or your family?" Jakob asked.

Benjamin drew back. "Angry? At Ruth?"

Jakob rested his elbows on his thighs and enclosed his mouth in tented fingers for several beats. Claire felt her stomach twist in response.

"When we were told about the note your sister received, you neglected to say anything about the stolen pie boxes or" — Jakob shifted a quick gaze at Claire — "or the broken milk bottles. Had we been told of those incidents as well, I wouldn't have been so quick to write it off as a harmless teenage prank. But you didn't."

"Stolen pie boxes? Broken milk bottles?" Benjamin turned to his brother. "Eli? Do you know of such things?"

Eli toed the ground.

"Eli!"

Eli's eyes narrowed, and his jaw tightened.

"Mr. Snow has done things . . . to Ruth's store. To strike at our family." The young man's voice roared through the night like a freight train gathering momentum for the mountain climb ahead.

"Why did you say nothing?" Benjamin accused. "Did you think I could not help, Eli?"

"You would look the other way! As you did with the money he stole."

Benjamin's jaw tightened in matching fashion. "I did not look the other way!"

"You made me stand up . . . in front of church . . . and seek forgiveness for defending my family!" Eli said as he waved a gloved hand in the air.

"You threatened a man, Eli!"

"Mr. Snow is no man! He is a crook!"

"Was a crook," Jakob's even-toned voice cut through the argument playing out in front of them. "*Was* a crook. Walter Snow is dead, remember?"

"As he deserves," Eli hissed.

Claire closed her eyes and tried to block out the statement, but it was too late. The words were out there, and they'd been spoken by the person who appeared to be Jakob's chief suspect.

Benjamin opened his mouth to dress down his younger brother but shut it when Jakob waved him off. "Do you not hear what I'm saying? This fire couldn't have been started by Walter Snow. He's dead."

"But the stolen pie boxes . . ." Eli raked an angry hand down his face. "And the shattered milk bottles. He was not dead for those."

Claire felt Howard's stare and put words to its meaning. "He was for the paint."

The weight of three additional sets of eyes turned in her direction.

"Paint?" Jakob repeated.

"There was no paint," Eli countered.

Howard's shoulder brushed against Claire's in a show of solidarity. "Someone threw paint on Ruth's front window just the other day."

A strangled sound emerged from Eli's lips as he pushed past Jakob on the stairs. When he reached the top landing, he pointed at the front window. "There is no paint."

"That's because I cleaned it off myself, son. And I can say, with absolute certainty, that there was much too much of it to have been anything but deliberate."

"But I know of no paint."

Claire took a deep breath, then released it into the night, aware of the potential implications of her words yet knowing they needed to be said. "Because she didn't want you to know, Eli. She didn't want to upset you any more than you already were."

Jakob dropped his head into his hands only to lift it once again. "How come this stuff wasn't reported?"

"I meant to tell you about the paint," Claire offered. "I really did. I even took pictures with my cell phone to show you. But I guess it slipped my mind in light of everything else going on. I'm sorry."

If he accepted her apology, he didn't show it, choosing to focus on the Miller brothers instead. "I am here in Heavenly as a police officer. The Ordnung doesn't prevent you from speaking to me."

Any residual anger drained out of Benjamin. "I did not know of anything but the note."

Jakob looked up at Eli and waited.

"I do not know why I did not come to you." Eli leaned against the window in defeat.

"Well, it needs to stop. I can't help you if I don't know what's happening." Jakob pushed off the step and stood. "If we'd known, we would have stepped up patrols around the shop. That alone might have been enough to discourage whoever is doing this from trying to burn your shop to the ground."

Benjamin broke the silence that followed,

his words bringing a catch to Claire's heart. "Will you help us now?"

Jakob nodded, any emotion he may have felt at the unexpected request firmly in check. "Can you think of anyone who may have some sort of an ax to grind with either Ruth or your family at large?"

"No."

Eli's response took a beat longer but matched that of his older brother.

"Have you seen or heard from anyone involved in that altercation you had outside that bar a few months back?"

Benjamin stiffened at Jakob's question but said nothing, opting to wait for Eli's answer just like everyone else.

"No!"

"How about that Englishman who filed a complaint after you cut him off in your buggy two weeks ago?"

"Eli?"

Eli averted his brother's eyes and directed his answer at Jakob. "I do not think so."

Without breaking eye contact with Eli, Jakob aimed his next question at Claire and Howard. "Anything going on among the business owners around here? Any sort of ill feelings or issues you think I should know about?"

"I don't think so, but I haven't had the

shop for all that long." Claire handed the question over to the patriarch of Lighted Way. "Mr. Glick?"

Howard anchored his hands against his upper arms. "Everyone gets along real well around here. Can't imagine anyone who'd set out to hurt Ruth like this."

Ruth.

The sweetest, most gentle human being Claire had ever met . . .

"Mr. Glick is right. Ruth is loved by everyone."

For the first time in nearly ten minutes, Jakob turned his gaze on Claire, his words sending a shiver of fear down her spine. "That doesn't appear to be the case any longer."

CHAPTER 20

They were silent on the way to the inn, the smell of smoke clinging to their clothes and hair.

"If Mr. Glick hadn't chosen tonight to stay late at his shop, Shoo Fly Bake Shoppe wouldn't be standing the way that it is." Jakob drove slowly down Lighted Way, peering up at each shop and each home that they passed. "The Millers were lucky. Very, very lucky."

She tried his words on for size. "I'm not so sure Eli sees the luck."

"That's what happens when you allow yourself to be blinded by things like rage or resentment." He released a sigh. "I was guilty of that myself for a time."

She glanced at him across the center console, the tense but handsome lines of his face intriguing in the dashboard light. "Oh?"

He met her gaze briefly before turning it back on the empty road. "I was so bitter about being banned by my family that I didn't embrace my police work in the way that I should have. I was doing what I wanted, what I'd been called to do, but I wasn't enjoying any of it because I kept looking back at the door that had been slammed shut in my face."

The honesty of Jakob's words left her momentarily speechless. She'd been in that place once, too. "So what changed?" she finally asked.

"Me. My attitude. When I started looking forward instead of backward, my vision became far less cloudy."

The car left the cobblestone surface of Lighted Way in favor of smooth pavement, the irony of the transition not lost on Claire. She leaned her head against the seatback and stared out at the passing scenery. "Too bad we didn't have that kind of hard-earned wisdom when we were Eli's age."

Jakob nodded. "That guy is his own worst enemy, you know?" The car slowed to a near crawl as Sleep Heavenly sprang into view at the bend in the road. "I mean, look at what happened tonight. What could very possibly have been avoided if he wasn't the loose cannon everyone knows him to be."

She looked up at the inn as they pulled into the near-empty lot, the soft glow of her aunt's wall sconces peeking out through the parlor draperies. There was certainly a measure of truth in the detective's assertion regarding Eli, but there were also gaps Claire had failed to fill simply because they hadn't fit with questions she'd been asked.

"I realize I haven't known him long, but there's more to Eli than just a quick temper." She shifted in the passenger seat as Jakob cut the engine.

Dropping his hands from the steering wheel, he looked from her to the inn and back again. "Oh?"

"He's also very caring and sweet."

"Tell me."

She glanced out the window at her aunt's home, a sense of peace and contentment settling around her for the first time since the call that had sent them running toward town. "He looks after his sister with such love and respect that you can't help but notice his devotion. In fact, as I've mentioned before, not a day goes by that his buggy doesn't show up at random times throughout the day just so he can see if she needs anything."

Jakob's nod was barely perceptible but it was indication enough that he was listening. And absorbing.

"Sometimes that help involves carrying in

a shipment of pie boxes that have just arrived. Sometimes it has him carrying the trash out to the bin out back. And sometimes it even has him manning the register while she attends to a special bakery order in the kitchen," she continued. "But whatever it is, he never seems to complain."

"So Ruth and Eli are close then?"

"As close as any siblings I've ever seen." And it was true. "Benjamin helps, too, but he is more behind the scenes. Like dropping off fresh milk each morning before even Ruth arrives at the store."

A wry smile crept across Jakob's face. "Ahhh, yes. Benjamin Miller. Ever the workhorse."

She took a deep breath and then let it release, the man's open sarcasm difficult to ignore. "You don't like Benjamin, do you?"

His smile turned into a soft laugh. "Is it that obvious?"

"Yes."

He palmed the lower quadrant of his face with his left hand, then let it slide down his chin to reveal a mouth that was no longer smiling. "Growing up Amish, we were not supposed to idolize anyone. Perfection belongs to God and God alone. But, that said, we all had people we respected. Mine was my father.

"My father was one of the hardest-working men I knew . . . and that's saying a lot when the only people you knew were Amish." Jakob slowly leaned his head against the headrest, his eyes wide yet unfocused. "All I wanted for so long was to be big enough to be just like him. To be the kind of man everyone respected. And, most importantly, to be the kind of man *he* could respect."

She held her breath as he continued.

"But, try as I might, he'd always come home from whatever barn we helped raise or every church service we attended talking about Benjamin Miller." His voice morphed into one much deeper. "Ezekiel Miller has got a real hard worker in his son Benjamin. Why, you should see what he did today . . ."

The emotion that played across his face broke her heart. Reaching across the center console, she touched his cheek with her hand, the softness of his skin catching her by surprise. She pulled her hand back as he turned his startled eyes in her direction. "I'm sorry. I shouldn't have done that."

He stopped her hand midway. "Don't."

She glanced down at her lap, unsure of what to say.

He released his hold yet kept his focus squarely on her face. "Look, I shouldn't be unloading this on you. It's too much. Let's just leave it at the fact that there's some bad blood between Benjamin and me, okay?"

She wanted to argue, to urge him to continue, but she didn't. She'd broken the spell the second she touched him.

"Okay," she whispered.

An awkward silence settled around them only to be broken by the sound of Jakob clearing his throat. "So, uh, Ruth and Eli are close, you say?"

She worked her lower lip inward and nodded.

"Then why would Ruth keep so much from him? Why wouldn't she tell him about the paint? And why wouldn't they tell Benjamin?"

Grateful for the return to solid ground, she did her best to answer with what she knew to be true. "Like everyone else, I guess, Ruth hates to see Eli get so worked up. The way he got so upset over the pie boxes and the note . . . Well, I guess she wanted to save him the additional angst. Especially in light of the trouble he'd faced at home over his public threats toward Mr. Snow."

"So she looks out for him, too, then," he mused. "Okay, but why not tell the almighty big brother? Surely he could make it all stop on his own."

His tone hung heavy in the air only to be waved away by his right hand. "I'm sorry. That was over the top."

"I think Eli is trying to find his footing in the world. He wants to take care of things himself rather than always running to Benjamin for help." She picked at a piece of lint on her pants. "At least that's what Esther has said."

"I guess I can understand that. I mean, I know what it was like to be in that guy's shadow from three farms away. I can't even imagine what it must be like to live in it twenty-four/seven."

At a loss for how to respond, she merely nodded. And yawned.

Jakob glanced at his watch. "Hey, I'm sorry. I didn't realize how late it was. Your aunt is probably worried sick."

"Actually, she's probably fast asleep in preparation for a new round of guests slated for check-in tomorrow."

Slowly, he turned his head left, then right. "I was thinking the lot looked rather empty."

She pointed to the white sedan in the far corner of the lot. "That's Diane's car. It only moves when she has to pick up bulk supplies for the inn or on the rare occasion I take it for a spin. The rest of the time it pretty much stays put." Then, shifting her hand right, she gestured toward the tired-looking black pickup nestled under the largest shade tree in the lot. "And that one belongs to Mr. Streen."

Jakob snorted. "He's rather irritating, isn't he?"

"He can be, most of the time. But every once in a while, he surprises us by being really interesting." She searched her memory for some of the fun facts she'd learned over the past few weeks. "He's kept a list of every book he's read since he was ten years old. And in those fourteen years, he's read something like two thousand books. And the lion's share of those books were nonfiction."

"A bookworm, huh?"

"I guess," she said. "But this guy loves to learn, and he loves to share what he's learned, too. In fact it's from talking to him that I have to wonder whether the troubles Ruth has been facing could be some sort of a hate crime against the Amish."

"If Shoo Fly Bake Shoppe was the only Amish-run shop on Lighted Way, I'd be inclined to agree. But it's not."

She hadn't thought of that. But now that Jakob had pointed it out, she couldn't help but feel a bit stupid. "See? That's why I'd make a lousy detective."

It was his turn to reach across the seat, the warmth of his hand on her arm making her swallow. Hard. "Hey, I'm not saying the notion of a hate crime isn't a possibility. Especially in light of the fact that both the paint and the fire happened after Walter Snow's murder. I'm just saying that Ruth's shop isn't the only Amish store around here, yet it's the only one being targeted."

"Maybe it's not Ruth who is being targeted," she said, the notion surprising her as much as it did Jakob.

A shrill whistle escaped the detective's lips. "Wow. That's certainly something that —"

"Hey, I'm sorry. I have no idea where that just came from." She brought her hands to her face and rubbed at her eyes, the absurdity of her amateur sleuthing making her laugh. "Sleep deprivation, perhaps?"

"No. That actually has some potential . . ." And just like that, Jakob Fisher slipped into a world of his own only to emerge with a question. "If it's not Ruth they're after, then whom? Eli? Benjamin?"

She could only shrug.

Slowly, he traced his right index finger around the steering wheel. "The obvious would be Eli. I'm quite certain a kid like that has made his fair share of enemies —

not the least of which are the kids he got in that bar brawl with a few months back."

"But this stuff has only been happening for a few weeks," she countered.

"True." He pulled his hand through his hair and threw out another idea. "And what about Benjamin? Any chance he's made an enemy?"

"I can't imagine he has."

She felt the weight of his gaze on the side of her face for several long moments before he responded. "You think pretty highly of Benjamin, don't you?"

"I think he's very genuine."

"Genuine," he echoed quietly.

She resisted the urge to nod. She didn't need to push Benjamin's many attributes in Jakob's face. He'd had enough of that in his life already. Instead, she searched for a way to explain the man Benjamin Miller was today. "He's a quiet kind of soul, the way most Amish are, I guess. But there always seems to be a lot going on behind his eyes. I guess it's all the hurt he's been through."

"Hurt? What hurt?"

"His wife died not long after they married, and —"

The sound of Jakob's gasp brought her up short. *Elizabeth is dead?*

She met his eyes, the pain she found there

so strong it dulled all hint of a sparkle from their depths. "You knew his wife?"

The only sound that followed her question came from the crickets outside the car and the thump-thump inside her chest. But just as she began to feel as if it was best to leave him alone, he spoke, the agony in his eyes enveloping every word he spoke. "Like my father, Elizabeth preferred Benjamin to me as well."

CHAPTER 21

"You're up early." Diane Weatherly looked up from the assortment of measuring spoons and ingredients spread out across the counter and smiled. "What time did you get in last night?"

"After midnight." She wandered over to the breakfast nook and climbed onto the nearest stool. "Making your welcome cookies?"

"I am. Two couples are checking in this afternoon. One is from Nashville, Tennessee, and the other is from a small town in upstate New York. And both are retired."

It was impossible to miss the excitement in her aunt's voice. Even after twenty years of running the inn, the woman still got a kick out of what she did. And now that Claire was living in Heavenly, she understood it completely.

"You don't know, do you?"

Diane held a bottle of vanilla above her

mixing bowl and poured a teaspoon of the pleasant-smelling liquid with a practiced hand. "Know what, dear?"

"There was a fire at Shoo Fly Bake Shoppe yesterday evening."

A poof of flour rose into the air as Diane dropped the spoon into the bowl. "Is Ruth okay?"

"She wasn't there. No one was."

"Oh thank heavens." Reaching into the bowl, Diane extracted the spoon and set it on the counter, her cookie-making mission on hold. "So what happened? Did they leave the stove on?"

Claire reached across the counter and commandeered a chocolate chip from the plated pile to the left of the mixing bowl. "No. It was gasoline."

"In the *kitchen?*"

She popped the tiny morsel into her mouth. "The fire wasn't an accident."

Diane's mouth dropped open. "Oh no."

Oh no was right.

"I guess the broken milk bottles, stolen pie boxes, nasty note, and painted window weren't enough to get across whatever point someone is trying to make to the Millers."

The kitchen door swung open behind them, signaling the arrival of the only remaining guest. "Did you see this?"

Claire reached for the newspaper in Arnie's hand and set it on the counter, the front headline proof positive that a special edition of the *Heavenly Times* had been printed overnight while residents of the close-knit town slept soundly. She skimmed the first few paragraphs of the story, while Arnie and Diane leaned over her shoulder.

"Who's that with you?"

She followed Arnie's finger to the small photograph below the fold line. Despite the side angle, the worry she'd felt the night before was on display for all to see. "That's Howard Glick. He owns Glick's Tools 'n' More. He's the reason the fire was detected and put out so quickly."

"I never heard any sirens," Diane mused.

Arnie pointed at the second paragraph and the time of the fire. "I'm guessing that's because you were vacuuming every inch of this place at about that same time."

"You didn't hear it, either?"

"How could I?" Arnie reached forward and grabbed a handful of chocolate chips from the plate. "I was using headphones to block out your vacuuming."

Diane made her way back around the counter and secured the plate of chips from Arnie's overeager reach. "I have some fresh blueberry muffins in the basket by the stove,

Mr. Streen."

Arnie made a beeline for the basket, helping himself to three. "So what happened? That article doesn't say a whole lot."

She repeated what she'd told Diane thus far, adding the fact that she was worried for Ruth's safety in light of the increasing severity of the crimes.

"That's assuming it's aimed at her with intention to do harm rather than deflect attention." Arnie grabbed a knife from the utensil basket and cut off a sizable chunk of butter. He slathered it across all sides of each muffin before biting into the first one.

Claire stared at the man. "I'm not sure what you mean by deflecting attention."

"Well, throughout history, the most successful criminals have gotten away with their crimes by sending up smoke signals in other places." Arnie popped the second muffin into his mouth. "Keeps the heat off them while they cover their tracks from the bigger crime."

Pushing the paper to the side, she considered Arnie's words. "Okay, I get that. But what would the stuff at Ruth's bake shop be deflecting?"

Arnie ate the last of his three muffins and returned to the basket for two more. "That's easy."

"Oh?"

"It could be deflecting murder."

She heard Diane's gasp and knew it echoed her own. "Murder?"

Arnie shrugged. "Think about it. Some guy shows up dead in the alley behind your stores. And, lo and behold, it's the same guy who just happens to have ripped off a number of people, including Ruth's own family. But wait . . . One of her brothers got in trouble for making public threats of bodily harm to this very same dead guy. Hmmm . . ." Arnie scrunched up his chin and gave it a dramatic scratch. "It sure seems as if the stuff happening to this particular bake shop might be intended to make one poor Eli Miller look like a victim, too."

She stared at him, his freckled face giving way to a parade of images that lined up, one behind the other . . .

Stolen pie boxes . . .

Broken milk bottles . . .

A carelessly written, nasty note . . .

Splattered paint . . .

When she got to the fire — a fire that had done remarkably little damage in light of its potential — she felt her stomach twist into a knot. Each and every incident thus far was relatively easy for someone like Eli to pull off. All he'd have to do is show up early — or late, as in the case of the fire — before anyone else was around. And if he were seen, no one would think it odd. After all, why would they? Eli's devotion to his sister was admired by all of the shopkeepers on Lighted Way.

She drew in a second and longer breath. Was Arnie right? Was Eli staging everything to deflect focus for the murder?

"You can't be right, Mr. Streen." Diane's voice, steady and firm, rose up amid all of Claire's worry, wiping it away with her usual no-nonsense approach. "Two of those incidents happened before Mr. Snow's murder. That alone proves it has nothing to do with deflection."

Claire clapped her hands. "Yes! Aunt Diane is right. Only *three* of those things happened before the murder, not just two."

"He had to know this Snow guy was gonna come back at some point, right?"

She met Diane's confused gaze and followed it back to the redhead. "Huh?"

"Wasn't his wife still here?"

She nodded, along with her aunt.

"Then, I think it stands to reason that he couldn't stay away forever."

The meaning behind Arnie's words finally sunk in. "Oh, c'mon," she pleaded. "You're trying to say that Eli set these little pranks in motion *before* the murder?"

"I think it might be more accurate to say *in preparation* for the murder."

She looked back at Diane, waiting for her aunt's infinite wisdom to counter yet another round of Arnie's amateur sleuthing, but nothing came. Instead, Claire struck out on her own. "Assuming you're right, Mr. Streen — and I'm not saying you are — wouldn't all that . . . that preparation, as you call it, be a bit over the top?"

"The timing of the first three pranks threw" — he pointed a buttery finger at Diane and then Claire — "the two of you off just now, didn't it?"

Before she could answer, he continued, his mouth working around yet another muffin in the process. "If a person's eye is steady on the prize, he'll do whatever it takes to get it. Like me with wanting to go to grad school. If I hadn't wanted it bad enough, I wouldn't have all these scars." He lifted his battered and crumb-coated hands into the air. "But shucking oysters all day long for two years is the only way I could make that happen. And let's not forget your detective, Claire . . ."

"My detective?" she repeated.

"That's who you were out in the parking

lot with last night around midnight, isn't it?"

She felt her mouth gape as Diane turned to her with questioning eyes.

"I . . ."

"He worked his way back home, didn't he?" Arnie lurched forward across the kitchen in search of a glass. "Though, now that I'm saying it, he might not be such a good example, seeing as how *his* hard work is never going to pay off with anything more than slammed doors and the silent treatment to end all silent treatments."

All she could do was blink and swallow.

And then blink and swallow some more.

Arnie Streen was downright infuriating. He'd demonstrated that within ten minutes of checking into Sleep Heavenly. But this time, she didn't want to just walk away, muttering her frustrations under her breath. This time she wanted to stand her ground and argue back until the man was begging for mercy.

The problem, though, was where to start.

"I think you're way off base where Eli Miller is concerned." There. That was a good start . . .

He plunked his fresh-from-the-dishwasher glass on the counter and then filled it with the orange juice Diane had surely squeezed just prior to Claire's arrival in the kitchen. With little more than three gulps, eight ounces disappeared in the blink of an eye. "I wonder whether your detective would agree."

Diane looked at Arnie and then gestured toward the cookie ingredients spread out on the counter. "Mr. Streen, if you've had enough for the moment, I will see that your full breakfast is ready to be served in the dining room at nine o'clock as usual. In the meantime, I must get back to my work."

If he picked up the edge to Diane's voice, he didn't show it as he pivoted on his feet and headed for the same swinging door that had allowed him into their midst in the first place. "French toast with a side of eggs and bacon this morning, right?"

"Yes."

"Good. I'm starved." He paused, his hand in the center of the door, taking in first Diane and then Claire with a turn of his head. "And Claire?"

The stool creaked softly beneath her as her shoulders slumped. "Yes, Mr. Streen?"

"If I'm right about Eli Miller, as I suspect I am, your detective is going to have his work cut out for him trying to get answers out of a community hell-bent on pretending he doesn't exist."

CHAPTER 22

For the first time since opening her shop, Claire didn't stroll down Lighted Way with a spring in her step. She didn't drink in the distant *clip-clop* of horses or wave at the smattering of fellow shopkeepers who swept their front porches in anticipation of yet another day in Heavenly. No, this time she walked with her head down, her thoughts anything but peaceful and happy.

Try as she might, she simply couldn't shake the seeds Arnie Streen had planted. Nor could she forget the way she'd brushed off Diane's questions about Jakob. She hadn't meant to be evasive; she really hadn't. But she just wasn't ready to dissect feelings she wasn't even sure she had. Especially when her stomach was a mess with worry over Eli's potential role in Ruth's ongoing troubles.

Instead of lifting her face to the morning sun the way she normally did, Claire lifted her nose and sniffed. The smell of old fire still peppered the air like a post-campfire with a side order of faint gasoline.

She stopped in her tracks, her feet rooted to the ground by reality.

Had Howard Glick not been on the ball, Heavenly Treasures could have burned just as easily as Shoo Fly Bake Shoppe. The alleyways between most of the stores were just large enough for a buggy to fill. A slight breeze or a few early drops of gasoline, and she'd be looking at the same mess Ruth was faced with that morning.

She continued her walk, her destination clear. Esther was on tap to open with her at ten o'clock. The double coverage would enable her to turn her attention elsewhere for as long as it was needed.

When she reached the sidewalk that led to the bake shop, she turned and made her way up the porch steps, the lingering smell of smoke growing stronger as she reached the wide-open door.

"Ruth? Are you here?" She took a few tentative steps into the main room of the bakery and stopped. Everything in the room was as exactly as it appeared earlier in the week — the wood-planked floor mopped to a fine glow, the wood-trimmed glass case sparkling in the early-morning rays cascading through the open windows, and the freshly picked wildflowers featured in the basic vases strewn about the room. The only difference was the repugnant odor, a first for anything connected to Ruth Miller. "Ruth?"

The soft pitter-patter of Ruth's simple black ankle boots preceded Eli's twin into the main room. "Good morning, Claire."

She studied her shy friend closely, noted the tired eyes, the strands of hair that had strayed from the confines of the head cap, and the soot-stained dress. Yet somehow, someway, Ruth Miller still looked as if she belonged on the page of a beauty magazine.

"I'm so sorry, Ruth. I truly am. I . . . I can't imagine who would do such a thing to you and to this shop."

A flicker of pain darkened the young woman's ocean-blue eyes momentarily only to disappear behind a show of false bravado. "It is my mistake. I did not check carefully."

"What are you talking about?" Claire asked. "This wasn't your fault."

"But it is. I know someone is angry at me. And I did not check. This . . . this" — Ruth brushed her hands down the front of her lavender dress — "*mess* would not have happened if I had."

Claire took a step backward, unsure of

what to say. Granted, she hadn't stayed through the night after the fire, but she'd left with Jakob. What else could have happened to change the facts of the fire so drastically that Ruth would be standing there, taking the blame on herself?

"I was in a rush," Ruth continued. "I wanted to bake a cake for Dat's birthday. I must not have checked the lock."

"Ruth. Someone poured gasoline in your kitchen and then lit a match or flicked a lighter. How on earth is that your fault?"

"They could not have started a fire if I locked the back door."

She heard the words, even saw the expression on Ruth's face, yet it was still incomprehensible. Ruth Miller was the most meticulous person she'd ever met. Her shop was always clean, her display case always stocked, and her customers always pleased. Leaving a door unlocked simply didn't fit the picture. At all.

"Eli is furious."

Claire teed her hands. "Wait a minute. I don't care whether you locked the door or not. That doesn't change the fact that someone went inside without permission and tried to set your shop on fire. You can't blame yourself for that."

Ruth's bottom lip quivered.

"Ruth, please. Tell me you don't really believe this was your fault."

Slowly, the girl looked up and met Claire's eyes. "I really thought I used the lock. Like I do every night."

Claire took hold of Ruth's hand and gave it a squeeze. "Let's think, okay? Walk me through everything you did when you were closing yesterday."

"I was out of pies. Cakes, too."

She smiled in hopes of lightening the tension that hovered around Ruth like a pesky mosquito. "Well, that's not any different than any other day for you, is it?"

Ruth's cheeks reddened at the compliment. "I do not know."

"Oh, yes, you do."

"I had cookies left. I put them in a bag as I always do." Ruth's eyebrows scrunched in thought, then returned to their normal positions as she continued. "I wipe the display counter. I wipe the window. I wipe the door. Then I wipe the kitchen counter and stove. Oven door, too. Then I take my bag, I take my key, lock the door, and I leave. It is what I do each day."

"How sure are you that you did all of that yesterday?" she asked even as her thoughts worked through each step Ruth mentioned.

"I must not have locked the door."

Claire bobbed her head to the left until she recaptured Ruth's gaze. "I'm not asking what you think you did based on the fire. I'm asking you what you *remember* doing."

Ruth looked over her shoulder at the kitchen doorway, then turned back. "I locked the door."

"You said you take the key and lock the door each night, yes?"

Ruth gave a quick nod.

"Where do you take the key from?"

The faintest hint of a smile twitched at the corners of the Amish woman's mouth. "I will show you." Turning on her heel, Ruth led the way into the kitchen, the blackened walls and heightened odor eliciting a soft groan from Claire. "I found box in Mr. Snow's shop one day. It was made by" — Ruth's cheeks tinged red once again — "Samuel Yoder."

Before Claire could inquire as to Ruth's reaction to the man's name, the moment was gone, lost in an uncharacteristic flurry of words for a young woman who normally spoke very little.

"See? Isn't it lovely?" Ruth lifted a tiny treasure box from the counter across from the stove and held it out for Claire to see, its carefully carved floral design covered by a fine layer of soot. At Claire's nod, Ruth pulled the box close once again, wiping at the soot with a damp cloth. "We can not have decoration unless it has purpose. That is why I keep the shop key inside."

Claire walked to the back wall of the kitchen and squatted beside the spot where the fire started, her knees narrowly missing the finely crafted hope chest she'd uncovered in her stockroom. "The fire department certainly moved fast, didn't they?" Then, without waiting for a response, she glanced up at Ruth and the treasure box. "Open it."

Ruth hesitated a beat before doing as she was told, her long graceful fingers slowly guiding the lid up and over.

At Ruth's widened eyes, Claire skipped the question and went straight for the answer. "It's not there, is it?"

"No. It is not."

Claire turned her head and took in the origins of the fire, the darkened wall and still-damp floor a reminder that something was wrong. Very, very wrong. "Where do you put your key after you lock the door each night?"

"I put it in the flower pot outside. But do not tell Benjamin. He would not approve."

"Why?"

Ruth squared her shoulders. "He worries.

He says I should bring the key home."

"He's probably right," she said. "So why don't you bring it home?"

"Because it is long walk if I forget the key the next day."

Claire rested a hand on the top of the hope chest and hoisted herself upward. When she regained her balance, she made her way over to the door, gesturing for Ruth to follow. "Would Eli be mad, too?"

"No. He is glad. He does not want me to walk home for the key."

A nagging doubt began to gnaw at her stomach. "Does Eli know where you keep the key?"

Ruth took the lead as they entered the alley and looped around to the back of the bake shop. "He found the pot. Showed me the best place to keep the key." When they reached the pot in question, Ruth reached into the soil and extracted a small wooden box. "You can not see it because of the dirt."

Claire took the box from Ruth's outstretched hand and opened it to reveal the key. "Is this it?"

"Yes." Ruth blinked once, twice. "I did not think to look this morning because the policeman let me inside with Mr. Gussman's master key."

Ruth had locked the door. The key was

exactly where it should have been. Yet someone had gotten inside without breaking a window or forcing the lock.

She closed her eyes against the image of Arnie, hands on hips, giving her an I-told-you-so face. "Ruth . . . Can I ask you something?"

At Ruth's nod, she proceeded. "Why didn't you tell Benjamin about all of the things that have been happening around here? Especially after he saw that note last week?"

The quietly stunning woman pushed the key box back into the dirt. "Eli did not want to worry him."

Claire considered that nugget from various angles. "I mean at first. When you discovered that the shipment of pie boxes had been stolen and all those milk bottles had been broken. Why did you go to Eli first? Is it just because he's around the shop more often?"

Wiping her hands against one another, Ruth removed the dirt from her skin. "I did not go to Eli. He came to me."

"He came to you?" she echoed against the sound of Arnie's voice growing still louder in her head.

Ruth nodded and then led the way back around the side of the shop and into the kitchen. "He is one who saw the bottles first. The note, too."

Stage it and find it . . .

She shook her head free of the troubling thought, forced herself to focus on the things she knew. "But he didn't know about the paint, right?"

"Not until the fire." Ruth's lips dipped downward. "He was upset last night. Upset that I did not tell him."

Claire thought back to the previous night. Tried to remember Eli's reaction when she told Jakob about the paint. But her focus had been on the detective, not Eli. Had he been shocked at the news of the spattered paint? Or did he have time to feign surprise before anyone became suspicious?

She didn't have the answers. Instead, what she had was Arnie's accusations and a growing sense of dread.

CHAPTER 23

She supposed her turn left instead of right was an avoidance tactic, but it's the only way she could think to handle her mounting suspicion where Eli Miller was concerned. To turn toward the store and greet Esther with a smile required an acting ability she didn't possess at the moment.

Instead, she opted for a stop at Glick's Tools 'n' More and the inevitable gabfest that always came with its owner. Outside, the shop was a veritable carbon copy of both Shoo Fly Bake Shoppe and Heavenly Treasures. Inside, though, was a completely different matter.

Where Ruth had display cases for her tasty treats and Claire had tiered shelves offering a vast array of homemade items for the home, Howard Glick had sawhorses and Peg Board–lined walls filled with every tool known to mankind. And maybe even a few more.

In each corner of the room, a project was displayed for customers to view, with a work area set up nearby for the express purpose of trying out the required tools under Howard's supportive and endlessly patient eye.

Yes, Glick's Tools 'n' More was, without a doubt, every man's dream of what shopping should entail. Likewise, it was a blessing for all of the other shopkeepers on the street, who reaped the reward of having so many wives with uninterrupted browsing time on their hands.

It was truly a win-win for everyone involved.

She took two steps into the store and stopped, her eyes drawn to a wooden picture frame featuring an array of baby-inspired carvings in each corner.

"See? I can catch me a few women in this store, too." Howard poked his head around the register and grinned. "Course that doesn't happen all that much because most men shoo their wives toward your store the second they see a storefront dedicated to tools."

"You can make a frame like this?" she asked, fingering the lines of the stroller and baby rattle.

"So can you. If you've got the right tools."

She couldn't help but laugh. "Ever the salesman."

Howard rose from his folding chair behind the counter and made his way over to Claire, tugging his hunter-green work apron across his burgeoning belly. "That's 'cause I've gotta be. Gotta make up for all that lost revenue over the past few months."

She paused her hand atop the carved teddy bear and glanced at the man over her forearm. "Lost revenue? I didn't know you were having problems."

"It's getting better. Slowly." Howard reached across the demonstration table and neatened the stack of unfinished frames on the nearest work table. "But my books are still off because of Walter. Stuff like that takes a while to correct, as I'm sure you can probably imagine."

She let her hand drop to her side as she worked to make sense of Mr. Glick's words. "Walter? What did the situation with Walter have to do with you?"

Howard shrugged in time with his sigh. "The Amish trusted Walter Snow. They trusted he would hold up his end of their deal and pay them for their work."

"But he was a crook," she pointed out.

"Not at first he wasn't. In fact, he behaved himself for nearly a year — selling their furniture pieces and giving them the agreed-upon percentage." Howard walked to the next demonstration table and centered the wooden magazine rack that was on display. "So when the checks started lessening somewhat, and he explained it away as people bargaining down his prices because of the economy, they didn't think anything of it. After all, he'd never given them any reason to doubt his word."

She followed him to the third station and the homemade tool box it held. He ran his hand across the handle in an effort to wipe away the layer of sawdust that surely came from a customer trying out the project's appropriate tools.

"What changed?"

"He kept giving them less and less until Benjamin Miller realized something was wrong. I guess he saw a customer carrying one of his rocking chairs, and he asked how much the woman had paid. He compared that answer to the next statement, where Walter claimed he'd gotten only half of that amount. Benjamin put two and two together, and Walter closed up shop on the heels of some very disturbing threats made by young Eli."

And with that one name, she was right back where she'd started when she reached the end of Ruth's walkway and opted to head left instead of right. She leaned against a pole in the center of the store and studied her fellow shopkeeper. "Do you really think Mr. Snow ran because of Eli? Or do you think he ran because he didn't want to give up all that money he stole?"

Howard moved on to the Peg Board, his hand expertly removing tools and replacing them onto their correct hooks. "I imagine it was probably both, though we won't ever know for sure now."

She closed her eyes at the memory of the crime-scene tape stretched across the alley after Walter Snow's body had been discovered. It was the kind of image that didn't go with Heavenly. Not the Heavenly she needed it to be, anyway.

"Were Eli's threats really all that bad? I mean, he was mad, right? His family had been bilked of a lot of money. Maybe he was just letting off steam." The words flowed from her mouth as if grateful to finally be unleashed.

"Letting off steam would be to yell at him for stealing. Maybe even screaming until your face turns red. But that's not what Eli did. Not even close." Howard disappeared behind the counter only to return carrying a box filled to capacity with smaller plastic boxes with various sizes of nails. "Eli told Walter that he was going to rip him limb from limb if he didn't return every cent of the money he owed the Millers and all the other Amish families who'd been hurt by Snow's scheme. And he said that after he was done, he was going to throw Snow's body in the lake."

So much for letting off steam . . .

She swallowed hard in an effort to keep herself from asking the question that begged to be asked. But she couldn't resist. She had to know. "Do *you* think Eli killed Walter?"

Howard pulled three plastic boxes from the carton and fed them down the thin silver pole that held them at eye level. "I think it's a good possibility, although it's not one I'm terribly excited about."

"Oh?"

"I like Eli." Howard withdrew three more boxes and arranged them on a neighboring hook. "He's a right fine young man most of the time. He's got good manners, he is helpful at times I'm too stubborn to ask for it, and the way he looks after his sister is commendable."

They were all the same reasons she hoped Eli was innocent, too. Minus the one about a starry-eyed Esther, of course.

"Why did you say he's a fine young man *most of the time?*"

He deposited the rest of the nail packages onto their appropriate hooks and carried the box back to the counter, where he proceeded to break it down with ease. "Well, he's a hothead. I'm not sure more than two or three days can go by before he's out back hollerin' about something or another. Some kids laughed at him in the buggy that afternoon, some guy yelled at him for his horse going too slow, that strange duck from your aunt's place hanging out in your shop too much. It's always something, I tell you."

"Strange duck? You mean Arnie?"

Howard nodded. "Yeah, that's the guy."

She followed him to the counter and leaned her forearms against the Formica top. "Why would Arnie upset Eli?"

"Because he's got a crush on Esther, that's why."

"Arnie? Yeah, I know that. How could I not?" She took note of the bulletin board behind Howard's head and skimmed the various notes pertaining to the Lighted Way Business Owners' Association.

"No, I meant Eli. He fancies Esther, too."

She felt her mouth gape. "He does? Then why doesn't he say something? Esther is crazy about him!"

Howard's belly moved when he chuckled. "Because that hothead is shy where feelings and women are concerned. He'll look after 'em and make sure they're safe, but tell 'em he's got feelings for 'em so some awkward guy will quit hanging around? Nope. Not gonna happen anytime soon."

"Men."

"Spoken like a true woman." Howard patted his stomach and then dropped onto his folding chair once again. "Eli will come around, eventually. We men usually do. Unless, of course, he's in jail for murder."

She waved the notion away. "Do you think Eli is smart?" It was a question she hadn't meant to ask but it came out nonetheless.

Howard leaned back and kneaded his chin between his fingers. "I don't think he's terribly book smart. Few are when they've only received formal education until they're thirteen or so. But here's the thing . . . If I were to be stuck on a deserted island with someone who was book smart or clever smart, I'd pick the latter every single time. You can't teach clever. You either have it or you don't."

"And you think Eli is clever?"

"As clever as they come. Why, just the other day, when that school bus showed up

with all those summer kids on it, I was trying to figure out how to keep them from
clamoring to try all the hands-on stations."
Howard turned a sheepish eye at Claire. "I
guess I didn't want to take a chance those
kids would break something or, even worse,
hurt themselves and set me back even
further than Walter's nonsense did. So Eli
grabbed that sign" — Howard pointed at
the wooden plaque hanging in the middle
of the store — "and flipped it over. Before I
knew it, he'd managed to etch the word
demonstrations into the back side. It was
crude on account of having to use his left
hand, but it worked." Howard laughed at
the memory. "Course that meant I was hop-
ping all over the store, demonstrating each
and every tool over and over again, but it
was better than the alternative."

Howard crossed his arms in front of his
chest and tipped his chair back on two legs.
"Eli can work his magic on reality anytime
he wants as far as I'm concerned. Though,
given time, I'm not so bad with that sort of
thing myself."

It was an answer she didn't want. Yet it
wasn't one she could dispute, either. Eli
Miller was, indeed, a clever soul, able to
work his way around all sorts of situations
when he wasn't simmering over some pur-

ported injustice or another.

The real question was whether he could work his magic on reality in other situations as well . . .

"Well, I guess I better head to the shop. Esther is probably wondering what hole I dropped into this morning." She pushed off the counter and turned, her gaze falling on the carved picture frames once again. "Hey . . . you never finished telling me how the stuff with Walter affected this place."

Howard pulled his arms from his chest and raised them into the air, linking his fingers behind his head. "Remember how I said Walter Snow was honest for a while?"

She nodded.

"Well, once a person's trust is shaken in one seemingly honest person, it tends to be shaken toward others as well."

"You lost me."

"See those frames by your elbow?" Howard thrust his chin in her direction, then pointed it further right. "And those saws over there?"

She followed the direction of his chin to a bin of wooden saws. "Yes."

"And those work tables down yonder?"

Turning, she looked across the store to the stack of basic work tables just waiting to go home with customers eager to start their own workshops at home. "Okay . . ."

"Those are all Amish made. As is half the merchandise in this store. I lose those suppliers, and I don't have much to sell, do I?"

The meaning behind his words finally met their mark. "They stopped giving you things, too? Because of *Walter?*"

"Yep. Because of Walter." Howard unhooked his fingers and let his chair fall onto all four legs. "Sure, Benjamin and the others knew they were getting every dime I owed them. But they pulled back their wares anyway. I suppose they were smartin' from the betrayal, and I guess I can understand that. But by doing that, they made me one of Walter Snow's victims, too."

It was all so much to take in. Too much, actually. "I guess I better get going." She walked to the door and stopped, her mind virtually numb to anything resembling deep thought. "Eli really messed up threatening Walter Snow in the way that he did, didn't he?"

"I imagine it's cast a spotlight on him, that's for sure. Funny thing is, there's probably a few of us who'd have helped him get the body down to the lake. We just weren't dumb enough to say it out in the open with half a dozen witnesses standing around to hear it."

CHAPTER 24

Claire could feel Esther's eyes as she moved around the store taking everything off the shelves only to return it all to the exact same spot. She didn't dust anything, didn't re-arrange anything, and didn't change any of the pricing.

She simply made work for the sake of making work.

So she could avoid conversing with Esther about anything other than the weather and the relatively slow customer traffic.

It wasn't that she didn't have plenty to say or countless things to ask. Because she did.

She just didn't want to hurt Esther in the process.

"I feel so bad for Ruth. She has had too much."

Claire took a breath and held it for a count of ten. If she responded with more than a head nod, she'd be putting herself on a slippery slope. If she didn't, she'd come across as uncaring.

"I agree."

"Eli said there has been more — things he did not even tell Ruth."

She drew her hand back from the pyramid of votive candles she was restacking and started the count again. "Oh?"

"He said he found a nail stuck between the stones in the alley."

The counting ceased at the second six. "A nail?"

Worried lines deepened around the corners of Esther's eyes. "Eli said it could hurt the horse."

"Maybe someone dropped it."

"Eli said it was fixed in place. He said it could not have fallen in such a way."

Giving up on the pyramid, Claire moved on to the next shelf, her mind at a loss for what to do with the two trinket boxes that would justify taking them down in the first place. "And when did he say this happened?"

"Last week. After" — Esther looked down at her hands — "after Mr. Snow was found."

"When did he tell you this?"

A rosy glow fanned its way across Esther's cheeks. "This morning. I . . . I heard his buggy in the alley. I went out to see if he was okay."

It was hard to see Esther's face when she spoke of Eli. To see the hope in her eyes. It was even harder knowing that both Arnie and Mr. Glick believed he was capable of murder. "Why did he tell you about this nail now if he found it last week? Surely you've talked since then, right?"

"Eli is strong. He likes to fix things by himself."

Fix . . . or create?

She shook the accusation from her mind and forced herself to focus on the pair of trinket boxes and the lack of display options available to her. "Then why tell you now? And why you and not Ruth?"

"He worries for Ruth. He does not want her to worry more." Esther bent her arms up and tied the strings of her head cap, the move surprising Claire as much as anything else so far that day. Granted, Esther was Amish. But Amish or not, Jakob's niece had a bit of a rebellious streak where her clothes were concerned. "He needed to tell someone. He told me."

The pride in Esther's eyes at the notion Eli had shared a secret with her was impossible to ignore. Claire swallowed once, twice. "I'm . . . glad."

Esther's eyebrows rose toward her head cap. "Is it something I said?"

"What?"

"You look sad."

Because I am, she wanted to say. But she couldn't. Not without subjecting herself to questions she didn't want to answer. Instead, she merely shrugged, hoping the gesture and the noncommittal nod would throw Esther off the scent.

She held up both boxes. "Any creative ideas for how to display these?"

"You do not like Eli, do you?"

She turned to face Esther, the trinket boxes clutched tightly in her hands. "I never said that."

"You do not want to speak of him today."

Slowly, she lifted one box and then the other before setting them both back on the shelf. "I don't know what to say."

"I know of how people speak. I know some think Eli harmed Mr. Snow. But I know he did not."

She wanted to move but couldn't. She was in a bad place, and she knew it. The key was to remain calm. To keep her thoughts and her fears to herself until she had something more concrete. Then again, if Esther could vouch for Eli, her fears would be moot, wouldn't they?

"Do you know where he was when Mr. Snow was murdered?"

Esther shook her head. "I can not say for sure. But I know Eli. I know he could not do such a thing."

As fast as the glimmer of hope had waltzed in, it waltzed back out again, leaving her with nothing good to say. "Esther?"

"Yes."

She took in a breath of air and released it slowly. "I need you to hear me out. As your friend, okay? Someone who cares about you dearly."

Esther smiled so big that it nearly broke Claire's heart. She wanted to protect Esther, to keep her from getting hurt, yet, at that moment, the only one capable of hurting her was Claire. It was a task she didn't relish.

"Why are you so sure Eli didn't murder Mr. Snow? That man stole a lot of money from Eli's family."

"Eli would not do that. He would not hurt Ruth that way."

The reason gave her pause. Eli was devoted to his twin sister. Everyone knew that. Even Mr. Glick had referenced the brother's care for his sister during their talk. Then again, it was that same reason Esther gave for Eli's inability to commit murder that could be the reason why he would.

She took in a second, deeper breath as

her mind seized on a suspicion that started long before Arnie ever opened his mouth about trumped-up pranks in the name of deflection.

"You said you hid that love letter under the register because you didn't want Eli to be angry, right?"

All remaining hint of a smile disappeared from Esther's face in the blink of an eye.

Claire continued, her gaze never leaving Esther's troubled one. "Was that the only letter, Esther?"

"I can not speak of that," Esther whispered.

She took hold of Esther's shoulders and gave them a little shake. "Did Walter write more love letters, Esther?"

"Yes."

"Did Eli know of them?"

Esther squeezed her eyes shut but not before a tear escaped down her cheek. "I do not know. It is possible."

"I wonder if that's why he hasn't told you he likes you."

Esther stumbled backward and bumped into the counter. "Eli likes me?"

"Mr. Glick says he does." She closed the fresh gap between them and ran her hand along Esther's forearm.

"And he does not tell because of notes?"

"I don't know," she said honestly.

"But they were not for me," Esther whispered.

She caught her friend's troubled eyes and held them. "What wasn't for you?"

"The notes."

"Esther, I saw the one I showed you. I found it under the register where you put it."

"I had to hide it."

She ran her hand down her face in an attempt to make sense of what she was hearing. But it was no use. "But you just said they weren't yours, right?"

Esther's nod was so slight she wasn't sure she'd truly seen it.

"Then I don't understand any of this, Esther. I saw that note with my own two eyes. It was a love letter signed with a *W.* I asked you if it was from Walter, and you didn't deny it. Yet now you are?" She heard the shrillness in her voice and knew it was only serving to unnerve Esther even further, but she couldn't help it. She was growing more and more frustrated with each passing minute.

Bending at the waist, Esther dropped her head into her hands and let out a quiet moan.

Claire reached out and guided the young

woman's face upward. "Esther. Please. I can't help you if you don't tell me what's going on."

"I'm afraid."

The simple statement stirred something inside her, and she pulled a trembling Esther into her arms. "I know you're afraid to talk to Jakob. That you're afraid you'll get in trouble if you say anything to him at all. But if you do, it won't be as your mother's brother or as your uncle. It will be as a police officer . . . an *English* police officer."

"I am not afraid of that."

She took hold of Esther's arms and stepped back until they could see each other. "Then what are you afraid of, Esther? What aren't you telling me?"

Without waiting for an answer, Claire grabbed hold of the simple bow beneath her friend's chin and pulled, leaving the ties to dangle in true Esther fashion. "You are strong, Esther. You know this. So please, tell me. We'll figure it out together."

The trembling stopped as Esther looked down at the ties of her head cap and back up at Claire, a mixture of resignation and determination lighting her tired eyes. "The letter was from Mr. Snow. He left many. They were all the same. Love letters. Only they were not for me."

She stared at Esther, trying desperately to understand but falling short. Way short. "But you crumpled it up. You shoved it under the register so I wouldn't find it."

Esther shook her head.

"You didn't crumple it?"

"I did."

She groaned. "Ugh! Esther, please. You're making my head hurt."

"I crumpled the note. I put it under the register. But it was not so you would not see it."

"Then why else would you shove it under there?"

"So Eli would not see it."

She covered her eyes with her hands in an effort to block out the image of a ping-pong match with her brain as the ball. "But you just said the note was not for you. If that's true, why on earth would you have to hide it from Eli?"

"Because it was for Ruth."

She heard the gasp as it escaped her mouth. "Ruth?"

"Yes."

"Are you sure?" she asked.

"Yes."

She cast about for something to say. "Did Ruth know about them?"

"Yes. She was afraid of what Eli would do."

"Did she like Walter, too?"

Esther made a face, further loosening whatever grip Claire had on reality. "What? What's with that face?"

"Ruth sees only Samuel Yoder."

"Did Walter know that?"

"I tell him. Again and again. But he did not listen. He said they were meaned to be."

"Meant to be," she corrected gently. "But if she'd told Eli or Benjamin about the notes, they could have made him understand."

"Ruth does not like to worry Benjamin. She says he has too much to worry about already."

"So why not tell Eli?" But even as she asked the question, she knew the answer. Eli despised Walter for cheating his family of money that was rightfully theirs. He'd been so angry by the man's actions that he'd threatened to kill him in front of countless witnesses. Yet Esther didn't believe he would have followed through on his threats. And maybe she was right. But this latest wrinkle had the potential to change everything.

"Eli will allow no harm to Ruth."

"How would a love letter harm Ruth?"

"Mr. Snow is an English man. A married English man. If Samuel found out, if the district found out, Ruth could be shunned."

"But Ruth didn't do anything wrong," Claire protested.

"Mr. Snow was to say she did."

And then she got it. Walter had threatened to tell a lie — one that could sever Ruth's ties with her family, her community, her everything.

"And you're not positive Eli didn't know about the letters?"

Esther fiddled with her hands. "One is missing."

"Missing?"

"It came in the mail. To Ruth's shop."

She took it all in, questions firing from her mouth in rapid succession. "When did it come? What did it say? Where was it when it disappeared?"

"It was the week before Mr. Snow came back. It talked of love for Ruth. He wanted to marry and have babies. I brought it here, where Eli could not find it. But when customers came in, I lost track of it. I could not find it the next day."

"That doesn't mean Eli has it . . ."

"That is the day he fixed the back door for you." New tears formed in Esther's eyes, making their way down her cheeks. "If he read the letter, he would be angry. Very, very angry."

CHAPTER 25

She'd seen the worry in her aunt's eyes
when she'd asked to borrow the car after
dinner. And she could understand why.

Claire wasn't one to disappear in the
evenings unless it was her night off. Instead,
she tended to spend the post-dinner hours
doing traditional homebody things like
reading and crafting. But, lately, she'd been
staying away from the inn more than ever.
One night she'd gone walking and met Ben,
one night she'd gone walking with Jakob . . .

Tonight, though, she truly wanted to be
alone. Maybe then she could begin to sort
through all of the information she'd as-
sembled about Eli and Walter. It wasn't that
she had any burning desire to play amateur
sleuth, but when stuff started falling in her
lap, it removed any real choice in the matter.

Sure, she could take everything she had to
Jakob and dump it all off on him. But what

happened if something she said set him off on a path that could hurt an innocent person? That, she couldn't handle.

After dinner, when all the dishes had been washed and put away, she'd considered sharing her thoughts with Diane. After all, if she'd learned anything over the past few months at Sleep Heavenly, it was that Diane Weatherly was one smart, level-headed woman.

Who also just happened to be an innkeeper at a bed-and-breakfast with guests who roamed freely around the house . . .

She pulled out of the parking lot and headed east on Lighted Way, the cool evening breeze lifting her hair from her face and scattering it every which way. The English side of Heavenly was attractive enough, with carefully kept homes and yards. One and two automobiles per household were parked in each driveway she passed. The glow from an occasional bug zapper or porch light whizzed past her window along the quarter-mile stretch between Sleep Heavenly and the shopping district.

She slowed as the tires left the pavement in favor of the cobblestone section of Lighted Way. Here, light streamed into her car from the parade of gas-powered lamps that lined the street, their only competition coming from the lighted display windows of her fellow shopkeepers. She glanced left toward the toy shop, with its rocking ponies and plethora of brightly colored balls, and then right toward Glick's and all its man-friendly tools. She slowed still further as she approached Shoo Fly Bake Shoppe, straining to make out any sign of someone lurking. The reassuring shadow of a police car at the mouth of the alley let her know she wasn't alone in her vigilance.

A smile crept across her face as she caught a fleeting glimpse of her own front window, the placement of Amish-made items having its desired effect — at least on her.

"I'd shop there," she whispered before laughing at herself for sounding like a nut.

She continued on, passing Yoder's Fine Furniture and the general store before heading out into Amish country. Here, there were no street lamps or televisions flickering behind open curtains, no blue-green glows flickering from trees as curious bugs met with their demise. She slowed to accommodate the occasional rut in the sparsely graveled road. The hum of the engine disappeared against the symphonic backdrop of crickets and bullfrogs, and she felt her shoulders relax for the first time all day.

When she'd wrapped her hand around her aunt's key ring back at the inn, she'd been unsure of where she was going. All she'd known for sure was that she needed a little time to herself. Yet the second she'd pulled out of the parking lot and headed east, her destination was decided.

She passed one farm and then another before turning left, the midsize sedan making the climb with ease. The covered bridge vibrated beneath her wheels as she entered and then exited out the other side. When she reached the point where the road narrowed and wound off into the woods, she put the car in park and cut the engine.

For a moment, she simply sat there, surveying the clearing in front of the car, marveling at just how beautiful the Amish countryside was no matter the time of day. Then, squaring her shoulders, she pushed open the door and stepped onto the soft earth, depositing her aunt's keys into her front pocket as she did.

It was different this time.

Instead of shielding her eyes from the last of the sun's rays, this time she found herself looking up at the hundreds of stars that twinkled against the night sky. Instinctively, she picked out the Big and Little Dippers and the occasional airplane temporarily masquerading as a star, her breathing soft and rhythmic to her own ears.

Eventually, she picked her way across the moonlit prairie grass until she found the rock she'd perched on with Benjamin earlier in the week. Scooting toward its center, she looked into the valley below, locating the Millers' farm in short order. Two of the three farmhouses sported faint glows — candles or gas-generated lamps, no doubt. But the third house was dark.

She tried to imagine what was happening in each home. Perhaps the grandparents' home was the dark one, their increased age making them retire to bed earlier than everyone else. The larger house to the right of the barn was probably where Eli and Ruth lived with their parents and younger siblings. The light poking through their windows was minimal — maybe just enough for everyone to sit around the table and visit.

Bobbing her head to the left, she took in the third and smallest farmhouse — the one Benjamin probably took over when he married his late wife, Elizabeth. A pang of something tugged at her heart as she envisioned the quiet, gentle man wandering around the farmhouse all by himself, still mourning the decade-old death of his wife. She couldn't imagine that kind of pain. Nor could she imagine Jakob's pain. From what she could gather from his brief comments the night before, he had loved Elizabeth, too.

Only she'd chosen to marry Benjamin.

Pulling her knees to her chin, she wrapped her arms around her legs and stared down at the house, her thoughts veering off in odd directions . . .

Had Elizabeth known Jakob loved her yet chosen Benjamin instead? Or had Jakob kept the extent of his feelings for the Amish girl to himself? And was Elizabeth the true reason he left the Amish community to pursue police work?

And as a detective, would Jakob be able to solve Walter Snow's murder?

She hugged her legs close and revisited the things she'd learned that day, all thoughts, all questions eventually leading to one place.

The love letters.

Walter Snow had a monumental crush on Ruth Miller. One only had to look at the crumpled note Claire had found to know that. But what she didn't know was whether those letters played any part in the former shopkeeper's death.

And if so, did they hand Eli an even stronger motive for committing the crime?

The snap of a twig somewhere off to her right made her legs drop to the rock. Turning her head toward the sound, she strained to make out the shape of an animal but saw nothing. Her heart rate accelerated in her chest as she heard a second snap, this one closer than the first.

"Hello?" She slid off the rock and got ready to run through the tall grass to her car. "Is anyone there?"

A form emerged from the shadow cast by her car and stopped. "Miss Weatherly? That is you?"

She knew that voice.

"Benjamin?" she squeaked. "Is that you?"

"Yes. It is me." He stepped closer until he was completely visible from the light of the half moon. "I did not expect to see you."

She reached into the pocket of her jeans and pulled out her keys. "I'm sorry. I didn't mean to crash your special spot. I . . . I just kind of ended up here."

He raised his palms into the air. "I do not own this land."

"But it is where you come when you want to be alone." She stepped around the rock. "Had I seen your horse and buggy, I would have turned around."

285

"I made the choice to walk. Now I know why." Benjamin swept his hand toward the rock. "Please. Do not go."

She looked from the car, to the rock, and back to Benjamin. "Are you sure?"

"I am sure." He patted the spot she'd vacated and waited for her to reclaim it. When she did, he sat beside her, his simple black shoes dangling over the edge. "So why did you come?"

She opened her mouth to speak, to let all of her worries and fears out into the open, but closed it as reality sunk in. She couldn't talk about Esther and Eli, or Walter and Ruth. Not now. Not with Benjamin.

Instead, she searched for something that would sound semi-believable. "I've been giving some thought to getting a place of my own, and I guess I just needed to look at it from all angles, decide whether it's something I want to do now or wait for another year or so."

"Will you leave your store?"

"No! Never!" She pulled her knees up once again until her chin rested on them. "I love it here in Heavenly. I don't ever want to leave."

He bowed his head forward. "That is good."

"I just don't want to take a room from my

aunt for any longer than necessary," she explained. "My being there gives her one less room to rent."

"But you help, yes?"

She nodded. "I do. And she loves having me there. It's just that, well . . ." Her words slipped away as she looked into the valley again, her eyes drawn to the farmhouse she equated with Ben. "I guess I want to have a place of my own one day."

Benjamin shifted on the rock, then extended the index finger of his right hand toward the very parcel of land she'd been admiring from afar. "Do you see the farmhouse there? The one that has no light? That is mine."

So she'd been wrong. The absence of light she'd attributed to Benjamin's grandparents was actually due to his long walk. "Did you ever consider moving back in with your family after your wife passed?"

"I did not. I was a man, not a boy."

It was the same basic reason she'd given to Diane the few times the possibility of moving was discussed. It wasn't that she didn't love the inn — because she did. And it wasn't some sort of burning desire to get out from under her aunt's watchful eye. She treasured their time together, valued her aunt's opinions and experience.

She just wanted to do what grown-ups were supposed to do.

"Does it get lonely sometimes?" she asked, addressing one of her aunt's chief concerns for her.

"When I go inside and close the door, it is because I need time. I have many responsibilities. For my sisters and brothers. It is nice to sit alone at night."

"Yet you still come here . . ."

He braced himself back against his hands and looked up at the sky. "I am worried. For Ruth. And for Eli."

She caught her breath and waited for more.

"Eli . . . He does not know when to be silent. He does not learn from his mistakes. I worry his actions will hurt Ruth."

"How so?"

"He wants to be man. To earn respect. So he does not tell of problems at the shop. But he gets angry and says things he should not. He angers people. That anger is now on Ruth."

She jerked her head right, Benjamin's strong jawline visible in the light of the moon. "You think that everything that has happened is because someone is angry at Eli?"

Benjamin's head nodded beneath his hat. "I do."

"Who is angry at Eli?"

"Yoder . . . Stoltzfus . . . Lapp . . . Beilers . . . Troyer" — one by one he ticked them off on his fingers, the list continuing as he finished one hand and moved on to the next — "and Schrock."

The list of Amish names surprised her. "But why? Why are all of those people angry at Eli?"

"He made things worse."

She dropped her legs to the rock and spun around to face Benjamin. "What things?"

"He scared Mr. Snow. Mr. Snow ran. Took their money with him." It was a simple explanation and one she couldn't believe she'd missed. Suddenly, it made sense why someone would lash out at Shoo Fly Bake Shoppe.

Or did it?

The Amish were supposed to be pacifists. It was his failure to act as one that had earned Eli a spot in front of his elders as he asked for forgiveness for his behavior toward Mr. Snow. Surely they wouldn't condone things like stealing pie boxes, breaking milk bottles, spattering paint, and starting a fire.

She said as much to Benjamin.

"I do not believe they would do those

things. But they are not the only ones angry at my brother. There are others who are not Amish."

It was a point she couldn't argue. In just the short time since she'd opened Heavenly Treasures, she'd heard countless stories of Eli losing his temper with everyone from tourists to local teenagers — and everyone in between. Most people probably shook it off or maybe used it to further their ignorance of the Amish people. But most was not all. And it only took one bad apple to take things too far.

The notion was both appealing and unappealing at the same time. For if Benjamin was right, the pranks could continue, possibly even escalate beyond anything they'd seen so far. If he was wrong and Arnie was right, the stain of Eli's actions would reach far into his family.

She lifted her gaze toward the stars that peppered the sky and found the brightest one she could see. "Do you see that star right there?" she asked, indicating the correct one with her finger. "It's the brightest one in the sky tonight, which makes it a wishing star according to Aunt Diane."

He followed the path made by her finger. "A wishing star?"

"She says that if you find that star and

stare at it good and hard, whatever you wish for at that moment will come true."

"Have you done this before?"

She felt his eyes on her face and knew he was waiting for an answer. She took a deep breath and released it slowly. "I have. When I first moved here. We had spent the evening talking about all of the hopes and dreams I'd had before I got married. The ones that faded to nothing as my husband lost interest in his vows."

Like clockwork, the mere mention of Peter enveloped her in sadness, and she fought to keep it at bay. "So I told her I'd always wanted to own a shop with all sorts of things to make people smile."

His silence while she spoke was different than Peter's had always been. Peter's had been because he wasn't listening, something he'd proven again and again throughout their nearly five years together. Benjamin, on the other hand, was listening to every word, waiting, like a child, for the rest of the story.

"You said this wish on a bright star?"

"I did," she said. "I know it's silly to believe that wish made it happen, but I do."

When he didn't say anything in response, she glanced in his direction and found him looking up at the stars. "Will you make a wish now?"

She nibbled at her lower lip but gave up as her smile won. "I could."

"Will you wish for a new home?"

"I'm not sure I'm ready just yet," she said, the words surprising even her. "I think I need my aunt's presence a little longer. I need our talks; I need her encouragement; I need her hugs."

Benjamin stared up at the stars. "That is good. Family is good."

"I agree." It was hard not to lose herself in the sincerity that was Benjamin Miller. But as was always the case when she dared to think of him, she heard Diane's voice in her head, reminding her to look at his vest, his hat, his pants.

"So what is your new wish?"

She closed her eyes against the one she couldn't have, the one she couldn't voice to anyone, least of all him.

"Miss Weatherly?"

She jumped at the feel of his fingers on her shoulder and the rapid heartbeat his touch inspired.

Vest, hat, pants — Amish . . .

Vest, hat, pants — Amish . . .

Swallowing against the lump that threatened to render her speechless, she searched for something, anything she could say that would deflect him from the knowledge that had to be written all over her face.

"I suppose I would make two wishes if I could."

He pulled his hand from her shoulder and gestured toward the stars, his expression difficult to read. "We must find two bright stars?"

She allowed herself to laugh, the sound echoing around them. "I suppose that would be best."

"That is one." Benjamin pointed to her star's biggest contender. "So now there are two. Two stars. Two wishes."

"Okay . . . here goes." She looked at the first star and closed her eyes, the wish coming easily.

"What? I do not hear?"

She lifted one lid and peeked out at Benjamin. "You want me to say them out loud?"

"Of course. How am I to know your wish if you do not tell me?"

She thought about explaining the practice of silent wishes and the longstanding belief that they wouldn't come true if you spoke them out loud. But when she saw the way he looked at her, with such curiosity and anticipation, she simply couldn't burst his bubble. Besides, he was Amish. He thought wishes and such were hooey anyway.

She repeated the lead-up to her wish, this time voicing her request aloud for Benjamin and all of the insects and animals around them to hear. "I wish to live a simple life surrounded by love and family."

Opening her eyes, she searched the sky for the second star but to no avail. "Uh-oh. I think your star was an airplane."

Benjamin cleared his throat and pointed above his head. "No. It is there."

"Oh, yeah, I see it now." She closed her eyes again and spoke her second wish aloud. "I wish for us to figure out who is doing these awful things to Shoo Fly Bake Shoppe before any more harm is done."

"That is a good wish."

She turned away from the stars to find him staring at her with a look she couldn't quite identify. "You liked that one?"

"I liked both."

CHAPTER 26

Claire had just let herself into the stockroom via the back door when Esther started crying, tears streaming down the young woman's cheeks with reckless abandon.

"Esther, what's wrong?" Claire dropped her purse and keys at her feet and grabbed hold of her employee's soft hands. "Are you hurt?"

Esther's breath hitched once, twice, three times before she was able to shake her head.

She peeked around the girl and into the main room of the shop. "Did something break?"

"N-no."

When she was satisfied that she wasn't missing something in plain view, she focused on Esther once again. "Is it your mother? Your father? Are they sick?"

"It is not Mamm or Dat." The girl wiggled her hands from Claire's grasp and clutched them to her chest as tear after tear continued to fall. "It is Eli."

She heard herself gasp, the sound bringing Esther's tears still faster. "Was Eli arrested for Walter Snow's murder?"

Esther's eyes widened with horror. "You think they will do that?"

She took a step back to steady her breath. "Esther, please. Just tell me what happened."

"Last night he came to Eli's house. He asked questions." Esther swiped at the tears as they left her cheeks and dropped onto her dress. "He . . . He said Eli should not leave Heavenly."

"By he you must mean Jakob."

"Benjamin could not be found. He was not there to help Eli."

Guilt flooded her body as she realized where Benjamin had been. "Does he know now?" she finally asked.

"I do not know. Eli did not say."

She tried to absorb what she was hearing and to say something to wipe the fear from Esther's face, but she came up empty. "When did you see Eli?"

"He was just here. He told me what has happened." Esther reached for Claire. "He asked for you."

She shook her head and forced herself to focus. "Wait. I'm confused. I thought you were talking about Eli, not Jakob."

"It is Eli I speak of."

"Eli was looking for *me?*"

"I tell him you are smart. I tell him you are kind to the Amish. I tell him you are friends with Jakob." Esther spread her arms in pleading. "I tell him you can help."

Claire spun on her heels and headed across the stockroom, doubling back as she reached the wall. "Esther, I can't help Eli. I'm not a police officer. I don't know about any of this stuff, any more than you do."

"But you can learn," Esther insisted. "You learned about this shop. You learn about the Amish. You learn about so much. You can learn about this, too."

She made a second and third trip across the stockroom before stopping midway through her fourth go-round. "Esther, I don't know what you want me to say. I mean, I want to help . . . I really do. But I don't know how."

Esther bridged the gap between them. "Just speak to him. Maybe it will help."

"But you said Jakob already did that. Last night, right?"

"That is right."

"Then what can Eli tell me that he hasn't already told Jakob?"

"Your ears are not Jakob's. You do not

have" — Esther cast about for the right words — "resentment as Jakob does."

She wanted to argue, to insist Jakob would be fair in his pursuit of the truth, but Esther didn't give her a chance. "We need help. Please, Claire."

There were times in her life when she'd second-guessed decisions she'd made — recipes she'd tried and hated, job interview questions she could have answered differently, a marriage proposal she never should have accepted. But none came as quickly and swiftly as the bout that started screaming inside her head before she finished uttering the words Esther had begged to hear.

How, exactly, she was going to help Eli was anyone's guess. Including hers. But a promise was a promise, so she was determined to try if nothing else.

The fifty-year-old man behind the counter covered the phone with his hand and chinned her toward the door on his left. "Detective Fisher said you can come on back."

Hiking the strap of her purse higher on her shoulder, she thanked him and proceeded toward the specified door, her thoughts already skipping ahead to what she could possibly say that would make Jakob share the facts of the case thus far.

Several sets of eyes glanced in her direction as she made her way down an interior hallway that passed a handful of cubicles and a half-dozen or so offices. When she reached the correct office, as evidenced by the gold plate bearing the detective's name, she knocked on the open door frame.

Jakob looked up and smiled. "Well, isn't this a nice surprise." He pushed back his chair and stood, then swept an open palm toward the chair across from his desk. "Please. Come in."

She pulled her purse onto her lap as she sat and raised his smile with one of her own. "I'm sorry to bother you at work but . . ." Closing her eyes, she ran through the various ways she'd planned to ask about Eli and his standing as a suspect and settled on the only one that felt right. "I was wondering if we could talk about Walter Snow's murder and whatever role you think Eli Miller may have played in it."

His smile still in place, Jakob plucked a pencil from the wooden holder on his desk and turned it round and round between his fingers. "Esther has asked you to help, hasn't she?"

"Yes."

"And that's because Esther is worried I

won't be fair on account of my supposed bitterness toward the Amish in this area, right?"

She watched his fingers slide down the pencil only to flip it over and start once again from the top. It was the kind of motion that could distract her if she allowed it to. "Look, Jakob, I truly believe you're going to see this case through to the right conclusion wherever that may lead. I really do."

His smile faltered ever so slightly, but he recovered it so fast that she had to question her eyesight. "That's nice to hear, Claire. Thank you."

She forced herself to remain on task, to not be distracted by the memory of his hand on hers . . . "But, right or wrong, Esther and Eli are concerned. They were just toddlers when you left. They know only what they've been told."

"Which, in my case, was probably nothing until I showed up in Heavenly again."

She considered his words and discounted them. "Actually, I'm not sure that's true. Not where Esther was concerned anyway."

His eyebrows rose in interest, yet he said nothing.

"The first time she saw you, she seemed to know who you were. So Martha must have said something along the way."

He dropped the pencil back into the holder and rose from his chair once again. Wandering over to the corner window, he stood looking out at the midday hustle and bustle of tourists that was synonymous with Lighted Way. "I'd see that as a sign of encouragement if she weren't asking you to snoop around in the case."

She heard the hurt in his voice and felt the renewed desire to help bridge the gap between the detective and his family. "Maybe if I help her, and she sees that you are good and honest, something will change."

"Nothing will change because the Ordnung will not allow it. But I do want her to know those things about me." Slowly, he turned from the window and made his way over to a whiteboard that covered one entire wall of his office. He pointed at a series of notations he'd written down the left-hand side of the board with Eli's name at the top.

1. *Motivation:* Revenge over stolen money.
2. *Opportunity:* Was at Shoo Fly Bake Shoppe daily. Routinely parked buggy in alley where victim was found.

3. *Method:* Strangulation. Suspect had to be both strong and angry in order to choke the life out of another human being with his bare hands. See Motivation.

She read each line several times. It all made sense on so many levels, yet something was holding her back from jumping on the bandwagon with both feet. "Are there any other suspects you're even considering?"

Jakob pointed to a similar list on the opposite side of the board that named a half-dozen or so other Amish men who could work for the same motivation he had down for Eli, but the opportunity wasn't there, nor was the well-documented temper of his primary suspect.

"What about the other people who were hurt by Walter Snow's scheme?"

He pointed to the Amish names a second time. "That's why they're all here. But I just can't believe any of them would act in a vengeful manner. It's just not what they believe."

"It's not what Eli believes, either."

"But that hasn't stopped him from bar fights and threatening to rip a man from limb to limb."

She couldn't argue with that. To do so

would be pointless. "I'm talking about the non-Amish people who were hurt by Walter's scheme."

Jakob pinned her with a curious stare. "What are you talking about? Did he pull the same scheme on other vendors, too?"

"That I can't answer. Though it's my understanding that his shop offered only Amish-made items." She shifted her purse to the floor and then stood awkwardly by Jakob's desk. "No, I'm talking about the other shopkeepers who were made to suffer the carryover from shattered trust."

It's not that she actually thought someone like Howard Glick or Al Gussman was capable of murder, but she also didn't believe that Eli's culpability should be a slam dunk, either.

"How did it affect them?" he asked.

"Once you've been burned, you're not as likely to trust the next guy, I guess. And when a person's business thrives largely on goods made by the Amish, losing that connection is going to hurt a shop's bottom line." She hadn't really thought much about it when Howard first mentioned the struggles his store had endured in the wake of the scandal, but now that she was repeating it out loud, she couldn't help but give it its proper due.

Jakob ran a hand down his mouth and then looked back at the board, adding a third column in the middle. "What do you know about your fellow shopkeepers?"

"I wave to them each day. We get together once a month to brainstorm ways to draw in more customers. And we tell our customers about each other's shops in an effort to spread the wealth. Beyond that, not all that much."

He picked up a dry-erase marker from the metal sill below the board and uncapped it, glancing at her over his shoulder as he did. "Any of them have particularly strong hands?"

CHAPTER 27

She leaned against the exterior wall of Heavenly Treasures and tried not to look at the spot where Walter Snow's body had been found. It wasn't that she was all that squeamish when it came to crime TV or whodunit-style movies, but knowing a chalk outline had been drawn practically outside her doorstep was somehow very different.

Instead, she willed herself to focus on the young man pacing back and forth in front of her as if his life depended on it.

And maybe it did.

"Eli, when was the last time you saw Mr. Snow?"

He stopped pacing long enough to consider her question. "When I said those things."

"You mean when you threatened to tear him from limb to limb and dump his body in the lake?"

Eli held his finger to his lips and looked

nervously toward the screen door that separated them from the interior of Heavenly Treasures. "Please. I do not want Esther to hear those words."

She tilted her head to the left and studied the male version of Ruth with increasing curiosity. "Why not? I'm quite certain she knows you threatened him."

"But she does not know the words. Those things I said brought trouble for me. I do not want to do anything else to make Esther turn away. She is good woman. One I hope to marry and have children with one day."

Her mouth hung open. "You want to marry Esther?"

"Very much."

She dropped her voice to a near whisper and beckoned Eli to come closer. "Then why don't you court her? Why don't you let her know you like her?"

Eli looked toward the door again and then matched Claire's volume the best that he could. "Esther's Dat knows of what I said. He was not happy. I must show him I am a good man for Esther first."

She inhaled sharply at the fervor in the young man's words, her desire to help purely out of loyalty to Esther shifting into one based on something she now believed in her gut.

Eli Miller was innocent. He had to be.

Sure, he was a hothead with a lot of growing up to do. But he was also a man who exhibited a rare devotion to his sister and harbored a desire to become a better man for the woman he hoped to marry.

"She doesn't believe you had anything to do with Mr. Snow's murder." She knew it wasn't her place to say it, but she felt an overwhelming need to throw the guy a bone.

"That is good. But it is not enough. I need to show her I am the better choice. That staying in this life is the better choice."

"Better choice? I don't under —"

"Shhh!" Eli raised his finger to his lips and walked quietly to the back of the building just in time to see a stray cat dart behind the trash bin. "I worry about Ruth. I hear sounds and think there are more pranks."

"I know. I poke my head into the alley many times throughout the day just to make sure no one is hanging around." She traced his steps to the end of the alley and stopped. "I asked Jakob if he had any leads on the store, and, as of yet, he has nothing. But I know he is turning over every stone he can find."

Eli looked left and then right, lowering his

voice once again. "I think Jakob is good man."

She took a step backward in surprise. "You do?"

"I know I am wrong to believe that. But I do."

There was so much she wanted to say in response, but she let it go. There would be a time and place when further discussion about Jakob was warranted. But now was not that time. She needed to get to the bottom of a few lingering questions first.

"Do you remember that day you fixed my back door?"

He nodded. "I do."

"Did you go into the main room at all while you were inside? Maybe to strike up a conversation with Esther?"

"No."

"Are you sure?" She wanted to ask him whether he saw Walter's love letter to Ruth but kept it to herself. There was no sense setting him off unnecessarily.

Eli leaned against the back wall of Shoo Fly Bake Shoppe and lifted his nose to the tantalizing aroma of apple pie spewing its way out the back windows. "I wanted to. She was so pretty that day."

"Why didn't you?"

"Because I did not want to cause a problem for Esther."

She wandered over to Ruth's back step and sat down. "Why would talking to you cause a problem for Esther?"

"I did not want that woman to speak of my words. I do not want Esther to know. She will make the wrong choice."

There was the choice thing again . . . "Eli, I don't understand what you're saying. Please, walk me through this, help me to understand."

Eli shoved his hands in his pockets and toed at the cobblestone beneath his feet. "I was afraid that Mr. Snow's wife would tell Esther what I said. So I stayed in the back room and fixed the door. I left when I was done."

She wrapped her hands around the edge of the step and stared up at Eli. "Wait. Are you saying that Nellie Snow was in my store that day?"

Eli gave a single nod. "You did not know?"

Pushing off the step, she paced the same path Eli had covered not more than ten minutes earlier, her thoughts shifting from apprehension to pity as an entirely different scenario emerged where Ruth's missing love letter was concerned.

She found Esther right where she'd left her

before heading into the alley to talk with Eli. Only instead of shifting from foot to foot, finger drumming had become the young Amish woman's nerve manifestation of choice.

"Esther, we need to talk."

The drumming paused. "Did the talk with Eli go poorly?"

"It went fine." She stepped behind the counter and thumbed through the stack of mail the carrier must have delivered while she was in the alley. "In fact, the more I talk to him, the more I believe in his innocence."

Esther's hands flew to her mouth but not before the shriek of joy she tried to stifle echoed its way around the shop. "I do not know what to say. I am so happy. But" — her hands fell to her sides as she took in the various mail piles Claire was working to assemble — "you do not think he saw the letter?"

"If you truly had it on this counter as you say you did, then I'm not sure how he could have, considering he never came into this room that day."

Relief tugged Esther's shoulders downward. "I am glad."

She continued to separate the day's mail into three separate piles — bills, junk mail, personal letters — while mentally replaying her conversation with Eli. When she got to the part about Nellie Snow, she looked up at Esther. "Esther, why didn't you tell me Nellie Snow was here that day?"

Esther's brows angled down toward her nose momentarily. "Ms. Snow?"

"Yes. Walter's wife. Eli said she was here that day. You know, the day he was fixing my back door."

"I do not know." Esther grabbed a cloth from a drawer to Claire's left and headed across the shop toward the shelf of candle holders and picture frames that tended to collect dust faster than either woman could fathom. "It is hard to remember each visit."

Claire tossed the last two invoices onto their dedicated pile and turned her full attention on Esther. "Each visit? You mean she's been in here more than just that one time?"

"She comes many times." Rising up on tiptoes, Esther lifted a simple wooden picture frame from its base and wiped along its top and sides. "But she does not ever buy."

"Then why does she come?"

Esther replaced the frame on its stand and reached for another. "I do not know. To think of her husband?"

She tried to absorb what she was hearing,

to put it in its proper context. "So if she doesn't buy anything, what does she do? Does she just stop by to talk?"

Frames done, Esther moved on to the candle holders. "She does not come now. Not since Mr. Snow was found. But when she did, she talked a little. Before you cleaned his mess, I would hear noises in stockroom. That is how I would know she was here."

Claire braced her hands on the counter as the reality of what she was hearing truly sank in. "Wait. Are you saying she would go through the things her husband left behind when he took off?"

"Yes."

"So she'd waltz in the door, walk past you, and simply disappear into the stockroom? And you *let* her?"

Esther peered at Claire across the top of the candle holder. "I would hear noises. That is how I would know."

"Noises? In the stockroom? But you keep the back door locked when I'm not here, right?"

"I do."

"Then how could she get into the stock-room without you seeing . . ." The remainder of her question was pushed to the side as a theory began to form in her head. "Do you know if she had a spare key to the store from when Walter was a tenant?"

"Perhaps."

"Did you ever question her reasons for being in there? Did you ever tell her to get out?" But even as she asked, she knew Esther could never do that. It was not the young woman's place to correct an elder — Amish or otherwise. "You know what? Don't answer that. It doesn't matter now."

When the last of the candleholders were dusted, Esther made her way back to the counter. "Sometimes she would walk in here. Look under the shelves and the rug. And one time, she used the stool to check" — Esther pointed toward the drop ceiling above them — "there."

"Did she ever say what she was looking for?" Claire asked.

"She did not."

"And she hasn't been here since Walter was found, is that right?"

"That is right."

Claire sank onto the stool and rubbed at the ache she felt building behind her eyes. There was too much information coming way too fast. And trying to make sense of it all? Forget it.

"She would be glad to see the stockroom now. No more mess."

Esther's words trickled their way around the roar in her ears and brought her up short. "What did you just say?"

"She would be glad to see the stockroom. No more mess."

"But Walter was murdered after I cleaned the stockroom," she insisted.

"Ms. Snow has not seen it clean."

Claire shot her hands into the air in an attempt to slow things down. "Are you saying she hasn't been in since before I finished the stockroom?"

Esther nodded.

"So when was she last here?"

"It was the loud day."

She waited for more but nothing came. "You mean busy? With customers?"

"No. Loud. *Tap tap.* Again and again."

"Tap tap?" Claire pushed off the stool and cupped her hands around Esther's upper arms. "Are you talking about the sounds of Eli's hammer as he fixed the back door?"

She watched as Esther closed her eyes and then smiled shyly. "Yes. That is right."

"Oh my gosh, that's it!" She took in a slow and steady breath and then released it through pursed lips. "The last time Nellie Snow was in my store was the same day Ruth's letter disappeared from this counter. Maybe *she* took it!"

Esther's lashes parted to reveal eyes that held no hint of the smile she'd worn seconds earlier. "If she saw the letter, she must be so hurt."

Claire pulled her purse from the bottom shelf and flung it over her arm, her thoughts leading her down a path she couldn't ignore. "Esther, if Nellie saw that letter, I'm betting she felt a lot more than hurt."

CHAPTER 28

No matter how many different ways she tried to put the pieces of the puzzle together, the same picture kept emerging.

Time and time again.

But if she'd learned nothing else over the past few years, she knew that things were not always as they appeared. Success and money had nothing to do with happiness. Hustle and bustle didn't mean better. And *simple* wasn't synonymous with *boring.*

So it was possible that a blinding hurt didn't necessarily lead to anything beyond a basic retreat for the sake of licking one's wounds. Any thought to the contrary was just that — a thought.

She had absolutely no proof that Nellie was behind the vandalism at Shoo Fly Bake Shoppe. To go to Jakob with her harebrained suspicion prematurely would make her look like a total and complete nut. Besides, he had more urgent matters on his plate than trying to follow a trail of what-ifs and just-supposes.

That was something she could do.

"Why, don't you look pretty as a picture this afternoon, Claire."

Tilting her chin toward her chest, she took in the fitted white trousers and royal-blue short-sleeved sweater she'd paired with her favorite wedge heels. She'd been so busy trying to play detective that she'd forgotten all about her appearance. "Thanks, Mr. Glick."

He lifted his chin toward the steps she'd just descended. "Been a quiet day for you, too?"

"In the store, yes. In my head, not so much." She waved at the words as soon as she said them and hoped it would be enough. The last thing she needed was to get caught in a discussion that would keep her off task. "And you?"

"Same for me. But Al said there's a tour bus comin' in tomorrow with forty-five single seniors."

It was hard not to smile at that report. After all, the seniors who were inclined to take a bus tour tended to spend money. Toss in the fact that they were single and thus not rushed by a potentially impatient spouse, and, well, the hope for finishing out the week strong began to look a little bit more likely. "We could certainly all use that."

"Don't I know it." Howard rocked back on his heels and slid his thumbs down the inner side of his rather dapper-looking suspenders. "So where are you off to?"

"I thought I'd drop by Gussman's General Store and pick up a few items before Esther and I close up shop for the evening." It was true enough, even if the reason she gave was secondary to the real reason she wanted to pay a visit to her landlord. "Are you heading that way, too?"

"I'm headin' over to see Samuel Yoder at the furniture shop. Been so busy the past few weeks that it's been a while since I've looked in on him. But now, my part-timer is finally up to speed enough that I can steal away for a few moments to rectify that. Perhaps we can walk together?"

She forced a smile to her lips and nodded politely. If she'd waited just five minutes longer or gotten to the bottom of Esther's words five minutes sooner, she'd have been able to craft a mental list of questions that needed to be answered. Instead, she found herself making small talk with a man notorious for elongating conversations whenever possible.

"Did you hear 'bout the glue on Ruth's front stoop this morning?"

"Glue?" Claire stopped midstep and froze. "What glue?"

Gleefully aware of the fact that he held information Claire was not privy to, Howard merely nodded and waited.

"I talked to Eli this afternoon. He didn't say anything about glue."

"That's because he didn't know."

She turned to the west and shielded the sun's afternoon rays with her hand. "I would have thought, after the fire, Ruth would be more forthcoming."

Howard cleared his throat and then leaned forward, his breath warm on her cheek. "Seems Detective Fisher was out at Ruth and Eli's home last night asking some mighty pointed questions. Ruth is no dummy. She knows her brother is a suspect in Walter Snow's murder. She don't want to add to his stress any more than necessary."

It made sense. But still . . .

"Did you at least tell Detective Fisher? Because he should know."

"I called and left a message. Seems he's out at some meeting for most of the day. Nate, the dispatcher, said he'd have the detective call me when he returns."

So the vandalism continued . . .

"Is Ruth okay?" she asked.

"You know how she is. So quiet and sweet. She just keeps saying she must have done something wrong. Can't seem to wrap her mind around the notion that some people are just mean for the sake of being mean sometimes."

"Or for the sake of a vendetta . . ."

Howard snorted. "A vendetta? Against Ruth? For what? Making the best apple pie from here to the western seaboard?"

She had to know if she was right. And the question she had for Al Gussman wasn't the only one she had. "Mr. Glick, what do you know about Nellie Snow?"

"Walter's wife?" Howard stepped back until he made contact with the lamp pole. "I don't think she's the innocent little wife who got the wool pulled over her eyes like everyone else 'round here seems to think. In fact, if I was a bettin' man, I'd bet she was in on the whole money-stealin' scheme from the get-go."

"Then why didn't she disappear with him when he took off?"

Lifting his hand to his chin, Howard rubbed at his day-old stubble. "I think it was part of the act. I think that louse was actually protecting her — if you can believe that."

No, she couldn't. Not when she knew what she knew about the vow-challenged Walter Snow. To Howard, though, she offered only a noncommittal shrug and a verbal need to get to Gussman's General Store and back before closing time.

But even as she left him at the steps of Yoder's Fine Furniture and made her way across Lighted Way, she knew she was far from being able to say what Nellie Snow did and didn't know about the plan to extort money from the Amish. That kind of investigative work was beyond her limited capabilities. But short of hooking the jilted woman up to a series of wires designed to smoke out truthfulness, there were a few things she could find out on her own.

Like access.

She pushed open the door of Gussman's and took a moment to breathe in the feeling of yesteryear that called out from every shelf and every aisle that lined the old-fashioned store. Just as her favorite childhood storybook had depicted with its colorful illustrations, Al used large wooden barrels to display things like candy and sugar. Bolts of fabric in standard colors were stacked side by side with their patterned counterparts and shelved along the wall behind the cast-iron register.

"Good afternoon, Claire. What can I do for you?"

She peeked around a freestanding shelf in the center of the room to find Al sitting atop a ladder, removing cans of tomato paste from a cardboard carton. "How did you know it was me?" she asked.

"Easy." He pointed beyond the shelf to a small mirror she'd failed to notice during previous visits. "Thanks to that, I can see everything I need to see from just about anywhere in the store." When he placed the final can on the top of his makeshift pyramid, he tossed the empty carton to the ground and climbed down from the ladder. "If you'd like me to install one of those for you in your place, I can do that. Just let me know."

"Thank you." As far as landlords went, Al was top-notch. He provided a weeklong grace period for all rent payments, he tended to fix problems within hours rather than days of notification, and he was a master at drumming up publicity for all of the shopkeepers along Lighted Way.

"How are those back-door hinges doing since Eli worked on them?" He carried the empty carton behind the main counter and then met her in the center of the store.

"He did a great job. I haven't had any

more problems."

"I'm sorry that call came in while I was on vacation."

"It worked out fine. Eli was very helpful." She reached across her chest and played with the straps of her purse. "I'd like to ask you something if I may."

"Sure. Shoot."

"Did you ever come across that spare key you wanted me to have for the shop?"

He swiped a hand down the front of his work apron and shook his head. "You know, it's the darndest thing, but I can't seem to find it. Are you needing one for another employee? Because I can always have one made."

"No. I still just have Esther, and the first spare is fine for her." She shifted from foot to foot before proceeding full speed ahead with the question that had been nagging at her ever since Esther had mentioned Nellie's little visits. "Is . . . Is there any chance the previous tenant still has a key?"

Al made a face. "I don't see how he could. He left his key ring on the counter when he skipped out on the rent. Both them keys you have were on there."

"Is there any chance his wife had one?"

"Nellie? I don't — hmmm. You know, that just might be what happened. I can ask her next time I see her. Seems she's taken up jogging through here in the evenings, though she seems to run out of steam by the time she reaches your place."

"Run out of steam?" she repeated.

"Yeah. As in come to a complete crawl. Though what she expects when she's trying to jog while carrying a tote bag is beyond me."

Glue and paint can fit in a tote bag. So can a gas can if it's not terribly big . . .

A numbered list fashioned after the ones she'd seen on Jakob's whiteboard filtered through her thoughts, begging to be filled in. Obliging wasn't all that hard. Jealousy made a mighty strong motive for all sorts of murders, so why couldn't it be a motive for destructive acts? And a halfhearted attempt at fitness with a tote bag that just so happened to slow Nellie down outside the scene of the crime after shop hours certainly opened up opportunity . . .

"So what kind of odds would you place on her having a key to my shop?" She wasn't trying to sound like a broken record, but the answer was important.

"Now that you've mentioned it as a possibility, I'd say the odds are quite good. But, like I said, I can ask her."

There was no need. The high probability

was enough for her. "Actually, don't say anything just yet. She's dealing with enough right now. Besides, key or no key, it still doesn't explain how she'd have gotten into . . ." The words trailed from her mouth as the notion of a tote bag faded to black behind yet another, different spare key.

By the time she returned to Heavenly Treasures, Esther was already gone, the carefully scrawled note taped to the locked door an unnecessary apology in light of the time. But that's what she got for falling prey to Mr. Glick's charm on the way back out of Gussman's, too.

"So much for hurrying," she mumbled as she bypassed the front door in favor of the one off the alley.

"Is something wrong?"

Her key clattered to the walkway as she spun around, Benjamin's piercing blue eyes making her balance all the more precarious. "Oh, Ben . . . jamin. I . . . I didn't see you there." She took in the empty alley, then looked back at the man. "Where is your buggy?"

"Eli drove Ruth home. He will come back for me."

"Why are you out here?"

Her hands grew moist as his gaze remained trained on her face. "I did not get the key from Ruth."

She broke eye contact under the guise of retrieving her own key. "That's okay. Ruth keeps it . . ." And then she stopped, Ruth's words filling her head.

"I put it in the flower pot outside. But do not tell Benjamin. He would not approve."

She cleared her throat, then inserted her key into the back door and turned the knob. "You can wait in here if you'd like. I can't imagine Eli will take all that long."

"Thank you." Benjamin followed her into the stockroom and stopped. "I have wanted to thank you for giving the chest and chairs back to Ruth."

"Of course I'd give them back. They didn't belong to me. I'm just so sorry it took me longer than I'd hoped to sort through everything Walter left behind." She tossed her key onto the small desk she used for all paperwork pertaining to Heavenly Treasures and headed toward the main room. Something about sitting under the stars with Benjamin the previous night had changed everything. Every breath he took, every sound he made . . . She heard it all. "Were you able to sell them somewhere else? Because if not, maybe we can find room for them here." She hoped her voice didn't sound as raspy as it felt against a throat that was suddenly parched.

"Yes. The chairs will sell at Yoder's. But not the chest. That is for Ruth. For her pots. And for her pans."

She worked to steady her breath, to remain on task. Yet it was hard. Benjamin's sheer presence made it hard. She wasn't ready to be with anyone but herself. She needed time to heal, to learn to celebrate all of the things that made her special. Maybe that was why she felt these stirrings for Benjamin. Because, deep down inside, she knew they could never amount to anything.

Allowing herself to feel something for Benjamin was safe.

Allowing herself to feel something for Jakob was not.

"Ugh," she whispered as she stepped behind the counter and over to the register. Now was not the time to get sidetracked psychoanalyzing herself. Now was the time to see whether the hunch that hit her in the middle of Gussman's General Store was right . . .

Slipping her hand along the side of the register, she felt around until she found the magnetized key holder that had come with the register *and* the building. Then, with the holder between her fingers, she wiggled her arm back toward her body until she'd cleared the narrow opening.

She counted to ten in her mind and then flipped the case open, her eyes registering the absence of a key at about the same time her mouth and feet started moving. "Benjamin, I need to go. I have to find Jakob. *Now.*"

CHAPTER 29

She chased the last of the homemade mashed potatoes around her plate and then smiled up at her aunt.

"Mmmm. You have no idea just how badly I needed that exact dinner in this" — she gestured around the parlor with her fork — "exact room. So thank you for that."

Diane took the empty plate from Claire's hands. "The second I heard your voice on the phone, I knew something was going on. So I made up a plate from tonight's menu and set it aside in the refrigerator for your return."

"And Mr. Streen didn't try to eat it?" she asked, only half jokingly.

"Oh, he tried, alright. But I was able to distract him away with news of a documentary on the Amish that was getting ready to come on the television."

"Impressive."

"Yes, yes I am." Diane spun on her sensible shoes and headed toward the open doorway that led back toward the kitchen. "Don't go anywhere. I'll be back as soon as I put this dish in the sink and make sure all of the guests are set for the night."

"Trust me — I'm not going anywhere." She pulled her feet off the floor and nestled her way into the corner of her favorite couch, hugging the closest throw pillow to her chest as she did. All day long, she'd been running around, trying to see whether her suspicions were correct. And she still didn't know.

Not for certain, anyway.

But she'd done everything she could with what she knew. The rest was up to Jakob.

It was hard not to remember the way his face lit when they walked up to the police station at the same time — him from a series of meetings in a neighboring town, and her fresh from what she believed was the moment of proof regarding the problems at Shoo Fly Bake Shoppe.

And it was equally hard to ignore the warmth that spread throughout her body when she saw the way he smiled at her.

Jakob Fisher and Benjamin Miller were two very different men. Yet, for some reason, both spoke to her in ways she never expected. One was possible; one was not. And smack-dab in the middle of both of them was her wounded heart.

But just because she wasn't ready for a Jakob or a Benjamin of her own, it didn't mean she couldn't be friends with the real versions, right?

Her mind made up, she laid her head back against the couch and closed her eyes, the rhythmic *tap tap* of Arnie's fingers on his keyboard in his room at the top of the staircase lulling her into the first sense of peace she'd had all day.

"Oh no. You can't fall asleep until you tell me why you were at the police station." Diane breezed into the room and plopped down on the couch beside her niece's feet. "Did they solve the murder?"

"I don't know. Maybe . . ."

"*Maybe?*" Diane deadpanned. "Do you realize, I was alone at the table with Mr. Streen this evening?"

She braced herself for the inevitable as Diane continued. "Do you know that I was subjected to a thirty-minute lecture on the ins and outs of oyster shucking all because I asked whether he liked seafood?"

Lifting her hands, Claire covered her eyes dramatically. "The guilt! The guilt! Oh, how can I ever make it up to you?"

Diane lifted Claire's feet with one hand

and then slid herself underneath them until they rested on her lap. "You can tell me why you were at the police station. Without leaving anything out."

So much for peace . . .

"I think I figured out who's been doing all of those awful things at Ruth's store."

"Please tell me you haven't bought into Mr. Streen's deflection theory." Diane looked toward the staircase and then back at Claire. "I mean, it's not that I think it's totally impossible, but no matter what Eli could possibly be trying to cover up, he wouldn't do anything to hurt Ruth."

"I agree."

Like a balloon with a slow leak, Diane released a long, steady sigh. "Good."

"I think it was Nellie Snow."

"Nellie Snow?" Diane echoed in disbelief.

"She found out that her husband had a thing for Ruth, and I think it sent her over the edge."

Rubbing Claire's feet with her slow, methodical hands, Diane considered Claire's suspect. "I know he cast more than his share of lingering looks Ruth's way, but that's been going on since Walter opened his shop. Why would Nellie wait until Walter left town before she'd lash out? That doesn't make any sense."

"Would it make sense if those lingering looks escalated into something more concrete?" she posed.

Diane's fingers stopped massaging the bottom of Claire's socked feet. "Are you implying that Ruth was somehow involved with that man? Because I've known that young woman virtually her whole life, and I don't believe that for a second."

"I don't believe that, either," she said, staring longingly at her aunt's all-too-still magical hands. "But I do believe *he* was involved with *her.*"

In the blink of an eye, Diane lifted her hands up and away from Claire's feet completely. "You're actually making me long for further discussion on oyster shucking, dear."

Claire struggled into a seated position and tucked her feet underneath her body as she tried to explain her statement. "Walter had apparently gotten in the habit of writing little love notes and letters for Ruth and leaving them in places she would find — the milk box, under the welcome mat, in the crack of the side door. She was apparently so worried Eli would go crazy that she solicited Esther's help in hiding them — hence the crumpled note I found under the register that one day. But when he left town with everyone's money, he mailed her a love letter from wherever it was he'd gone. Esther set it on the counter when a customer came in, and then it disappeared. She was afraid Eli had seen it. Afraid, at least a little, that maybe it *was* Eli who snapped and killed Walter . . . because of the note."

"And now?"

"And now we realize it is much more likely that Nellie found the note."

Diane *tsk*ed softly under her breath. "How awful for her."

"Yes, it is. But that's about the time everything started next door. The stolen pie boxes, the broken milk bottles, the spattered paint, the nasty note, and then the fire. And that's where I started to realize it was far more probable than possible that Nellie was behind everything.

"I think she still has a spare key to my store. And by having that, she had access to Ruth's spare key and the opportunity to start that fire."

A hush fell over the room that Claire understood perfectly. It was how she'd felt when the pieces began to fall into place for her.

After several long minutes, Diane finally broke the silence. "I don't know what to say."

"I just hope I'm right. Because if I am, then everything can go back to normal. At least as far as Ruth and her shop are concerned." She released her hold on the pillow as a flash of car lights shone through the partially drawn parlor curtains. "Looks like your guests are back from their dinner."

Diane shook her head and rose to her feet, bridging the distance between the couch and the window with several easy strides. "They got back about fifteen minutes before you did." Nudging the curtain open a bit more, her aunt cupped her hands around her eyes and peered out into the night. "I think we're about to find out if your suspicions were right."

"Huh?" She let her feet drop to the floor as she scooted forward toward the edge of the couch. "Who is it?"

"Detective Fisher."

She lifted her hands to her hair and finger-combed it into place.

"You look lovely, dear."

She opened her mouth to protest, to insist she wasn't fixing herself for Jakob's benefit, but in the end, she couldn't. Diane would see through her words in a second. Instead, she squared her shoulders and met him at the screen door.

"Detective Fisher, what a surprise." She

flipped on the porch light, bathing him in brightness. "Is everything okay?"

"May I come in for a minute? I'd like to talk to you if I could."

"Of course you can." Pushing the screen door open, she stepped to the side to allow him entry. She looked up at him and felt the admiration in his eyes, an admiration she was at a loss on how to acknowledge. "I, um, why don't we step into the parlor. Diane will be happy to see you . . ." She led the way into the very room she'd just left only to find it completely empty. She spun around to face Jakob, keenly aware of a dryness in her mouth and a dampness in her hands. "She was just here a minute ago."

He gestured toward the couch and asked her to sit with him for a minute. When she obliged, he got to the reason for his visit. "You were right. Nellie Snow was behind everything that's happened at Shoo Fly these past few weeks. She denied it at first, even tried to pin it on Ruth as some sort of bizarre need for attention, but when questioned about the missing letter, she caved."

She sat perfectly still in an attempt to absorb everything he'd said. "So that part is over?"

He hesitated, then leaned back to afford a better angle with which to peer into her eyes. For several long moments he simply studied her, his gaze taking in her hair, her face, her royal blue sweater, her legs . . . When he returned his attention to her face, she shivered.

"I'm sort of hoping it means that all of it is over," he said.

"What do you mean when you say all of it?"

"I mean the whole thing." He rested one hand on his thigh and rubbed his freshly shaved face with the other. "The vandalism, the fear, the murder case. All of it."

She felt her mouth drop open at the implication. "Wait. You mean you think Nellie is responsible for her husband's murder, too?"

"We're certainly looking into the possibility."

"But how? He was strangled with bare hands, wasn't he?"

"She had cause to be blinded by rage."

"Wow." It was all she could say given the circumstances.

"Wow is right. Now I'm just worried whether I have any business being a detective in this town when you're out there doing your thing."

She caught the teasing sparkle just before the dimples appeared yet felt the need to explain nonetheless. "I wasn't trying to play amateur sleuth; I really wasn't. It just sort of happened."

"Claire, it's okay. It's awesome, actually." He lifted his hand from his thigh and dropped it along the back of the couch, grazing her shoulder as he did. "Like . . . you."

"Like me?" she echoed.

"Yeah." His gaze locked on hers. "Like you."

"Claire?" The moment broken, she turned toward the sound of her aunt's voice. "Benjamin Miller is here to see you."

Jakob's dimples disappeared along with the sparkle that had lit his eyes in such mesmerizing fashion just seconds earlier. In their place was a sense of resignation, maybe even defeat. She looked back toward her aunt as Benjamin stepped into her view, his black hat and pants almost stern against the warmth of the foyer.

"Miss Weatherly. I have come to thank —" Then, just as quickly as the words started, they stopped, Benjamin's lips clamping shut as the identity of Claire's companion registered in his mind. "Jakob."

"Benjamin."

Claire looked to Diane for help, but, once again, her aunt was gone.

"I did not mean to interrupt."

She stepped forward in an effort to ease the tension. "No, no. You didn't interrupt anything. We were just talking." The quick intake of air behind her made her second-guess her words, but it was too late. "I mean, we —"

Jakob moved around her to assume a stance more suitable to his profession. "I just came to tell Claire that she was right about Nellie Snow. And, as a result, your sister and your family can rest easy knowing there will be no more fires and no more property damage."

"I have heard. Eli told me. That is why I am here, too. To say thank you to Miss Weatherly. And, I suppose to you, too, Jakob."

Claire gasped.

Jakob nodded, then held out his hand, shaking Benjamin's firmly when it was offered in return. "And I want you to know how sorry I am to hear about Elizabeth. I had no idea."

"You could not have known."

"I could have if I'd been told." Then, without waiting for an answer, Jakob gave a single clap of his hands and moved toward the door, his focus settling somewhere just over Claire's head. "Well, I best leave you two alone. Enjoy your evening. And thanks again, Claire, for all your hard work. I'll keep you posted as things progress."

And then he was gone, his back disappearing into the darkness just beyond the porch. She'd hurt him, that was obvious. But she hadn't meant to downplay his presence in front of Benjamin. She really hadn't. She just didn't want Benjamin *or* Jakob to get the wrong impression.

"My star worked, yes?"

Benjamin's voice broke through her wool-gathering long enough to leave her feeling more than a little confused.

"Star?"

"The one I found. You said you wished for the problems at the shop to end. And they did."

She couldn't help but smile at the wonder she saw on his face as he looked at her. "I guess you're right."

"Maybe your star will work, too. Maybe you will live a simple life."

CHAPTER 30

She was sitting on her window seat looking out across the darkened fields and hills of Heavenly when she heard a soft tapping at the door. The sound, coupled with the late-night hour, surprised her out of her thoughts.

"Come in," she whispered.

Diane padded into the room in her fuzzy white slippers and pushed the door shut in her wake. "I saw some light coming from under your door and wanted to make sure you're okay."

It was a simple inquiry that required a simple answer, yet simple seemed to be escaping her at that moment. In fact, the simple, basic day-to-day rituals that had been such a comfort to her after moving to Heavenly had faded into the background in a life that had suddenly become complicated again.

Instead of enveloping herself in her

present life at the inn, she'd begun to think ahead — to an apartment she'd yet to rent or even a house she'd yet to buy. Suddenly the simple joy that came from wandering downstairs to hunt through Diane's vast book collection for the next great read she could devour wasn't enough. In its place was worry about the rent payment she didn't have and the make-believe room she really didn't have to paint and decorate.

Instead of enjoying the friends she'd made in Esther and Ruth, and Jakob and Benjamin, she found herself worrying about their lives and their relationships.

Instead of taking time to learn who she was and what she wanted in life, she found herself right where she'd been when she'd first met Paul — so wrapped up in trying to read Jakob's reactions and Benjamin's thoughts that she wasn't fully aware of what her own feelings were saying.

And all of it had changed so subtly, she hadn't seen it coming.

Yet there it was.

There *she* was.

So she tried her best to explain it all to her aunt, to describe how she felt about the changes she hadn't seen coming and her worry over how to stop them and reverse course back to the first few weeks in Heavenly. When everything had been so new, she didn't have time to worry about much of anything.

"But don't you see?" Diane said when she was done. "Don't you see that by thinking ahead to renting or buying your own place, you've accepted this town as your home?"

She hadn't thought of it that way . . .

"And don't you see that by wanting to help your friends, you've come to care about them as if they're your family?"

Without waiting for a reply, Diane relinquished her place on the edge of Claire's bed and set about the task of fluffing pillows and readying sheets for the sleep Claire would have to succumb to sooner or later. "I don't see how wanting to put down permanent roots and caring about the people around you can be a bad thing."

"I know you're right, I really do, but . . . Well, I guess I'm afraid of losing myself before I've even had a chance to truly figure out who I am and what I like." She hoped she didn't sound like an idiot, but she'd finally found a way to verbalize the knot of fear that was starting to reattach itself to her soul the way it had when she first left Paul.

Diane finished her professional aunt duties and, grabbing Claire's hairbrush from the vanity, made her way over to the window seat.

"I think you're shortchanging yourself more than you realize. You know what you need in a relationship because your heart finally spoke up and demanded to be heard. It took you a while, but you finally listened. Your heart has had its say, and it's not going to fade quietly away only to be ignored all over again. Just listen to what it says, and you can't go wrong."

She encased her aunt's free hand with her own as it stroked the side of her cheek the way she'd treasured so much as a child. "But what happens if I can't hear what it's saying?"

"You will when you're ready. Just like you were when you left New York, when you made the decision to open the store, and when you took what you knew about Nellie to Jakob."

Disengaging her hand from Diane's, she looked out into the darkness once again. "I think I hurt Jakob this evening, and I feel awful about it."

"What happened?"

"I downplayed his presence when Benjamin stopped by." Her heart ached as she recalled her words and his reaction to them as if it was happening again at that very moment.

"Why?"

Ah, the million-dollar question. "I'm not sure."

"Is it because you want Benjamin to see you as available?"

"I'm not sure," she said honestly. "Maybe."

"But you know it doesn't matter whether he does or doesn't, right?"

She turned from the window to meet her aunt's worried eyes. "I'm trying to know that."

"And Jakob? Do you have any feelings for him at all?"

There was no denying the tingle she felt every time his skin brushed hers, no ignoring the way a simple touch of his hand warmed her entire body . . .

"I'm not sure," she repeated. "Maybe."

"Then maybe you need to get to know him better. Learn more about each other."

It sounded so simple when Diane said it. But that's because it was through Diane's eyes, not hers. She was living it; Diane was watching it. "Jakob Fisher is a good man."

Diane gathered Claire's hair in her hands and brushed it from top to bottom, the repetitive motion comforting in its simplicity. "And a person would have to be blind not to see that he's a bit smitten with you, dear."

She pressed her forehead against the glass, the sensation of the brush as it moved through her hair making her long for safer topics . . .

"Jakob thinks Nellie could be behind Walter's death now, too. But instead of jealousy — as her motive was with Ruth — it would probably have been blinding rage that made her snap and kill her husband.

"And I guess it makes a ton of sense if you think about it. She was so sure he was going to come back for her after he skipped town. But instead of coming back, he sends a love letter to another woman . . . a woman nearly half her age."

Diane stood silently behind her, the woman's reflection in the window offering a sense of strength and courage that had been lacking in the room prior to her arrival. It was as if everything in life would work itself out one way or the other as long as Diane Weatherly was on duty.

"But Walter was strangled wasn't he?"

Claire closed her eyes against the image of Nellie squeezing the life from her husband with her own bare hands. It was hard to imagine on some levels but certainly not out of the question for someone who had been publically humiliated in so many ways. "Yes he was."

"But how could Nellie have strangled someone nearly twice her size?"

It was the same question that had surfaced when she'd heard of Nellie's potential role in Walter's murder, so she gave the same answer she'd been given. "She had more than a few reasons to be blinded by rage."

"Agreed." Diane set the brush back down on the vanity, then leaned forward to plant a kiss on the top of Claire's head. "But Jakob is missing one undisputable fact."

"What's that?"

"Nellie couldn't have strangled that no good husband of hers to death even if she tried."

She left the window seat and followed her aunt to the door, the late-night hour and the busyness of the day finally taking its toll. "How can you be so sure?"

"Because Nellie Snow's hands are so riddled with arthritis she can't even open a bottle of water by herself."

CHAPTER 31

She was almost finished with her bagel and coffee when Arnie burst through the door with a stack of papers in one hand and a camera in the other.

"Hey, mind if I tag along to the shop with you this morning? I want to get a few pictures of the town and maybe a few of Esther, too."

"Sure, you can tag along." She lifted the blue and yellow mug to her lips and drained the last remaining drops of the lukewarm liquid. "But you know as well as I do that Esther won't allow her picture to be taken by you or anyone else."

Arnie's scrawny shoulders hitched upward. "Yeah, I know. But maybe . . . if she thinks I'm taking a picture of something else — like maybe one of those hand-painted milk buckets or something — I can snap one of her without her even knowing."

"No."

Securing the camera around his neck, he reached for the bread basket beside the refrigerator and peeled back its floral cloth cover. "Hey. Where are the muffins?"

She pointed to a larger basket not more than six inches from where she sat. "Diane made a larger batch this time, so they're in that one."

"Cool."

"So what's with the papers? Is that your thesis?"

He tossed the stack of pages onto the breakfast bar and snatched four muffins from the basket. "It's the first draft. Finished it last night while your boyfriend and his nemesis were sizing each other up in the parlor just below my room."

She felt her anger rising but shook it off the best she could. Correcting a man like Arnie wasn't worth it. He wouldn't listen anyway. Instead, she mustered up the closest thing to an apology she could find out of loyalty to her aunt's role as innkeeper. "I hope we didn't disturb you too badly."

"Nahh. That's what headphones are for, you know?"

Reaching in front of her, he plucked her knife from her napkin and buttered his muffins across every side he could find. When he was done, he stuck the knife in his mouth and licked it clean. "So you think Esther will give in to her feelings and come to your aunt's bonfire with me tonight?"

She wanted to laugh, she really did, but she couldn't. Because for the first time since she'd met him, she actually felt a little sorry for Arnie. He was living in a dream world where Esther was concerned, just as she was living in one over Benjamin.

Esther was no more going to walk away from the Amish for Arnie than Benjamin would walk away for Claire. It simply wasn't going to happen for either one of them.

Fortunately for her, though, she wasn't even sure whether she liked Benjamin as anything more than a friend who just so happened to make her feel like someone special. Arnie, on the other hand, not only liked Esther but actually believed she liked him, too.

Claire, however, knew differently.

"Hey, you were wrong about your whole deflection theory with Eli and the problems at his sister's shop." She slid off her stool and carried her empty mug and plate to the sink, where she proceeded to put both in the industrial-sized dishwasher. "He had nothing to do with any of it."

"And you know this because . . ." Arnie prompted as he crammed the first muffin into his mouth.

Returning to the breakfast bar, she ran a damp paper towel across the surface of the counter while he moved on to his second and third muffin. "I know this because the person behind everything confessed."

"Humph. Well I'll be darned. I guess the thought of covering his tracks never even occurred to that buffoon at all then, huh?"

"Eli Miller isn't a buffoon. He's actually a pretty nice guy." And she meant it. Any misgivings she'd harbored about the young man's temper in the beginning had faded in favor of his more enviable qualities. "I don't believe he had anything whatsoever to do with Walter Snow's murder. I really don't."

"Suit yourself." Arnie wiped the sleeve of his shirt across his mouth and then reached into his pocket to pull out his vibrating phone. "Aw, darn. You go on ahead without me. I gotta take this. It's that Amish midwife lady that Diane tried to hook me up with when I first got here."

"But I thought the first draft was done."

"That's before I knew she was going to call. I've only been waiting for three-plus weeks." He flipped open his phone and held it to his ear as he headed into the hallway and toward the stairs, his voice lingering long after his presence. "Does it take you this long to respond when someone goes into labor? Because if it does, you might want to consider another career path . . ."

Grabbing her purse and Diane's keys, Claire took off in the opposite direction, eternally grateful to Diane's friend for freeing her from having to spend another moment with the insufferable Arnie Streen. After all, less than four hours of sleep was enough of a liability for the day all on its own.

She made quick work of the parking lot before turning east and heading toward town, her mind already thinking ahead to everything she wanted to accomplish. Martha had new items for the store, as did Esther, and all would need to be priced and displayed before closing. Beyond that, she needed to track down Jakob and apologize for her behavior. If he accepted it without issue, she'd invite him to the bonfire she suspected her aunt of finagling as a way to bring Jakob and Claire together.

And maybe it would be fun.

By the time she reached the shop, she found herself hoping he would accept both her apology and her invitation. The laid-back setting promised to provide the kind of low-pressure fun she needed. And if she could convince Esther and Eli to come, too, the whole thing would be even better.

"Claire! Claire!" Esther was across the room and blocking her path before she'd barely cleared the door. "Did you hear the news?"

"You mean about Nellie and the stuff at Ruth's?"

Esther nodded emphatically.

"Yes, I heard."

"Maybe this means she is one who — who murdered Mr. Snow."

Recalling her aunt's words from the night before, she rested a friendly hand on Esther's arm. "I wouldn't get your hopes up about that just yet."

Esther's shoulders sagged. "But I want to hope."

"I know." She sidestepped her friend and headed toward the counter and the promise of new handcrafted items from Esther's mother. "So? What did she make this week?"

"Mamm did not feel well today. She said she will come Monday."

She tried not to show her disappointment, but it was hard. One of her favorite parts of the job was seeing all of the beautiful things the Amish made. "Then I'll look forward to Monday."

"I have things." Esther escaped into the stockroom only to return moments later with a large brown paper sack. "I hope you like these."

Claire took the sack from Esther's hands and plopped it on the counter. She reached inside and pulled out four hunter-green and cranberry checkered cloth napkins with a matching table runner. "Oh, Esther, these are lovely."

The young woman reddened at the praise, but Claire could tell she was pleased. A compliment was a compliment no matter who you were. "I am glad you are happy."

Scooping up the newest additions to her ever-growing inventory, Claire wound her way around the various displays she'd set up around the shop. When she reached the section where she tended to keep things like tablecloths and other items for the kitchen and dining room, she glanced back at Esther. "I was thinking about what you said last night. About Nellie Snow searching both the stockroom and this room looking for something. I wonder if maybe she was looking for the money her husband stole."

"But she could not find what he did not leave."

She turned back to the napkins and table runner, arranging them in a way that best showcased the exquisite work that had gone into making them. Esther was, without a doubt, on par to be as crafty and creative as her mother.

"I wonder if he hurt her, too."

"He did. Everything about those love letters to Ruth had to hurt Nellie terribly."

"No," Esther corrected gently. "I mean her wrist. Like mine."

A vague memory poked its way into her conscious thought and made her forget about everything except Esther. "You mean when he was in here that last day?"

"Yes."

"Why was he angry again?"

"I do not know. He spoke only of things I could not answer."

"And you didn't tell Eli, right?" The details of that day were starting to assemble themselves in her brain although the overall picture was still fuzzy.

"He was with Benjamin. On the bakeshop porch. That was the day Ruth got the hate note."

Any cloudiness that remained as to the details of that day began to lift, enabling her to fill in a few gaps of her own. "So you just waited in here for me to come, right?"

"I . . . Yes."

Something in the way Esther hesitated sent a chill down her spine. "Esther? What aren't you telling me?"

All color drained from Esther's face as Claire repeated her inquiry.

"He came back," Esther whispered as tears began to stream down her cheeks.

She felt her stomach lift toward her throat and fought it back down. "Did he hurt you again?"

When Esther did not answer, Claire grabbed hold of the young woman's shoulders and gave her a gentle shake. "Esther! You have to tell me."

Slowly, and with great effort, Esther walked her through Walter's return, his encore performance very similar to the first except for one point. "He grabbed me like this" — with a shaky hand, she reached around the back of her neck and lurched it forward, the memory as much as the motion intensifying the pace of her tears — "and pulled me close. He said he would hurt me more if I did not tell where the chest was."

"Chest? What chest —"

"And that is when I heard the noise outside the window." Esther pointed toward the shop's westward-facing window and its view of the alley between Heavenly Treasures and Shoo Fly Bake Shoppe. "He heard, too. And that is when he ran. He did not come back."

"Do you know who was out there?"

Esther began to shake uncontrollably as the tears turned into gut-wrenching sobs. Pulling the young woman close, Claire simply held her until the sobbing stopped and her breathing steadied. "You think it was Eli, don't you?"

"I do not want to believe that."

Neither did Claire. But more than any monetary injustice, Eli was a protector. He proved that on a daily basis with his sister. Knowing what she now knew about Eli's feelings for Esther, coupled with the strong likelihood he'd witnessed the scene that had just been described, any and all doubts about Eli's' innocence came screaming to the forefront.

The motive may have changed from the one Jakob had written on the whiteboard, but the opportunity and the strength to carry out the crime were all there vying to be noticed.

"Will you tell Jakob?" Esther asked between hiccups.

She knew what Esther wanted to hear, knew what she wished she could say. But she couldn't.

"I think I *have* to," she whispered.

CHAPTER 32

She could feel Jakob's eyes watching her every move as she handed out graham crackers, marshmallows, and chocolate to Diane's guests. And although there was a small part of her that wanted to pretend it wasn't happening, a larger and more unexpected part found the attention to be oddly comforting.

She'd stopped by the station after talking with Esther and told him everything she knew and even more that she feared. He'd listened to every word she said and even took some notes, but in the end he'd managed to make her feel as if there was still a chance Eli wasn't the one.

How much he truly believed that, she couldn't say. But for that moment, it had been enough. Like seeing a life raft on a ship and taking comfort in the fact that it was there if needed.

Despite the heaviness she felt in her heart

over Esther, Claire had still managed to find a moment to apologize for downplaying their time together in front of Ben. She hadn't offered a reason for what she said, and she hadn't tried to explain it away. Instead she simply told him what she felt in her heart — that although she'd enjoyed their brief time together, she was still trying to discover who she was inside. Hearing that Jakob not only understood but could also relate erased any residual tension she felt between them. And when he accepted her invite for that night's bonfire, she'd known their friendship was intact.

What, if anything, was ahead for them in the future would remain to be seen.

"How about you?" she asked, as she waved the plate of s'more fixings inches from his nose. "Care to make one, too?"

"Absolutely." Jakob leaned forward, his hand finding its way around the plate like an old pro. "In fact, I'll even make you one if you just want to sit back and take it easy."

"That sounds wonderful." She took the empty beach chair to Jakob's right, balancing the plate on her legs as the guests swarmed their way toward the roaring fire.

He gestured toward the flames with his cooking fork. "If it's okay, I'll give the troops a little space before I start trying to push my way into position."

"I understand." She leaned her head against the chair and looked down at her hands. "I guess by now you know about Nellie's arthritis, right?"

Jakob rolled his marshmallow between his fingers and gave a slight nod. "I do. It's so severe, we didn't even need the statement from her attorney putting her in his office at the approximate time of her husband's demise."

"Too bad Eli is too young for arthritis."

"I know what you mean. Although, if you think about it, there are lots of things that could impact the mobility of a person's hand."

"Like what?" she asked.

"Like a neurological disease of some sort or maybe a third-degree burn. You know, that sort of thing. Breaks, too."

"Oh. So nothing about being Amish then, huh?"

"You mean other than the fact that violence of any kind is against everything the Amish stand for?"

"Touché."

He poked the tongs of his cooking fork through each of their marshmallows and carried them to the fire, the rest of the guests seemingly oblivious to their conversation. "Hey, you've gotta know that I'm hoping just as hard as you are that Eli isn't our man. I really am. But it's not looking all that good for him right now."

All she could do was nod and stare at the flames lapping around her marshmallow as something Jakob said teased at her subconscious.

"Heck, we can't even place him anywhere *but* the bakery for the bulk of that day."

"I know. I saw him there, too."

"What do you remember about those times that you saw him?" Jakob asked from his spot in front of the fire.

She thought back over that day, remembering her surprise at the notion that someone would target Ruth with a nasty letter taped to the front door of the bakery, warning people to eat elsewhere. But as clearly as she remembered the things that were said, she couldn't really picture Ruth. No, the people she most remembered that day were Benjamin and Eli . . .

Eli pacing across the porch with one hand in a fist and the other sporting splinted fingers.

And Benjamin dressing him down again and again for his outbursts.

"Wait a minute!" she hissed. "That's it!"

He pulled their marshmallows from the

fire and brought them back to their chairs. "What's it?"

"His hand! Eli had hurt his hand not more than one or two days before the murder!"

With help from the chocolate and graham cracker, Jakob slid the marshmallow from the stick and handed the finished product to Claire, her words seeming to have little effect on the detective.

She tried again. "Don't you hear me? Eli had broken his fingers when he punched the wall over the stolen pie boxes. I told you about this when we were out at the swimming hole, don't you remember? He hurt his hand so badly, I had to help him pull a milk jug from the box outside the bake shop on the very day we're talking about!"

Jakob stopping working on his own treat as he seemed to finally hear what Claire was saying. "How come I haven't noticed any splints?"

"Because he's taken to wearing gloves in what I suspect is an effort to downplay his temper around people like Esther's father. You know, kind of an out of sight, out of mind thing, I guess."

"And his hand was that bad?"

"Yes! In fact, that same day, after Benjamin went off to show the nasty note they'd found to Mr. Glick, Howard had to split a few pieces of wood for Ruth's cooking stove because Eli couldn't grasp the ax with his fingers all messed up like that!"

"Are you absolutely sure of this?" he asked.

The first full-fledged smile of the day made its way across her face. It was going to be alright. Esther and Eli were going to get to be together. And all because Eli had punched a wall . . .

"I'm positive."

"So I'm minus yet another suspect, yes?"

She couldn't help but laugh at the sheer joy she felt. "It sure looks that way."

He hung his head in mock defeat only to right it at the telltale snort of a horse. "Are you expecting someone?"

"Not necessarily expecting but certainly hoping, yes." She rose from her chair and turned toward the open field behind them, the sight of Esther in Eli's open-top buggy bringing a mixture of relief and anticipation. "Can we tell them?"

She saw Jakob's nod out of the corner of her eye. "I'd like to be the one to say it, if that's okay. I'd like to bring at least one good thing to my niece's life."

An unexpected lump rose in her throat as Jakob made his way over to the young couple. She didn't need to hear what he was saying. Just watching the way they hung on his every word and the way they looked at one another was enough. But it was the gratitude in Esther's face toward the uncle she'd never known that affected her most deeply.

"What's that chump doing here?"

Claire turned toward the voice beside her, the disappointment in Arnie's face almost painful to see. "You mean, Eli? Esther asked him to come and I'm glad he did."

"Pardon me if I don't share that same sentiment."

For the first time since they'd met across the dinner table at Sleep Heavenly, Claire found herself willingly reaching out and touching the socially awkward man with a calming hand. "Please, Arnie. Jakob needs this time with his niece. It's important . . . to me."

"Here they come." As they approached, Arnie stepped forward to greet Esther, extricating her from her date and the detective with surprising ease. Claire watched as he led her around the far side of the fire, his hands joining in on whatever he was saying to the object of his affections. And as always, Esther was herself — quiet, sweet, and kind.

"Claire?" The whispered touch of fingers

on her bare arm brought Eli into view. "Jakob said what you have done."

"I didn't do anything except remember."

"That is enough."

She followed his gaze as it left her face, traveled across the soaring flames, and settled on the woman he loved. "You should tell her how you feel, Eli."

A hint of sadness rippled across the young man's face. "I can not. Esther must make a choice, just as Jakob did."

Confused, she looked to Jakob for the explanation he was unable to give, either. "You've made that statement before, Eli. But I don't know what choice you're talking about."

"Between worlds."

Jakob sucked in a breath. "Is Esther thinking of leaving the Amish?"

"No, of course not," she insisted as she too looked over the top of the flames to study her friend. "I . . . I don't understand why you'd even think she was considering such a thing, Eli."

Slowly, deliberately, Eli raised a hand and pointed toward the freckle-faced redhead who was doing his best to curry favor with Esther King. "He is English. I am not."

"You mean Arnie?"

Eli could only nod.

"You think Esther is interested in Arnie?"

Again, Eli nodded, only this time he shared the true reason he'd failed to tell Esther of his intentions. "He comes to the shop many times. She spends much time talking to him."

Taking his hands in hers, Claire held them tight until she had Eli's complete attention. "He is a graduate student in anthropology, Eli. He is studying the Amish. He talks to Esther to learn more about you . . . your beliefs . . . your customs. She is helping him because she is kind."

Again, his eyes drifted to the other side of the fire although his verbal attention remained focused on Claire. "He likes Esther."

Jakob stepped forward and into the conversation playing out between Claire and Eli. "Eli, all that matters is who *Esther* likes."

"He stands at the window. For hours sometimes. And she does not like —"

"Stop right there," Jakob said. "Say that again."

"He stands at the window. For long times. I do not know if she looks back."

"What window does he stand at, Eli?"

"The window in the alley."

Jakob cupped his hand over his mouth, then let it fall to his side. "Was he there that day? The day Walter Snow was murdered?"

"I do not know," Eli said woodenly. "I do not remember."

Claire stood silently, trying to make sense of what she was hearing while comparing it to what she knew. "I know he wanted to talk to Esther that day, but he said she wasn't able to talk — oh my gosh! Jakob, that's it! Arnie must have seen Walter yelling at Esther. He must have seen him grab her by the arm and neck!"

Eli stiffened. "Mr. Snow grabbed Esther?"

She looked again at Arnie and nodded. "Knowing how he feels about Esther, he must have been incensed. I certainly would have been." Yet even as she voiced her thoughts aloud to Jakob and Eli, she knew the freckle-faced man on the other side of the fire wasn't strong enough to strangle a flea, no matter how enraged he may have been. "On second thought, it *can't* be Arnie. I mean, look at him. There's not a muscle anywhere on that body. And he's as lazy as they come. He can't even walk to a garbage can that's six inches from his feet to throw a candy wrapper away. But when it comes right down to it, it's really no wonder he's lacking strength of any kind when his greatest form of exercise is talking endlessly on one of three subjects."

Jakob crossed his arms in front of his chest, his eyes trained on no one but Arnie. "And what subjects might those be?"

"Everything Amish, everything Esther, and oysters."

Jakob's gaze cut to her face. "Did you say oysters?"

"That's how he paid for grad school."

"By eating *oysters?*"

She laughed. "No, by *shucking* them, silly."

A beat of stunned silence was soon followed by the snap of Jakob's phone as he flipped it open and pressed a single, solitary digit. "I think we've got our man."

CHAPTER 33

If there was one thing that defined her walk to work that morning more than anything else, it was the sound of whistling.

From pedestrians . . .

From her fellow shopkeepers . . .

And from one very happy Eli Miller.

In fact, virtually every single person she'd come in contact with so far was either whistling or smiling. The fog of uncertainty that had settled around Heavenly with the discovery of Walter Snow's body had finally lifted.

Justice had been served not once, but twice — with the discovery of Nellie's wrongdoings and the arrest of Arnie Streen for murder. In fact, the relatively swift resolution to both problems seemed to lessen the lingering sting of Walter Snow's thieving ways.

The man had been a bad apple, plain and simple.

The best thing they could do now was move on — like Eli was trying to do, if his presence in Claire's store rather than Ruth's was any indication.

It wasn't that she minded the volunteering hands every time she needed to go to the trash bin or climb to the top of a shelf to retrieve a customer's sought-after item, because she didn't. At all. But she was also smart enough to know that the young man's presence had absolutely nothing to do with Claire and everything to do with the happier-than-ever Amish girl beaming up at him as if he was the greatest thing in the world.

That kind of adoration and that kind of respect and belief was sure to keep Eli on the straight and narrow, maybe even pave the way for him to become the same respected member of the Amish community that his older brother, Benjamin, had been for quite some time.

She knew that Benjamin had been looking for her before she arrived; Esther had already clued her in on that little fact, but it was okay. Diane was right. Benjamin was a wonderful man for someone else.

Someone Amish.

Now it was just a matter of her heart getting on board with her head. Whatever feelings he'd stirred inside her needed to remain a mystery — one that would be forever locked away in some corner of her soul.

As for Jakob and the way he made her smile from the depths of her being, that too would remain a mystery. At least until she figured out a little bit more about herself — her likes, her dislikes, her hopes for the future. Until then, she'd simply count him as one of the many blessings she'd been given since moving to Heavenly.

Like owning her own shop . . .

She shook herself out of la-la land and grinned at the Amish couple making puppy-dog eyes at one another across the register. "Earth to Esther, earth to Esther: come in, Esther."

A hint of crimson rose in the Amish girl's face, but the love-struck smile remained. "I am here."

"Is your mother still bringing me some new treats today?"

"She is."

"Good. I can hardly wait." And it was true. There was something about seeing the talents of such peaceful people that gave her hope. Like wishing on the brightest star in the sky or spending an evening in the parlor with Aunt Diane.

She thought back to the moment Arnie had been arrested, the shock and horror on her aunt's face nearly bringing her to tears. But as she'd tried to explain, again and again throughout the rest of the weekend, there was no way Diane or anyone else could have ever known what Arnie had done. He'd spent so much of his life living in the background that he'd become proficient at the skill.

But Diane had fretted anyway, convinced she, who had been nicer to Arnie than anyone had ever been, should have known something, should have done something. It wasn't until Claire had wrestled the conversation away from Arnie and onto his obsession with Esther that her aunt had finally let it go, her nurturing side clucking away at the angry way in which Walter had handled Esther.

"He was after something mighty important, Claire, to have risked going back inside your shop to see Esther a second time."

It was a statement that had nagged at her subconscious throughout the night only to rise to the surface again while watching Esther speak so happily to Eli . . .

"Esther?"

Esther ran a hand down the front of her aproned dress. "What is it, Claire?"

"What was it again that Walter was so intent on finding when he grabbed your wrist and then your neck?"

Esther flashed a reassuring look at Eli, then followed it with a calming hand to his cheek before addressing Claire's question. "He wanted the chest. He said it was in the stockroom."

"Did he say why?"

"No. Only that he must have it."

She closed her eyes in a mental review of the Amish-made furniture pieces she'd sorted through every chance she got during the first few weeks the shop was open. There had been rocking chairs and horses, bed posts and night stands, kitchen chairs and quilt racks. And there had been one chest . . .

"I gave that chest back to your brother, Eli."

Eli nodded. "He gave it to Ruth. For pots and pans. It almost burned in fire."

And then she remembered. She'd knelt beside that very chest when she'd checked in on Ruth the morning after the fire.

"Can I see it?" she asked Eli.

"Benjamin can make a chest for you."

She waved the appealing notion from her thoughts. "No. I want to see *that* one — the one that Walter was so desperate to find."

With a shrug of his shoulders, Eli led the way through the stockroom and into the alley, his hand wrapped tightly around Esther's. When they stepped inside Ruth's kitchen, he swept his hand toward the finely crafted chest that sat no more than a few feet from where Nellie had started the fire designed to punish Ruth.

She dropped to her knees and ran her hand across the chest, the smooth wood beneath her palm oddly comforting. "May I open it?" she asked over her shoulder.

"Please."

Lifting the latch, Claire used her fingers to raise the lid upward until it rested against the back wall and she was looking down at an assortment of baking pans that sparkled and shined. Then, with barely a hesitation, she began removing them from the chest, handing each and every pan to Esther until there was nothing left but the floor of the chest.

"There is a compartment. In the bottom." Eli moved in beside Claire and pointed toward a small recession in the wood. "The English use it for papers. For keepsakes."

Reaching into the chest, she pushed her fingers into the recession and slid them to the right, a split panel giving way to a shallow compartment below.

"What is that?" Eli shouted as he dropped to his knees beside Claire.

Her heart pounded double time in her chest at the sight of so much green. "I'm not positive, Eli, but I suspect that's the money Walter stole from the Amish."

Three hours later, every single dollar had been accounted for and sorted into envelopes bearing the names of several different Amish families . . .

Stoltzfus.

Lapp.

Troyer.

Beilers.

Yoder.

Miller.

And King.

She lifted the last envelope off the counter and handed it to Martha, the shock on the woman's face threatening to bring the same tears to Claire's face that Esther's already sported. "This belongs to your family."

With hands that trembled, Martha turned the envelope over and lifted the flap, her body sagging against the counter at the sight of the hundreds of dollars it contained. "I do not understand. I have not made enough things."

"This is not for the things you bring for

my shop. This is for the things your husband brought to Walter Snow."

Martha's head snapped up, her gaze volleying between Claire and Esther. "Walter Snow? But he . . . took our money."

"And now you're getting it all back. Right down to the very last dollar." The telltale jingle of an arriving customer brought an intake of air from Esther's direction. The sound told Claire everything she needed to know even as she kept her focus squarely on the girl's mother.

Slowly, Martha looked back down at the envelope of money, her hand shaking almost violently. "But . . . how?"

"Because one man spent the past three hours poring over Walter's records until he knew how much money belonged in each envelope."

Eli draped a respectful arm across Esther's shoulders and addressed his future mother-in-law in a voice choked with emotion. "He is a good man."

"He is a fair man," whispered Esther.

Martha looked from Eli to Esther and finally to Claire before turning to face the man they spoke of — a man standing just inside the doorway with a pained expression in his eyes.

For that moment, time seemed to stand

still, stymied by sixteen years of hurt and disappointment, bitterness and uncertainty. Claire held her breath and waited, the pounding of her heart rivaled only by the ticking of the clock above the register and Esther's occasional tear-induced sniffle.

But all of that faded away as Martha turned a watery gaze to the floor and addressed the brother she'd been raised beside until a life choice took them in separate directions, bringing them together again at that very moment . . .

Two people who were no longer the same yet had changed very little.

"Thank you, Jakob."

The employees of Thorndike Press hope you have enjoyed this Large Print book. All our Thorndike, Wheeler, and Kennebec Large Print titles are designed for easy reading, and all our books are made to last. Other Thorndike Press Large Print books are available at your library, through selected bookstores, or directly from us.

For information about titles, please call:
   (800) 223-1244

or visit our Web site at:
   http://gale.cengage.com/thorndike

To share your comments, please write:
Publisher
Thorndike Press
10 Water St., Suite 310
Waterville, ME 04901

11-12